THE PERIPHERALS

BOOK ONE: THE END IS THE BEGINNING

MARK ALDRICH

Wallace Street Press • Kill Devil Hills, NC

Cover Design: Chris Sorensen
Proofreading: Gretchen Tannert Douglas
Formatting: Chris Sorensen
Editing: Chris Urie
Author Photograph: Justin Patterson Photography

ISBN#: 979-8-9871069-0-7

Published by:

Wallace Street Press
P.O. Box 211
Kill Devil Hills, NC 27948

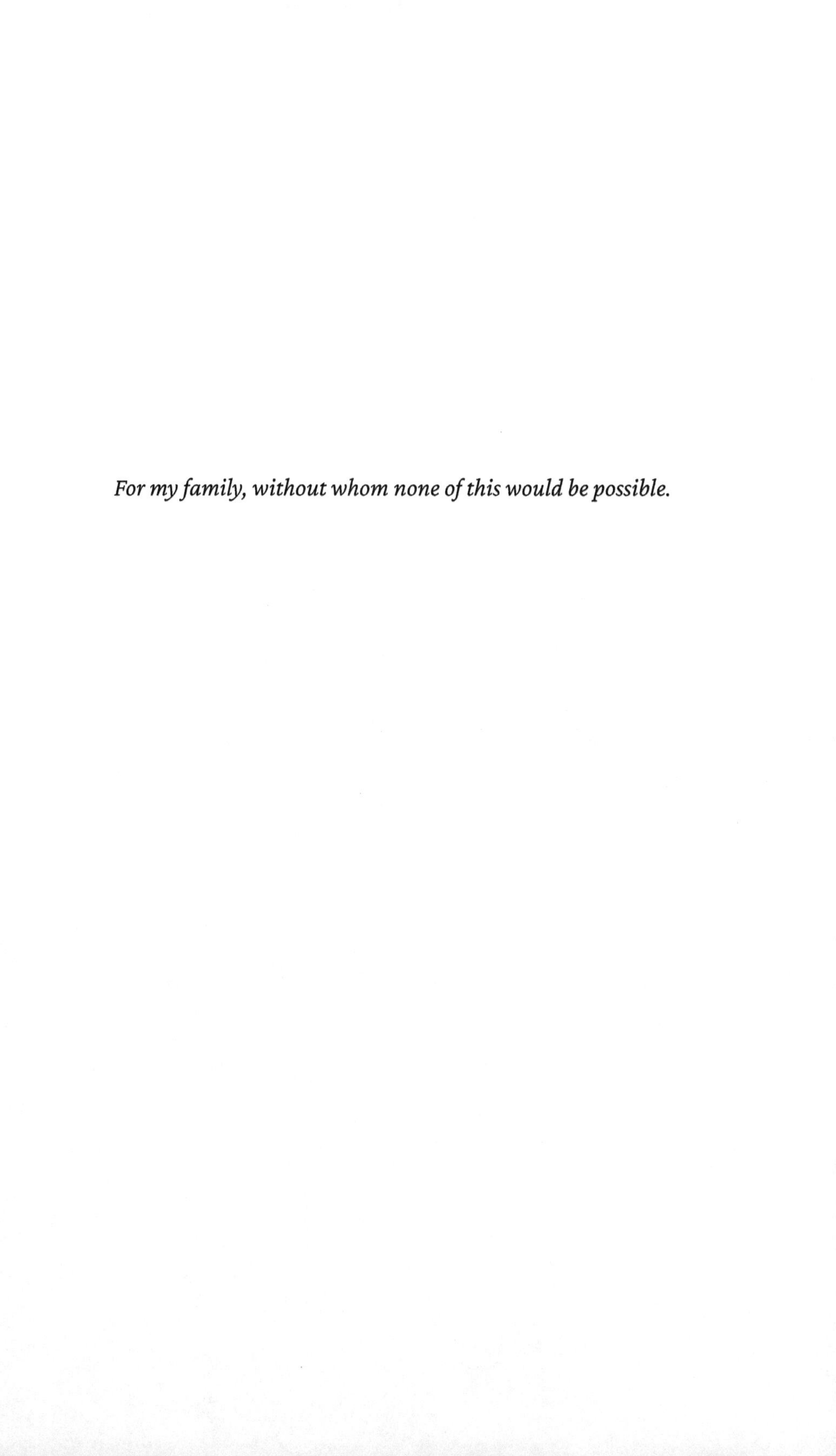

For my family, without whom none of this would be possible.

"When I hear music, I fear no danger. I am invulnerable. I see no foe.
I'm related to the earliest of times, and to the latest."
Henry David Thoreau

"If I cannot fly, let me sing."
Stephen Sondheim

PROLOGUE

1987

The eleven-year-old had been wrangling his friends and cousins for the better part of the morning, trying to get them organized into an impromptu variety performance for the adults of the family later this day. He was a bit of an anomaly in the group. No one else, either relative or neighbor, had ever shown any inclination toward performing. Or producing. Or entertaining in any way. Yet he had taken it upon himself to bring this together.

The children each chose something they wanted to present. Most of the small group used cassette tapes of their favorite songs played on a boom box and recreated their favorite music videos. The more adventurous wrote down skits or scenes that they'd watched on television. The eleven-year-old found all of that rather tedious, but soldiered on nevertheless. He had chosen to perform a classic scene from *I Love Lucy*. Long before his time, but he recognized the genius of it and desperately wanted to share, to get his extended family to see what he saw. He'd also written an original song, which he performed with two cousins. He didn't play guitar well, but knew what he wanted it to sound like and worked backward from there.

The family, the entire neighborhood, had always seemed to plod onward under grey skies. They all worked. Hard. And long hours. There was little time for entertainment. Art was unheard of in their circles, even frowned upon. They had more important things on their collective plates than something that didn't put food on the tables or pay the bills. The young boy had always known something was missing from their lives. That they could all be seeing, feeling, thinking... other things. Of course, he sensed this all on an instinctual level, but knew he wanted to do something to shift their grey clouds. Wanted them to see the possibilities that he saw. At the very least, he wanted them to be able to just... enjoy something.

And so, after their twenty-minute "show" in the kitchen of his aunt's house concluded, he felt a very small sense of accomplishment. He doubted that any of the other children had experienced it the way that he had. And the adults, especially the men and his dour aunt, had smiled and applauded politely at each of the acts. If they had looked askance at him dancing across the floor with a mop as his partner, he was willing to be seen as silly, if only one of them, even just one, would laugh. Surprisingly, his Uncle Ed had done just that. And that would be enough for today.

As he walked home after, leaving the other children to play their games in the backyard, he was pleased. Not with himself so much, but just that he had shared something, had told his story, revealed something of himself, and hopefully made their day, in some small way, different. He had enjoyed having all of the eyes on him. Not nervous or shy, the way some of the others had been. Not even self-conscious. Just himself.

He felt eyes on him now and turned to see if his aunt was watching him cross the street. She wasn't, though, her curtains drawn. He caught a movement out of the corner of his eye and turned quickly. He wasn't scared, more curious, but he most definitely felt someone was watching him. A bright light, as if he'd just rubbed his eyes, winked to his other side, but when he turned to it... nothing. He chalked it up to imagination and adrenaline and marched on his way.

He hadn't been wrong. He was being watched. By numerous sets of eyes. Some darker than others. It could be him. Possibly. He could be the one, they thought. For today, though, all they did was watch. They would be back for him. Later.

CHAPTER I

Present Day

S ean Curley opened his eyes abruptly at 7:58 a.m., two minutes before his alarm was set, which was not unusual for him. He was one of those people who always woke up just before an alarm. Light sleeper? Some innate sense of time? Just normally twitchy? Who knew? But this morning was different. He had the distinct feeling he was being watched. In fact, the dream that launched him into wakefulness was that of an unfamiliar face, inches from his own, shouting soundlessly at him. Not a relaxing start to what was bound to be a long day. He often remembered his dreams, but this one was unsettling and vividly real. Yet, eyes open, his room was empty. He was alone in his small, cluttered, overly expensive apartment in Astoria, Queens, New York City.

He took a moment to clear his head and allow his eyes to focus, then swung his legs out of bed and shuffled toward the bathroom. For most people, the hour wasn't early, but for someone who had been performing until eleven the night before, and then taken the long ride home on the subway, getting home after midnight, 8:00

a.m. came quickly. Normally, he'd allow himself to lie in later, but today was no normal day. His Broadway show of over a year was closing tonight, which meant a farewell to the window of stability it had brought to his usually nomadic life. And it meant an evening of goodbyes he'd rather not face. A cast, crew, and staff that had (mostly) become a second family over the intense time they'd spent together. Even worse, it meant a return to auditions, something he had not missed one bit. Which was the reason for his early rise and slight distraction. Sunday auditions were unusual, but no longer unheard of. Weekends weren't really a thing anymore. Especially in show business. All of this likely contributed to the usually observant Sean not noticing the quick shadow that flittered along the wall near the window as he made it to the bathroom and blearily brushed his teeth.

Morning ablutions done, he turned to his closet. Oh wow. He hadn't had to dress nicely for a while, he realized, as he sorted through his potential audition outfits. He made a mental note to go shopping for new work clothes as he settled on a dark pair of semi-casual pants and a button-down shirt, which remained untucked in an attempt to disguise the few pounds he'd put on over the last twelve months. Probably the closest he'd ever gotten to complacent.

Sean was firmly in the upper middle class of actors in New York. He'd likely never be a star (but never say never). He worked steadily but would never be wealthy. He survived and had made a name for himself in certain circles of the business. That meant he was doing better than most, and he was grateful. At forty-two, dreams of Hollywood riches and starlets (not that he'd ever really entertained them) were long gone. He was happy with what he'd accomplished. In fact, he'd done well. He was average height, average build. Having a good singing voice, solid acting technique, and genuine awareness of others opened many doors for him. However, it was his shock of red hair that set him apart, for better or worse. Some dismissed him as too... what? Irish? Too "other"? Standing out too much? At one point in his life, it had bothered him, but those days were long gone. He was comfortable with who he was, even if it cost him the occasional job. Better than being boring.

After a five-minute shower, downing a protein shake in the kitchen, and with a full water bottle in hand, Sean grabbed his backpack and headed for the door. He hoped to get back for a short rest before his 7:00 p.m. call for tonight's performance, but New York was unpredictable, so he packed for every conceivable scenario: rain, dance callback (please, God, no), singing callback in the afternoon (please, God, yes), coffee with friends, outfit for tonight. He briefly felt sorry for himself, and then remembered that women all over the city were doing the same with significantly heavier bags and more stuff to carry and decided to get over himself.

Keys? Check. Cell phone? Check. Umbrella? Double check. With that, he launched himself into another NYC day, albeit one with some expected emotional highs and lows. He focused on the audition as he turned left onto Thirty-first Avenue and made his way toward to the Broadway stop of the N train. His curtains twitched as he passed. He caught it out of the corner of his eye but convinced himself it must be a draft inside his apartment.

The train was late. No surprise there. Service had been getting worse over the last few years, and delays were built into his commute each day. At least it was just late and not out of service. That would have been a bigger issue. As he waited, he saw a woman on the platform he recognized from auditions. What was her name... Allie? Angie? He nodded hello but stayed focused on his audition material. She smiled and returned to her phone screen. He wondered if he'd see her at the audition. He also wondered why he'd never really spoken to her. She was attractive, friendly, and clearly worked (because time and hard luck removed most people in their age group by now otherwise). Suddenly, he hoped she was going to the same audition. Focus, Sean...

The train arrived. Luckily, it was not too crowded, and Sean found a seat. A rarity lately. He continued reading his audition material. This was for a regional theatre production of another old classic show. Not a dream job, but a show he loved (and could be cast in) in a beautiful part of the country. After over a year in the city with no breaks or vacations, it could be a welcome respite. Or it could mean missing the next Broadway audition. Choices. Ah, the glamorous life. The train stopped at Fifty-seventh Street and he saw Allie/Angie stand and make her way to the exit. So, she wouldn't be at the same audition. Too bad. As she passed, she smiled down at him and said, "Break a leg, Sean. Good to see you." She was gone before he could respond. Dammit, what was her name?

His stop was next, and he felt his shoes stick slightly to the floor of the subway car as he stood and made his way to the exit. Climbing the stairs to street level, he ran his song lyrics in his head a few more times. The audition studio was just across the street from the subway stop, so time was winding down to prepare. He knew as soon as he entered the building, he'd start seeing people he knew, and concentration would be tough. New York City may be an enormous city full of aspiring actors, but it was always surprising how many knew each other and how often they ran into one another. This audition would be a zoo.

He stopped at the street corner, waiting for the light to change. Suddenly, the girl from the subway's name flashed in his mind. "It's Abby!" he said out loud to no one in particular. Pleased with himself but distracted, he started to cross the street before the light had turned. Suddenly, he felt a hand on his shoulder pull him back just before he stepped in front of a cab streaking through the very yellow light. He stumbled slightly and turned to thank his good Samaritan, but no one seemed close or acknowledged what had just happened. Odd. He turned a full 360 but saw no one. This was turning out to be an intense morning so far. He hoped it settled down.

The light changed, the crowd of people surged forward, and Sean, with greater focus, crossed the street promising himself that he would pay it forward to someone if he had the chance later that day.

She watched him from just a few feet away. No one noticed her or her focus on the man crossing the street. He was the one she needed. They needed. She was convinced, but the others were not. They would be. With time. Something they had precious little to spare.

He was right. The audition was mobbed, and two other shows were auditioning in the same studio complex that morning. As soon as he emerged from the elevator, he started fielding hellos and well wishes, waving as he made his way past the other auditions. Most people were aware his show was closing that night, so there was the odd mixture of schadenfreude and empathy that could only make sense in an audition waiting room. He saw some seats down a side hallway and sought refuge there. As quiet a spot as he would find. Checking his watch, he saw he had twenty-five minutes until his audition time. He was one of those people who thought five minutes early counted as being late. Arriving on time WAS late. He took a deep breath, brought out his music for a glance, and tried to breathe deeply. No matter how many times you audition, how many shows you've done, how long you've been in the business, auditions are nerve-racking. Especially for Sean who was more sensitive and less secure than many of his colleagues.

The seat beside him creaked as someone took it and threw their bags on the floor. His brief respite over, he turned to say hello and burst out laughing. Next to him sat his current cast mate, Brandy Johns. Another veteran character actor of a certain age, they had grown close over the last year. Along with three other middle-aged character actors in their show, they had been dubbed The Grumbles by the show's fans because they played vaguely evil and perpetually annoyed characters. The five embraced the name. They had t-shirts made. They had fun.

Character actors don't often get attention, so they were happy for it. Brandy was the only woman in the group, but more than held her own. Small in stature, she made up for it with a piercing voice and a penchant for saying inappropriate things at all the wrong times. And all the right times. Basically, she enjoyed getting a reaction. And she was good at it. Her hair was cropped close, and she tended to wear brightly colored t-shirts, old jeans, and sneakers. Glamorous she was not. But she could tell a bawdy joke with the best of them and had a huge heart despite spending so much time denying it. She was spark plug both in stature and in temperament, but she would walk through fire for a friend, and even for most strangers. She would just deny it after the fact and get back about her business. She and Sean had an unlikely friendship, but somehow it just worked.

She took one look at Sean and opened with, "If you steal my job here, I'll have to cut you."

He laughed. "It's highly unlikely we'll be up for the same role."

"Maybe... but your voice is as high as mine so it's not impossible. Are you sure you're male?" she replied.

"Very sure," Sean said, but the grin on his face was evidence this was a common conversation between them.

Brandy sighed. "This is weird. I wanted us to run for at least five years. I hate auditioning."

"I know. Me, too. I'm definitely not ready for it to end. But no one asked me, so..." He left it hanging in the air.

"You bringing anyone tonight?" she asked.

"Nah... I figured it would probably be nice to skip out of the party early with you all and find a place to toast the run with just us. Maybe Beer Culture? Something more our speed."

"Also, you don't have a girlfriend, so that makes the decision a little easier, doesn't it, Red?"

"True. And thanks for reminding me. You bringing Mick?"

"He'll probably come to the official party and take off early. He knows we'll want some time."

"He's a good guy. Better than you deserve, that's for sure," Sean teased.

"Tell me something I don't know," she replied.

Just then, the audition monitor called Sean's name. It was early. Good thing he was there. He stood up, felt the butterflies, and tried to focus his nerves. He followed the monitor into the room, where his name was announced to the table of decision makers and the accompanist held out his hands for the music with a pleasant, if slightly tired, smile on his face.

Three minutes later, the door opened again, and Brandy saw Sean smile, mouth a "thank you" to those in the room, and just like that he was back in the hallway.

"That was quick. How'd it go?" she asked.

"Definitely booked it. Might as well start packing now," he said, rolling his eyes. "You know, I really would have liked to close our Broadway show before experiencing the joy of rejection again."

"Hey, what doesn't kill you makes you stronger," Brandy said.

"Thanks. You always know the right thing to say... Get some rest. Tonight's going to be a lot. See you then," he said as he started down the hallway toward the elevator.

"Not if I see you first!" Brandy called after him. They both had grins on their faces as Brandy rose to the sound of her name being called. Audition time.

Between the now-remembered sting of audition rejection and the looming bittersweet evening ahead, Sean was a swirl of emotions as he made his way toward the exit. Earbuds in, head down, and a definite vibe of "preoccupied, do not approach," he made it to the elevator and street level without facing any old acquaintances. No coffee dates today. He crossed the street toward the subway having decided that the better part of valor was to go home, regroup, and steel himself for tonight. His attention focused inward, he barely noticed the city thrumming around him. The eyes that followed his progress registered as little more than a tingle up his spine, which he attributed to a blast of air from the subway as he reached the top of the stairs. That hot, humid, stale air that could only belong to the NYC subway system. The good old MTA.

The long walk from the subway to his apartment back in Queens did little to calm his mind. In fact, the gloom settled in deeper as he realized one of his favorite restaurants had posted a closing notice. The neighborhood had changed so much in his fifteen-plus years there. Gone were many of the small independent shops and cafés. Single-family homes and duplexes were becoming extinct as luxury condos and apartments grabbed every possible lot. His humble one-bedroom apartment now stood next to million-dollar condominiums. It seemed every day he felt more out of step with the world around him.

"Geez, Sean, quit your whining!" he thought to himself as he took the steps into his building. "You're closing a Broadway show tonight. You've had a good run and you're not done with things yet. Get a grip, grab an iced tea, and appreciate where you are for once." He waved absentmindedly to his super, Glen, as he entered. Glen muttered something in response but most of the time Sean had no idea what he was saying. Glen was actually from Queens, which made the indecipherable accent even more baffling. After so many years, Sean could interpret the gist of Glen's comments. A strange arrangement, but it worked, and they'd somehow formed an easy friendship without ever really knowing exactly what the other was saying.

Two deadbolts and a doorknob later, Sean was in. Apartment 2E. Home for so many years. It was a small one-bedroom. Very small. As in, people-in-almost-every-other-city-in-the-country-would-question-your-sanity-for-living-there small. But he'd gotten a great price on it many years ago and just... stayed. As an overly sentimental person, Sean tended to keep mementos from important events or occasions. Pretty much all of them. And a life in show business offers many such opportunities. Playbills, show posters, ticket stubs, opening night gifts, closing night gifts, fan art (yes, Broadway fans are very loyal and create all sorts of personalized gifts). All of this is to say, the apartment was cluttered. But every time he settled in to clear things out, he had specific reasons to hang on to every single item in his cluttered apartment. He was even sentimental about the small, cluttered apartment itself. Other than his childhood home, he'd lived here longer than anyplace else. It had also been home to his longest relationship to date. That had started well but flamed out horribly after many years. Hard to believe there had ever been another person here. How had she fit? That felt so long ago now...

He slipped off his shoes as he came through the door. He was surprised to see he'd left the light on by the door. Unlike him, but he chalked it up to audition nerves. He noticed the bathroom door slowly swinging shut as he made his way to the kitchen. He really had to check on that draft, although something in the back of his mind was sending up a warning. Of what?

He poured himself a cold drink and flopped onto the well-worn, slightly uncomfortable mess of a sofa that was long past its sell-by date but held fond memories. He had a few hours to go before leaving for tonight's closing performance so flipped on the television, set a reminder alarm so that he was in no danger of being late, and allowed himself the indulgence of tuning in to the sports news. The baseball regular season had finished, and the playoffs were in full swing. This year, happily, his Red Sox were included. Almost as happily, the Yankees were not. The Mets... well, he didn't even let himself think about it. Maybe next year. Hope and Mets fans spring eternal. The safety of home began to seep in, and he found himself relaxing and eventually drifting into a fitful sleep. The maelstrom of conflicting emotions having taken its toll, it was not restful and he dreamed vaguely of strangers watching him. A feeling he found hard to shake upon waking.

He woke with a small start, three minutes before his reminder alarm was set to sound. His neck was stiff from his awkward semi-sitting position on the couch, and he absently rubbed it to loosen things up. The news had shifted to a football pregame show. The Jets were warming up. That would be as bad as being a Mets fan. Maybe worse. The Patriots were on later and were having another great season. He decided to take it as a good omen for a successful closing night performance ahead. Still hard to believe it was ending. Endings. He'd never been really good with them, even the ones he knew were for the best. That overly sentimental streak at work again.

He checked his phone and saw he had a message from a real estate agent he'd contacted about an apartment he'd seen online. He called back quickly, and it was answered on the second ring.

"Coleen Egan, how can I help you?"

"Hi Ms. Egan. It's Sean Curley returning your call regarding the Weehawken apartment? You mentioned you had some questions?"

"Yes," she answered. "Thanks so much for getting back to me. Sean, your income levels seem in line with what we'd need. However, you listed 'actor' as your sole means of employment. Where else do you earn money? Annuities? Inheritance?"

"Um... no. Just acting. That's my job," he responded.

"Oh, I'm sorry. I didn't recognize your name off the bat. Have I seen you on television? In a movie?"

"Possibly... but I work mostly onstage. If you've been to a Broadway show..." he responded slowly, having heard this all before.

"Oh, wow, no. Not my thing. I had no idea you could earn real money doing that. I wasn't even sure you all got paid," she stammered, the salesperson in her trying to find a graceful way out of this.

"Not a worry, Ms. Egan. I'll forward some pay stubs to you so you can verify. I have to run right now, though," he said, ringing off.

He'd been hearing things like that all his adult life. Shaking his head, he put the phone down and started to get ready to head out, certain that he would be trying a new real estate agent going forward.

He heard his neighbors start in on each other next door. This was not unusual. It would take them a while to work into full rage mode and he hoped he was long on his way to the theatre before they reached that stage. He wondered what made someone stay in such a clearly dysfunctional relationship, then reminded himself about glass houses and all of that. Apartment living. Even if you didn't know your neighbors, you got to know your neighbors. Whether you wanted to or not.

He brought his glass into the kitchen, rinsed it, and placed it into the dishwasher, an indulgence left by the previous owner for which he was eternally grateful. He lived alone, rarely cooked for himself, and would have been just fine without one, but it was a touch of luxury, and a nod to his suburban childhood. The galley kitchen had precious little space. He probably should remove the dishwasher and put in storage. But he knew he wouldn't. Pleasure where you can find it.

He fished through his too small closet to find something suitable to wear tonight. He settled on something pretty close to what he wore most days anyway and brought it to the bathroom. The shirt was wrinkled. Very wrinkled. Single-guy-living-alone-who-doesn't-pay-attention-to-these-things wrinkled. He draped it over the towel rod while he showered for the second time that day, hoping the steam would chase away some of the creases. It was semi-successful, and he considered it a win. A quick shave and a comb through the hair, he headed back to the living room, never noticing a small handprint in the fog on the mirror. Smaller than his hands, for certain.

He had eschewed closing night cards for his fellow company workers. He never knew where to draw the line. If he included only actors and stage managers, that seemed exclusionary. He'd become close with many on the stage crew, so they deserved cards. They probably didn't care much about them, but they deserved them. He'd also befriended some in the front of house staff. And some in management. They all deserved something, but the scope of that project was too daunting. Ironically, his sentimentality here caused him to abandon the sentimental gesture entirely. He figured he'd buy a round of drinks for his fellow Grumbles before the night was over and that would be his gesture.

He put a blazer on as he made for the door. A blazer he wholeheartedly expected to take off not long after the post-show party started and would end up rolled into a ball in the backpack he shouldered as he checked for his keys, phone, wallet. The essentials. He paused halfway out the door. Had that been a noise coming from the back of the apartment near the bedroom? His pulse quickened a bit. He listened closely. Nothing. Maybe the dysfunctional neighbors at it again. But somewhere inside that warning was sounding. For the first time in many years, he felt that he was not alone in his apartment, and it was unsettling. But he had no time for this now. Two deadbolts and a doorknob later, he walked out into the evening chill and a night of goodbyes he didn't want to make. But first, a show. No business like it.

They watched him leave. Some were clearly still unconvinced. But she nodded to them, as if they must have seen what she saw. With so much at stake, some would take more convincing, but she was making progress. In truth, they had no other options. He had to be the one.

CHAPTER 2

The fans had already formed a loose line in front of the theatre and spotted him as he turned the corner onto Forty-first Street. The Nederlander Theatre was the farthest south of the Broadway houses and had far less foot traffic than many of the uptown theatres. But the fans were loyal, had been from the start, and were there to send their favorites off in style. He chatted amiably with a few that he knew by face and shared some hugs with a couple who had become friends. Social media, for better or worse, had created access like never before. Sean was very aware that a few of the stars were justifiably wary of some of the darker turns that access could take, but he recognized he was very unlikely to attract any kind of negative attention. Or much of any attention at all. He was handed a few cards and mementos from the line as he made his way toward the entrance. Through the throng of fans, he thanked them all and made his way down the lobby, turning right into a decidedly un-glamorous alley that led to the stage door. Most patrons never see Broadway behind the scenes. Most of the theatres are old, cramped, musty, if not downright dirty... antiquated. Refurbishment is mostly saved for the areas of the building the public sees; lobby, house, merchandise and refreshment stands. Given their age and original construction, almost all of them could use added restrooms. Especially ladies' rooms. Many a Broadway intermission had to be extended because the line for the ladies' was still too long.

Sean walked past the graffiti wall (which included signatures from actors in past shows at the theatre), paused in front of the door, breathed deeply, and entered.

"Ginge!" came the familiar shout from Paolo, their stage door-man, as soon as Sean took a step inside. "Big night, my friend! Break a leg!" Paolo was ceaselessly optimistic, and while Sean had initially thought it would get old, it never had. They had become friends, if not quite close friends, over the past year. He handed Sean a card as he passed the front desk and Sean began to question his "no card" decision.

"Paolo, my friend. It has been an honor. Can't believe this is it! See you after?" Sean said.

"Absolutely," came Paolo's reply. "I would not miss it for all the canto coins in Canto Bight!" That was the other thing about Paolo. He loved *Star Wars*. A lot. In fact, he was dressed in his best Jedi robes for tonight's closing. They'd all gotten used to it after a while. Even embraced it. Funny though, no one was really sure if he just loved the movies or thought he actually was a Jedi. Made no difference. He was endlessly upbeat, that Paolo. And universally appreciated within the theatre. Some things might be better unknown.

Sean maneuvered his way down the ridiculously narrow hallway toward the callboard where he initialed next to his name to let stage management know he was there. In the notes for the night, he saw that everyone was in the show for the final performance. Swings and understudies would be incorporated into the curtain call, and it closed with the simple message, "Congratulations. Job well done. It has been a pleasure. Let's go out the way we came in: at the top of our game." Sean felt emotions straining to come. In his throat. Out of his eyes. And blinked them back. Way too soon. He turned and made his way past a table full of flowers, cards, small gifts. A quick scan showed none were for him. Not shocking. He then began the trudge up the four flights of stairs to the dressing room he shared with the Grumbles. His knees wouldn't miss the stairs, but the rest of him would miss the cardio. He made a mental note to make sure his gym membership was renewed.

Reaching the dressing room door, he paused, took a breath and steeled himself. Dressing Room 9 had become a home away from home for them. So many hours spent here. During shows, between shows, after shows. They had seen each other through the ends of relationships, the loss of friends and family members, career highlights and disappointments. Eight shows a week, fifty-two weeks a year. It added up. He opened the door and went in.

"Ginge!" the call went up from around the room. Stewart Garland was closest to the door. He was the only black Grumble. Tall and sinuous, a few years back he'd been one of the hottest commodities in the theatre industry in most senses of the word. He had been a leading man in demand both onstage and off. More recently, he had happily settled into the aging character actor phase of his career, which somehow seemed more in keeping with his impish humor and frequent off-color comments (he got along famously with Brandy). Next was Sullivan Nichols. Sean had always thought they should call him "Sully," but everyone just called him Nick. Made little sense, but that was the way it was. He had a macabre sense of humor and a wicked laugh to go along with it. Follically challenged, he had a perfect look for television and was recognizable for numerous performances where he was shot, knifed, poisoned, run over, and in one memorable scene had his head explode. Endlessly curious, he often had his face in a screen looking up some little-known fact or event.

The next station in the dressing room sat empty. Ken O'Carroll was often the last one there. He usually strode in just at call time, often with an ice cream in his hands. (He'd once been late for the show because the line for ice cream was too long, and he refused to leave it empty handed).

Across the room sat Brandy. Her dressing room was downstairs, but she'd been given an unofficial spot in here where she spent most of her time backstage. Sean made his greetings as he walked down the line to his spot in the corner by the vaguely mildewy showers. Others might have complained, but he enjoyed being out of the way and being able to keep an eye on the others from a safe spot. Pranks were common. Better to have a (relatively) safe vantage point.

"Hello, gents! And that includes you, Brandy," he said as he settled into the leather office chair he had bought for the dressing room. They'd all bought one, thinking they would run for quite a while longer based on their good reviews. But the theatre gods had other plans and now none of them knew how they would get the damn chairs home. "What's the word? How are we feeling?"

Silence. No one turned to acknowledge him. No nods or grins. Not even a middle finger, which would have been almost as common and meant with affection (he thought). He sat down, puzzled, on alert. Something was up. Suddenly, all three turned to him and simultaneously threw wet washrags. Nick hit him square on, Brandy hit the back of his head, and Stewart, not surprisingly, hit the wall behind and three feet above. No small feat given that room was so cramped there was barely room to swing a cat. But that was Stewart.

Sean wiped himself off, gathered the washcloths for later revenge, and said, "Well, glad to know tonight won't be much different from every other night. Bastards... and that includes you, Brandy." But the smile on his face was a signal that he was glad they would try to avoid the trap of being overly emotional all night. Hours to go before the curtain will fall. Better to hit each other with face-cloths in the meantime.

Just then, Ken entered with a cup of ice cream in one hand and a vase of congratulatory flowers in the other. Long and lanky, his physique belied his sweet tooth, and the others gave him grief for a metabolism that seemed patently unfair. He looked as if he'd been torn from the same book as Sean, but slightly different. Sandy, almost red hair, and pale green-grey eyes gave away his Celtic lineage. "What'd I miss?" he called loudly as the half-hour call came over the loudspeaker. Made it with no time to spare. As one, they all turned and threw a second wet washcloth in his direction with much more success this time. Sean used one of the ones he'd suffered to join in. Ken threw a hand up out of instinct and dropped his vase of flowers (protecting the ice cream, naturally).

Nick miraculously shot out a hand and caught the vase before it hit the floor. "Broadway ninja, baby..." He grinned as he placed the flowers on Ken's station.

As they finished their prep for the show, they listened to the stage manager calls count down the half hour. At the five-minute call, they together shouted, "These are the best of times," something their director had said to them on opening night all those months ago. Silently, they filed out of Dressing Room 9, down the stairs, and onto the stage to bid farewell to a big piece of their lives.

CHAPTER 3

The performance went off without a hitch. If the hundreds of shows over the last year (and then some) had ingrained it into their muscles, there was something extra tonight. A focus, an intensity, a collective energy that elevated the entire night. The audience, which included many regular attendees, responded in kind and the theatre was electric from start to finish. After the curtain had fallen, most remained onstage sharing hugs, smiles, tears, memories. Eventually the buzz subsided and slowly they drifted off to collect their things from the dressing rooms. An almost manic melancholy took hold along with a denial of the finality of what had just happened. Most, especially the younger company members, changed into their best night out clothes and focused on the party ahead. The Grumbles and the other veteran company members took a deeper breath in recognition of the fact that these opportunities come around rarely. Focusing on gratitude and days of leisure (read: unemployment) ahead, they too got changed and made their way to street level to bid farewell to the faithful fans who would be lining the street by the stage door. Tonight, they would sign autographs. Tomorrow, their neighbors wouldn't know who they were.

The Grumbles were the first ones out the stage door. They required far less primping than the stars and the youngsters who hoped to get a glam photo on one of the Broadway websites. The crowd erupted when they emerged. A few patrons quieted when they realized who they were, but overall, the bittersweet thrill of the night kept the cheers raucous. They worked their way from one end of the crowd. Sean used his phone to run the length of the line making a video of the crowd. They erupted in cheers as he passed them. It was unlike him, but he was determined to appreciate the night. He hadn't taken one day of this experience for granted and wouldn't start now. He stepped back and watched his castmates soak it in and grinned. Not bad for someone who had grown up in suburban Virginia and never had dreams beyond the local community theatre.

As the Grumbles gathered their bags and started out toward the restaurant where the closing party would be held, Sean said, "Hey guys, I'll catch up to you. I want to run back inside for a sec." The others acknowledged him and started down the street. Brandy paused just past the line, a normal New Yorker now, beyond the fans and the velvet ropes. She glanced back as Sean slipped back into the theatre. She grinned to herself, shouldered her bag, and turned into the night.

Sean knew the house and stage would be virtually empty by now. The crew was on a short break downstairs before they began striking the set. A new show was already lined up to come in, and Broadway landlords wasted no time on sentimentality. Time was money.

The house lights had been dimmed and the stage was awash only in the glow of the ghost light. Sean had always loved taking a moment to himself on the darkened stage after a show closed. The ghost light was a solitary light left atop a stand center stage at night when the theatre would otherwise be dark. Sean knew that the reason for it was very practical: to keep anyone staying late safe and prevent them from tripping over set pieces or falling into the orchestra pit. He preferred the more romantic explanations for the ghost light. Some argued that, because every theatre was rumored to have at least one ghost, the light was left on to appease those ghosts, allowing them to enjoy the stage to themselves at night and stop them from cursing the theatre and the living who had taken their place. Another belief was that they were meant to scare the ghosts away by denying them the darkened theatre.

Sean paused and stood in the pool of light. He breathed it in. He took a photo with his phone. This could be his last night on a Broadway stage, and he wanted to remember this moment. He closed his eyes and heard only the faint shouts of the crew enjoying a late-night meal in the basement and, closer, the echoes of over five hundred performances on these boards. Memories came unbidden, and as he opened his eyes, he could almost see them drifting past. He was convinced that ghost lights served more than just practicality. They were far too poetic for that. He turned slowly in a circle. The house was dark. How many patrons had watched them from the now empty seats? Which theatre ghosts had shared the space? Were they watching him now? The theatre, which had been filled with music and cheers just a short while ago now lay empty. A shell.

He began to sing one of his songs from the show quietly. He'd always heard that characters in musicals sang when their feelings became too powerful and speaking wasn't enough, and realized that it applied to him right now. Furthermore, he realized it was the first time he had ever sung on this stage purely for himself. No one listening. It felt good, and he relaxed into it, enjoying the sensation. Suddenly, it seemed the ghost light brightened, throwing its glow farther into the auditorium. He turned and was caught by the brightness of the bulb. He squinted. Then a movement on the far side of the light caught his attention. Had he imagined that? An elegant, sinewy woman, neither young nor old, seemed to shimmer on the far side of the pool of light. She had short strawberry-blond hair, wide, catlike eyes, a button nose turned up at the end. Her mouth was full, generous. Her face seemed to be floating in the air, but as his eyes adjusted, he realized she was dressed in black. And then his breath caught sharply. She was beautiful but otherworldly. She seemed to have arrived from another time. He'd never seen her before. She took a tentative half step into the light, and he thought he saw movement behind her.

"Sean, I'm sorry to startle you. I need to explain..." she said, in one of the most musical speaking voices he'd ever heard. "We've been thinking it's time you see us."

The stage door rattled as someone shook it to reenter the theatre. Apparently, Paolo had locked the door after Sean had come back. He turned to the noise, then immediately back to the stage. She was gone. He stood for a long while, watching, waiting. Wondering if he had imagined it. Finally, he turned slowly away and headed toward the door. As he reached it, he thought he heard the single word, "watch." But when he looked back, the ghost light stood alone, holding the darkness at bay.

He left through the stage door. The air was brisk, and the street had cleared for the most part. The diehards lingered, hoping to catch cast members they may have missed. Sean didn't have the heart to tell them that most of them had left through a different door to get to the party quicker. He spent extra time taking photos and chatting with anyone who was still there. He went through the motions, but his mind couldn't let go of what he had experienced with the ghost light. Had he really seen that? Or was his imagination running away with him in the swirl of emotions that the show's closing was stirring? He stayed until the last fans had drifted away, but his thoughts remained elsewhere, replaying what he had witnessed. Unsettled didn't even begin to cover how he was feeling. Finally, he quietly slipped past the stanchions onto the sidewalk, pulled his collar up against the brisk October breeze, and disappeared down the block, anonymously merging with the other pedestrians.

He checked his phone for the address of the party. A restaurant he'd never heard of before. Not surprising. The Grumbles had a very short list of spots where they spent most of their nights out and their preferences were usually more low key than the rest of the company. Sure enough, he arrived at the address, saw no name above the door but did see a velvet rope with a doorman clutching a guest list in his hand and wearing a look on his face that somehow said both "don't mess with me" and "I enjoy being the gatekeeper to pseudo-celebrities but am far too cool to let you see that." Quite an accomplishment. Sean pointed to his name on the list, received a dubious glance from the doorman who clearly disapproved of his decidedly untrendy outfit, and passed inside where he was greeted by a dimly lit interior that forced him to squint, a small dining room of white tableclothed tables that sat mostly empty but for everyone's personal belongings—bags, jackets, the odd flower arrangement—being taken home from the theatre. A burst of noise from the back of the restaurant led him to where you will find most company members at parties of this nature everywhere—the bar. In the bar area, one wall was lined with tables holding buffet dish after buffet dish. What looked to have been a decent spread now stood nearly empty. Food went lightning fast at these affairs. Sean had been prepared for this. The actors rarely got much, if any, food because they took the longest to change and arrive. The glamour.

The Grumbles were holding court at the bar, exactly where he'd expected to find them. Almost all were drinking top shelf bourbon. This was an open bar on the producers' dime, after all. They'd spent the better part of the last year sampling different whiskeys after the show in the dressing room before they headed home. They knew what to order, and did so with fervor. Nick was the lone exception with a RumChata in front of him. It was a creamy liqueur that had been ordered as a joke and had become a favorite of Nick's. No one, not even Nick, could quite explain why. They had saved Sean a barstool and he dropped his bag on the floor as he sagged onto it and heaved a sigh. Brandy slid him a drink.

"Elmer T. Lee neat. We couldn't believe they had it. Open bar ends in fifteen, so get that down your neck and pick something else. We didn't manage to snag you any food. Actually, we didn't manage to snag ourselves any either. These damn parties... Where've you been?" She took a closer look at him and continued, "And what happened to you? You look even paler than usual."

Sean was having trouble focusing. He cleared his throat, tried to mutter a response, and found himself staring at the floor. He raised his glass absentmindedly to his friends in a silent toast and sipped his bourbon. "Damn, that's good," he muttered and downed the rest in one go. "Thanks, Elmer."

Brandy was still waiting impatiently for an answer, and as the drink brought some color back to Sean's face, she tried him again. "Seriously, you're freakin' me out a little. You OK?" she asked.

Sean was more successfully focusing now and responded, "Yeah... I'm OK. Just emotional saying goodbye to the theatre... It's a lot."

Brandy gave him a skeptical look. He shook his head slightly. She raised her hands in acknowledgement, an unspoken "here if you need me" and they turned to include the rest of the Grumbles.

Nick checked his watch and announced, "Nine minutes of open bar left. Make your last order a good one!" They each placed their orders, left generous tips for the bartender, and circled up. In solidarity, and acknowledgment of the occasion, they all ordered a fresh round of bourbons, even Stewart, who normally avoided the brown liquors, and Nick, who eschewed his beloved RumChata for the moment.

"To one helluva run, folks. Can't imagine a better group to share it with. There's no family like a show family. Once a Grumble, always a Grumble," Nick toasted, and they all raised their glasses in response.

"Grumbles forever," they all responded. Glasses clinked, eyes met pointedly over the rims, and they all drank. Stewart's face crumpled into a dried-apple collapse, evidence that he should have opted for his traditional margarita no matter the celebration.

They finished their drinks, replaying stories from the run of the show, until Ken leaned in and muttered, "Open bar is done. Let's go have the party we want."

They gathered their belongings, made heartfelt goodbyes, stopped by two of their stage managers, Timmy and Bekah, to let them know where they were going ("Culture, if you're in the mood"), and slipped out the front door. They met on the sidewalk in front as each was able to make their way through the crowd inside. Silently, they stood and let the sounds of the city wash over them. Things felt different. THEY felt different. It wasn't just being unemployed. Every actor experienced that and had learned to accept it or moved on to other endeavors. This was the loss of a chosen family. Knowing that this big, messy, improbable group of people would likely never be together again. They turned, almost as one, and all looked through the windows into the party, which carried on unabated.

"Shots?" Brandy almost whispered into the night air and just like that the moment passed. They turned and headed down the block, loosening ties, taking off jackets (Sean's finally made its way into his backpack), and generally breathing a sigh of relief that the worst, the inevitable, was through.

Eyes watched as the group headed west on the block. Most faded back into the shadows but two pairs, unaware of each other, separated themselves from the darkness and silently moved down the street after them, keeping a distance.

CHAPTER 4

Three short blocks later, the group walked down the few steps from street level into Beer Culture. This was more their speed. Homey, comfortable, honey-hued light bounced off the exposed wood and whiskey barrels that dotted the small space. Coolers of craft beer lined one wall (including "Grandpa's fridge," which was a vintage refrigerator holding nothing but beer your grandfather would have ordered. A Genesee Cream Ale always hit the spot, after all). Behind the bar was a selection of whiskeys, bourbons, and scotches. Everything a Grumble could ask for.

Paul Campanelli, bartender extraordinaire, made a beeline toward them as they settled into their usual corner. He knew them all well. Not only did he manage and bartend the unofficial Broadway bar, but he had also become one of the foremost fans of Broadway. He saw and loved everything and his genuine affection for the shows and people who made them endeared him to each and every one of them.

"Well, well, well," he called as he approached. "Welcome gents. I include you in that, Brandy." She nodded in appreciation. "Congrats on an amazing run. Sorry it's ended, but glad it happened. First shot is on me." The Grumbles made the appropriate noises of gratitude and commiseration.

Six shot glasses appeared on the bar and Paul joined them all in a toast. The whiskey was good, but not too good. And the pour was generous, but not too generous. In a word, just right.

A steady stream of well-wishers stopped by the group to express condolences and congratulations. Some were company members of other shows who knew their time would come, too. Some were bar regulars who had gotten to know them. Some were Broadway fans, commiserating on the loss of a show that they loved. The entire ecosystem of live entertainment was on full display—the workers who made their living there, the businesses that profited from that work, the patrons who helped keep them all employed. The entertainment circle of life.

The door to the street blew open and a massive figure stood silhouetted in the light from the street. Well over six feet and broad, the shadowed figure took a step into the room, shouted "Shots!" and let out a Big Sky-sized laugh. Dan Trout had arrived. A Montanan in NYC, he looked the part. He was wearing work jeans (the kind that had seen actual work), a plaid shirt, work boots (the kind that had seen actual work), and a faded John Deere baseball cap. His face was lined and weathered from time in the great outdoors. He wore a mustache that was flirting with the term "handlebar" but stopped just shy of being labeled. His eyes were bright, kind, mischievous. He also had been on Broadway more than anyone else in the bar. Twenty-one shows and counting. His Jameson and lager were on the bar before he reached it, but before he drank, he slapped every Grumble on the back and gave them congratulations.

The Grumbles shouted "Trout!" in unison, and hooked their index fingers just inside their cheeks.

"Gents, and I include you in that, Brandy, condolences, congratulations, commiserations—all the appropriate 'C' words to you. Helluva run. We've all been through this before; hopefully we'll all go through it again. To taking the road less traveled! Even if it means frequent unemployment, heartbreak, no stability, and a hard time getting a mortgage." With that, he downed his whiskey and followed it with a healthy pull off his can of lager.

"You suck," said Brandy. "You're right, but you still suck."

"To sucking!" Trout cried, and the group laughed and took a drink.

And so, the night progressed. Many drinks were had, more than Sean had planned, but in reality, it was always going to be this way. Very few tears were shed, most by Ken, and many stories were remembered. By 1:30 a.m., the group was losing steam and Sean decided to call it a night. He accepted the grief the group threw at him, knowing full well they would all be headed home within a few minutes. He motioned to Paul for his tab, but Paul just shrugged his shoulders and motioned that there was none. Sean approached him, "No way, Paul. We had a big night. You can't just put it all on the house."

"I'd love to claim credit for that, but the woman at the end of the bar picked up your tab. Just yours, don't let those other mucks get any ideas..."

"What woman?" he asked as he scanned the rest of the room.

"End of the bar. Blond hair. Black dress," Paul replied.

"I don't see anyone," Sean said.

"Right there..." Paul began as he turned to point her out and stopped mid-sentence. "Huh. Weird. She was right there. Last stool. Looks like she took off. Fan of the show maybe?"

Sean shook his head. It had been a long, stressful night and it was catching up to him. "Well, I'll pay it forward somehow. And let me know if you see her again. I'll have to return the favor if I can."

He left a generous tip on the bar. Paul saw it and shook his head, but Sean insisted. "Hey, take it now while you can. This is my last employed day for a while." He shot a more meaningful look at Paul and said, "Thanks, my friend," then moved to the group. He said his goodnights and they all promised to meet for drinks in a few days. They each hoped the others meant it.

Brandy pulled him to one side. "You call me if you need me. Even if it's just to talk. I can see something is up," she told him.

"I promise. I will," he said. And with that, he headed for the door, breathed deeply, told himself to keep it together, and was gone.

The street felt empty. Emptier than a NYC street should be, and his city sense sent out a warning. NYC felt safest when the mass of humanity was around you. He hailed a cab back to Astoria and home, trying to shake the feeling that danger was near. He almost texted the gang inside telling them to be careful but shrugged it off. The cab was likely the last indulgence of its kind until he found another job. One last fringe benefit of a Broadway job for himself before tomorrow, when he would buckle down, watch the pennies, and get to finding new work.

Ten minutes after Sean made his exit, the rest of the group sheepishly agreed it was time to call it a night. Even Trout, the most recent arrival, was sagging after doing his best to catch up with the others' drink total. They gathered on the street after saying their goodbyes.

"I don't think it's really hit me yet," said Stewart.

"Yeah. Probably tomorrow about 7:30 p.m. when I'm still sitting at home, it may sink in," replied Nick.

Ken tutted at them and announced that he was "Excited to take some time off, smoke a bowl or three, and find the next big show. Suck it up, boys! That includes you, Brandy." She grunted her acknowledgement, but clearly did not share the sentiment.

"OK. I'm off. Time for me to turn into a pumpkin," Trout muttered, and they broke for home with promises of a beer together soon.

Stewart and Brandy lived in the same building in Manhattan, so headed west on Forty-fifth Street together. The others all lived in NJ, as many actors did to keep costs down. Trout headed south. Nick tagged along, although they would part ways in a few blocks. Ken paused, watched them all depart, and decided "no time like the present" and pulled out a prop cigarette hollowed out and filled with pot. He lit up and began his walk to Penn Station and the train that would take him home. He was in no rush, as he'd timed his exit wrong and had just missed a departure. The pot did its job quickly and he felt any residual anxiety slip away as he began his walk. "Hey," he thought to himself, "change is good. Big things coming my way..." He didn't notice that the shadow in one doorway seemed darker than any others. And he definitely didn't see it detach itself from the building and move silently after him.

The eyes burned. The eyes hungered. The eyes followed the lanky figure loping down the street and moved, answering the irresistible instinct.

The night caught up with Sean as he sat alone in the back seat of the cab. All the emotion, tension, celebration, and heartache finally overtook him. He almost fell asleep listening to the rhythmic thump of the tires as they crossed the Queensborough Bridge but focused on the in-car video screen and watched a clip from the local news. Something about his show closing came on, and he turned the volume off. Enough of that. He made it home and through the front door, but barely. He managed to kick off his shoes before he fell onto the sofa, and that's all he managed. He fell into a deep sleep, disturbed only by perplexing dreams of strangers and a woman in black, and violence. Then the dreams stopped, and he knew nothing more until the sounds of a city morning woke him the next day.

CHAPTER 5

Morning arrived quicker than he wanted. Light streamed in through the window and caught him square on the face. That's what he got for falling asleep on the couch. He opened his eyes and was blinded by a combination of the bright sunlight and the dull ping in his head from the last drink. Or three. He closed his eyes again and let himself just be. Nowhere to go today, so why not. Nowhere to be any time ever, as of this moment. He settled deeper into the cushions on the sofa and stretched, feeling a sharp but gratifying crack from his stiff neck. He took a huge yawn and happily breathed deeply the smell of freshly brewed coffee. Always a favorite and much needed this morning of all mornings. Coffee... How could there be coffee? He hadn't gotten up yet...

His head cleared instantly, and his eyes flew open. On the coffee table in front of him was a cup of coffee and two Advil. He could see the steam rising from the mug, so this wasn't something he'd done the night before and forgotten there. He half sat up. Was still. Listened. Nothing. Silence.

"Good morning, Sean. I thought it was time we met," came a female voice from behind the sofa. Sean whirled around, nearly falling off the couch, heart hammering in his chest. And there she was. The woman from the ghost light the night before. Sitting in the easy chair to the side of his sofa. Suddenly he thought of the woman Paul had described who'd paid his tab. It fit. He clutched a throw blanket to his chest.

"Who are you? How did you..." he said as he checked the front door. It was still locked and chained. A quick glance at the window showed it to be down and latched. There was no other way into the apartment. How had she...?

"I'm sorry for the surprise, Sean. I have been trying to get your attention for some time and, frankly, matters have become more urgent in the last few hours. I was out of alternatives. Please, trust me. I'm not here to hurt you. In fact, I need your help. Badly. But first, have some coffee, swallow your pills, and take a deep breath."

"Lady, I have no idea who you are or how you got in, but if you don't get the hell out of my apartment, and now, I'm calling the police. I don't want any trouble. Just... get out!" he exclaimed, his voice rising throughout. He felt panic setting in.

"Breathe, Sean," she said, and her voice again sounded musical and calm. Sean noticed a slight lilt that reminded him of his time spent in Ireland long ago. And she sounded... familiar? "We've met before last night. Many times. Our paths have crossed and not by chance. And a time has come that requires something of you."

"Look, I have no idea what you're talking about. I've never seen you before last night. I don't know what you're after, but you won't get it from me. For the last time, go!" he said. But some of the panic had seeped out of his voice and he paused, something niggling in the back of his brain.

Her catlike eyes were bright blue, the brightest and most piercing he could ever remember seeing. And deep. Ageless but kind. Her generous mouth was curling up at the edges, not laughing or mocking, but with mirth, as if she knew things he didn't. She was dressed all in black. A short black jacket over a black shirt, with trim black pants and, incongruously, sturdy boots.

"I've been waiting for this for some time," she said. "And if you stop to really consider, I should seem known to you. We've circled each other for years."

"OK, you're starting to freak me out again. Please, just get out. I won't call the police. Just go..."

She remained perfectly still in the chair. Eyed him and sighed. Even that seemed melodic. "My name is Breena," she said quietly. "Does that seem as if you've heard it before? Be still and reflect, and I think you'll relax. We have so much to discuss."

And she was right. Something in the back of his mind responded to that odd name. Her tone and manner, so serene, put him at ease, and against all his instincts, he found himself responding to her. He settled back into the sofa, but now with muscles that were relaxing. He shouldn't feel safe. But he did.

"I've been with you for some time, Sean. You've seen me often but always fleetingly, until last night on the stage. I was the one who pulled you out of harm's way yesterday as you crossed the street. And yes, I paid your bill last night. I was there when you experienced your greatest loss, and helped you find your way home each time you felt lost after that."

He wanted to scream at her. Call her insane or a stalker. Rail at her until she left. But he couldn't, because what she said somehow resonated in him. Flashes of memories caromed through his mind. The hand on his shoulder yesterday. The times he felt desolate and some feeling of warmth or understanding took it away. And as he looked at her, he realized she had been there. He had seen her, often, but never retained the image. Never carried it beyond the moment. He called up memories of her passing on the street, in a crowd, on a bus, on an airplane, in an audience. Something in what she was saying echoed inside him. She had flung open parts of him that he never knew existed. It was terrifying. But somehow made perfect sense. His brow furrowed in confusion, he said simply, "Tell me."

And she began to speak. "I have known you for many years, but we've never spoken before last night. You've seen me often but don't remember. How can this be?" she asked, in response to the question forming on Sean's lips. "I ask you now to listen. I will be telling you things that make little sense to you. That you will disbelieve. But hear me through and listen openly... I belong to a race some call the Tuatha Dé Danann. We have also been called the Sidhe. Thousands of years ago we retreated from the world of man, your world, as we recognized that your numbers and aggression were soon to become overwhelming. There was treachery involved, but the decision to go was ours and ours alone. In your myths, we disappeared into the underworld. In others, we transitioned into what many cultures consider myths—fairies, leprechauns, elves, in Africa the Aziza, the Mayans called us Alux, the Vietnamese Tien. We were gifted with what your kind called supernatural power and used that, along with poetry, song, oration to create a balance, a relationship with the world around us. But we never truly retreated. We found a way to inhabit this world with you. We live in the places you don't perceive. Those lights that catch the corner of your eye, that movement just outside your sight. That sound you think you hear, but just barely. We've discovered places on the planet inaccessible to you, or over-looked, or simply unwanted, and taken them as our own."

Sean sipped his coffee warily, convinced that he would need to find a way to call for help soon. This woman, intriguing as she was, clearly needed help and he wanted to get her out before the situation became dangerous. He eyed the door. Still chained shut. His phone was in his backpack by the couch, but out of reach. She continued...

"Have you ever asked yourself why so many of your peoples have similar mythologies? Similar creatures, stories, horrors? Fairy tales that are identical but come from different parts of the globe? It's because they are all based in truth. In a history long lost to your collective memory. But while your kind forgot us, we remained. To watch over the beauty of the world. And to protect both the natural world, and in a way, yourselves. On the whole, your kind is younger, less wise, quicker to anger and destruction. We've sought a way to temper that. Balance it. And you. For the good of all."

Sean began to reach slowly for his bag and was surprised to find that it was now across the room. Well out of reach. She raised her eyes to him, almost with the expression of a disapproving parent who has caught a sneaky child. Strike that. That was *exactly* the look she gave him.

"Sean, please," she admonished. "I know this isn't easy. I know by your standards this all seems impossible. But silence that doubt and ask yourself if this rings true somewhere inside you. You've felt my presence even in the last few days, as I was close to you. A hand on your shoulder as you crossed the street, the feeling of someone watching you as you walked home, curtains swinging though there was no wind, a handprint in the steam on your mirror (you missed that one, by the way). How did I appear and disappear last night onstage? Paying your rather large, I might say, bill last night and leaving unseen? One or two of those things alone could be coincidence, but all of them? And now, look further back. We've lived on the periphery of mankind for centuries. It's been for the good of all. We even allowed you to demonize or infantilize us. Make us the objects of fear or children's fantasy tales. We allowed it because it kept everyone safe, in their places. Stop struggling, Sean. Listen to the parts of you you've ignored. For so long. We know you can. I know you can. It's why I'm here talking to you now."

From the depth of his backpack, Sean's phone began to ring. His favorite song, "One Last Drink" by a band called Enter the Haggis. Sean's head whipped around toward the phone and his hand began to reach for it. Breena gave the phone the merest glance and the ringing stopped. As Sean began to protest, she assured him, "Don't worry. It was the bartender from last night." Sean's mouth flopped open. Disbelief turning to... something else.

"Look, please just... go. I won't turn you in or anything. Just... leave me alone?" he asked.

"I didn't want to resort to this, but..." She disappeared from where she was sitting. One moment she was there, the next... gone. Sean turned to look behind him, to the sides. Nothing.

"What the hell," he muttered.

Suddenly, she was back. Sitting exactly where she had been. He tried to back as far away from her as he could, only stopping when he reached the arm of the sofa. She looked at him as if to say, *Believe me now?*

"I told you we could exist on the edges of your perception. Now you know I'm telling the truth." He nodded slowly, torn between fear and curiosity. "And now," she continued, "I expect you want to know why I'm here talking to *you.*"

"OK, that was a good trick. Or whatever it was. I won't say I believe you," he said. "Not yet. Maybe never. But... I can't seem to just dismiss you, and you'll be happy to know I'm no longer considering calling the police. At least for now. But yes, why on earth would you be here talking to me? I'm just a guy trying to survive in New York. Holding on, but nothing special. I'm just... here."

"Oh, Sean. That's partially why we're here. You are so much more than that. And so much more to us," she said, almost pleading for him to accept what she was saying. "First, I would hope that with a name like Sean Curley you know your family roots lie in Ireland."

He nodded.

"Historically, my people, the Tuatha Dé Danann, are most often placed there. And yes, we called that island home for some time. But we were spread wide across the lands. Your archeologists have found signs of us nearly everywhere. Most dating from four thousand of your years ago. In the Xinjiang province in China, they've discovered mummies with red hair from that time. In Egypt, the mummy of a nobleman named Yoya proved to have blond hair and even Nordic features. So did his wife. They were of us. I really wish they'd left him alone. By all accounts, he was very kind and deserved better. All of this is to say, the Tuatha originally had red and sometimes fair blond hair. What color is your hair, Sean?"

Quietly, he responded, "Red."

"That's right. Red. The Tuatha having relationships with ancients of your kind was not uncommon. Some amongst us believe that those of your kind with red hair are descended from these unions. Unproven, but there is some evidence. You're a well-read and curious man, Sean. I'm sure you know some of the unique characteristics those you call 'gingers' possess?"

"Yes," he responded in a quieter voice. "A few. I know it's rare. Very rare. I know we are more resistant to anesthesia. I found that out the hard way having my wisdom teeth out... I know we sunburn more easily. Obviously."

"More than rare, less than two percent of your population are gifted with it. And what color are your eyes, Sean?" She asked.

"Blue," he muttered.

"Yes, blue. The rarest of the rare. Less than one percent of your people have that color combination. Many think it's a sign of an ancient link to the Tuatha. At the very least, to royalty of some kind. Further, redheads need less sunlight. You actually produce your own Vitamin D, I believe you call it. It seems more than a coincidence that my people retreated underground (as the ancient stories go), or into caves as we removed ourselves from our interaction with you, and you yourself would seemingly thrive in that environment. Also, you sense temperature more keenly than others of your kind."

"You know an awful lot about this..." he said.

"Well, we've been interested in you for some time. And I wanted to be prepared. You store your collective knowledge in your technology," she said with a nod toward his phone. "We evolved differently. Our collective knowledge is more organic. We've shared this knowledge, these stories, for millennia. We simply... know."

"That sounds a lot simpler than what we've done."

"We're mythical to you, but we live in the same world. We've accumulated knowledge at the same rate. We just share it more directly."

"Of course. I didn't mean to..." he backtracked quickly.

She laughed and it was the most carefree sound he'd heard in a very long time. "To sum up, you have some sort of link to us and we to you. Likely we'll never know exactly what, but something is there. But you, Sean, specifically, have even more in common with us."

"Oh, good," he whispered. "I definitely want to hear more about this."

"Sean, what do you do for living?" she asked.

"I'm an actor...?" he slowly replied.

"And a singer, I believe, yes?" she asked.

"Well, yes..."

"Did you notice earlier when I told you that some of our strength came though poetry and music?"

Sean nodded slowly, his head spinning with information and the desire to reject these fantasies she was throwing at him. But somehow... he couldn't just dismiss them.

"You make your living telling stories, singing, speaking heightened language. Music. Poetry. Using your gifts to move people. Enlighten them. Entertain them. Teach them."

"I think that's giving what I do far too much credit," he demurred. "Did you see my show?"

"Over forty times, Sean. It's no accident that I'm coming to you now," she told him.

"Forty times... OK, wow. Did not expect that... Did you see *Mamma Mia*? Not much enlightening going on with that one. Fun though," he quipped.

"Focus, Sean. There's still much to get through," she said, doing her best to hide a smile.

Appropriately chastened, he nodded, pursed his lips, and looked for all the world like an eight-year-old who'd just been scolded.

"In your people's ancient times, our closest allies among them were called Seanachies. They were storytellers, wise men and women who kept your history alive through words and music. That tradition is as old as your kind and seen all over the world. In Africa they were called griot, in Hawaii the tradition of hula, yes *that* hula, served to preserve the collective wisdom through word, music and movement. Sound familiar?"

"Partially," Sean said. "Again, I think you may be giving what I do a grander purpose than it gives itself."

"I think my favorite example, though, is the aboriginal population of Australia. Their wise people called their oral tradition dreamtime stories. They were sacred and passed from one generation to another. Do you really not see the similarities?"

"Well, I see some similarities, but I just don't think what I do is all that connected to what you're describing…"

"Your culture, such as it is, has certainly moved away from the idea of stories and storytellers as sacred, but that perception, or lack thereof, does not diminish the truth. Storytellers wield a special power, and always have."

"I'm not sure you'd feel that way if you saw a 10:00 a.m. children's matinee," Sean persisted.

"Actually, that's the perfect example. You may not know it in the moment, and your society may not give it the weight it deserves, but that is exactly how the collective wisdom is shared. Passed on. There is immense power in that."

"If you ever consider becoming a talent agent, let me know," Sean joked.

A stern look from Breena put a stop to his deflection. "Sean, given everything I've told you, from your past to your unique traits, to the path your life has taken… can you see why we have been led to you? How closely you lie to our historical ties with your kind? We have watched and debated amongst ourselves as to exactly who most closely we should approach. Who was the ideal person to contact? And this is the first deliberate contact we've had with mankind for many centuries. I need you to hear that. Accept that."

All right," he said. "You've got my attention. I still don't know *why* you're contacting me though. I mean, I'm appropriately confused. Intrigued. Possibly delusional. But I have to ask what you want from me. Because there must be something."

"Good, Sean," she responded. "You're starting to think. Move past the initial surprise. And you're right. We do need your help."

"Stop," he said. "Wait. I'm confused. Well, even more confused. You keep saying 'we,' but you're the only one here. Why, if there are so many of you out there, do I only have you here? Seems like more of you could have made the arguments faster, convinced me quicker…"

"We did debate that, Sean," she responded. "We decided that the shock of too many of us would be too much to begin with, but you're right. The situation does require more than just me. And I am not alone."

With a slight tilt of her head, she seemed to be signaling someone. Or something.

A faint rustle behind him jolted Sean upright, and he turned toward the noise. Four similar people emerged from the shadows of the room—two women and two men. All dressed similarly to Breena, in all black. All lithe, otherworldly. They were compact, but definitely not short. Wiry, muscular, confident. They stood in a loose semicircle behind the couch, their hands held loosely at their sides. All wore curious expressions and tipped their heads in deference to Sean, who leapt backward in surprise and nearly landed on Breena in doing so. Her hands shot out to steady him and he felt something like electricity at the thrill of it. He turned just as quickly to look at her again. There were questions, so many, that died in his throat before they found voice, and as he looked at her, he knew, somehow and beyond doubt, that what she said was true. And nothing would ever be the same again.

CHAPTER 6

And that is how, mere moments later, Sean found himself surrounded by creatures he didn't know existed when he woke that morning. In fact, he had actively disbelieved they existed. It was surreal now for him to see them perched about his small apartment. They clearly were uncomfortable here, being meant for wider open, more ancient places. They all seemed wary, exposed. They each introduced themselves.

First was Kallan, who most closely resembled Breena. Taller than the others and wiry, he projected a stolid, competent air. His eyes were deep blue, and serious, almost somber. Kallan's voice was deep and earthy, with a hint of a Scottish burr that evoked images of the Highlands. He was cautious in his words with Sean, who couldn't shake the impression that Kallan had far less confidence that Sean would be able to help them. Sean shared that lack of confidence.

Next came Odette, a small, compact, dark-haired female. Her features were razor sharp and her eyes a glittering emerald that seemed to take in every detail of the room and everyone in it. Her voice and bearing felt more Teutonic than Celtic. Her words were clipped and direct. To the point. No nonsense. Precise, disciplined, she gave the impression of deep concern and seemed coiled tightly as if ready to launch into action at any moment. She had an air of physical strength and a willingness to use it. Sean made a note to do all he could to stay on Kallan's and Odette's good sides.

Alara was next, and she also seemed physically different from Breena. Shorter and with an olive complexion, the blackest of hair, and eyes which were a bright golden brown. Her voice fell on the room like a sprinkle of rain, and Sean felt instantly at ease with her. More than that, he felt safe and full of confidence and potential. She seemed kind, beautiful, generous. She clipped her words, he noticed. And there were rolled *r*'s and flattened vowels. Sean had no frame of reference for this, but to his ear she sounded more Eastern than the others.

Last, Breena introduced Bayard, the only one of the group whose hair came somewhat close to Sean's ginger, although it was more chestnut or auburn. Bayard had an open carelessness about him and a coltish energy that gave the impression he could dash off in any direction at any time. He seemed full of good nature and humor, but not quite as reliable as the others, as if he wouldn't turn down the opportunity for a joke or prank. His voice and manner were more florid, expressive. He would be at home in a Parisian café late at night, debating the merits of Proust and Camus or Jerry Lewis over an absinthe. The twinkle in his eye was more mischievous than the one in Breena's. Sean instantly liked him and wasn't exactly sure why.

They all had clear distinctions, seeming to hail from different parts of the world, but somehow, they also seemed similar. Connected. Not through their clothes or vocabularies, but through a certain sensibility. They seemed timeless, assured. The one thing they definitely did *not* seem was from New York City in this day and age.

Introductions out of the way, Kallan stepped forward and took control of the conversation. Sean was a bit taken aback by this, as his first contact had been with Breena, and he thought of her as being the leader. He quickly realized, however, that there was no leader in the traditional sense. They all seemed able to finish each other's sentences.

"Sean," Kallan said, "thank you for opening your home to us." Sean noticed the slightest emphasis on the word "home" and felt just how small his apartment seemed with all of them in it. "Trust me when I say that we wouldn't put you in this position if we didn't think it was absolutely necessary." Somehow, although the words themselves were cordial, they seemed to imply that Sean was not a participant that he would have chosen to include.

Alara chimed in, "Which is not to say, Sean, that we aren't thrilled to meet you and include you. We very rarely interact directly with your kind. In fact, for most of us, this is a first. Our way, for thousands of years, has been to avoid you. To watch over the things we hold important, but give mankind a wide berth. Not because of any particular negativity, but rather more to keep the natural order of things." As she spoke, Sean felt himself put at ease. Any tension caused by Kallan's brusque words melted quickly.

"Thanks, Alara. I appreciate you saying that. Is it OK if I call you 'Alara'? It seems almost presumptuous under the circumstances. Is that appropriate?" he asked, glancing around the room to include them all in his question. He received slightly bowed heads in response and took that as permission.

As he scanned the room, he became acutely aware of some of the more ridiculous mementos scattered around the apartment: a munchkin skull cap from a show he'd done years ago, a stuffed camel his father had brought him from a trip overseas, an Abraham Lincoln puppet he had used on a web series he'd created... Lord, how must he look to these graceful, powerful, otherworldly creatures? What a silly person he was.

He continued, somewhat abashedly, "So... have you all been watching me? Hovering in my... peripheral vision? Is that how this works? Also, I have no idea *why* you need me. What's happened, and what can I possibly offer to you in any kind of circumstance?" The questions tumbled out of his mouth almost unbidden. He was feeling overwhelmed. His senses accepted the beings sitting with him in the room, his mind trying mightily to reject their existence. This simply couldn't be.

"Sean, we know this is a lot. Just relax. Let us lead you through some things and I promise it will begin to make sense," Breena said as she reached to Sean and placed a hand lightly on his upper arm. He instantly felt relief—less anxiety. He noticed that Alara had picked up the stuffed camel and was absentmindedly petting it. The sheer absurdity of the entire situation crashed over him, and he sagged deeper into the cushions. He felt exhaustion, disbelief, surrender... and he let out a small, choked sound that was part laugh, part grunt.

Odette leaned forward in her seat and locked eyes with Sean. "Yes, Sean, at some point recently, we've all been near you. Watching you, looking out for you. Making sure you were ready to meet us and help. You've felt us, surely. One thing has become clear and that is that you are more attuned to us than most. Breena was the first one to notice and she has argued your case to us since. We agree. She was correct," she said.

"If you weren't all here speaking to me and so... bright and somehow inspiring, I'd think that was the creepiest thing I've ever heard. Creatures—people—that lurk in my periphery watching me, impacting my life." Sean said and noticed that Bayard was doing his best, and failing, to hide a grin. "But you're here. I can't deny that. My very own Peripherals here to look over me while also judging me. Awesome."

"Those thoughts are understandable. This is an unprecedented situation. But, Sean, something is happening. The natural order that we work to maintain has shifted, somehow," Kallan said earnestly. "And we don't think it's by chance. We believe, for the first time in our collective memories, that someone, or something, is intentionally disrupting things in a way that will endanger both our people and your own."

Bayard leaned in and spoke for the first time. "Sean, our elders felt the danger was serious enough to form a team—us—to get to the bottom of this. The more we learned, the more it became clear we would need help from you. Your kind. They empowered us to approach you to ask for that. Yes, we watched you. Yes, we may have interfered. For your own benefit. No, we did not judge you. Much." There was that grin again.

"So, you are… what? The best Peripherals there are, sent out to right the world? Like… Peripheral superheroes?" Sean said, trying to pass it off as a joke but genuinely trying to understand what the hell was going on here.

Bayard laughed loudly at that and flopped backward in his chair, earning a disapproving look from Kallan and Odette as Alara hid her mouth behind the plush camel and tried in vain to keep her shoulders from shaking with the laugh she was holding inside.

"Oh, my new friend, Sean, you have the wrong end of the stick there. We are the ones our elders deemed most expendable. We've been sent in a desperate effort that's not expected to succeed while the elders prepare our people for a full-on assault from… what we don't know. If we are, as you call us, Peripherals, we are the most peripheral of all of them. Those who would be missed the least if, as is expected, we fail."

Sean sat digesting this latest bit of information. "Great. So, what you're telling me, hard as it is to believe from looking at you, is that I've been sent a team of *Star Trek* red shirts to try to save the world with…"

He was greeted with blank stares. All except Odette, who quickly leaned in and said, "I very much enjoy that program. And yes, you have the right end of the stick now. We are, as you say, red shirts." Sean couldn't help but smile.

"But we were also the only ones who were willing to risk ourselves to help your people. The rest of our kind have written you off as lost. We'll do what we can to prove them wrong," said Breena.

"We think you're worth saving. Even more, that you may hold the solution."

As Sean sat back, trying to make sense of what he was hearing, the silence was broken by the ping of his phone signaling a message. Sean turned to Breena and raised his eyebrows, asking if he could answer it now. She nodded and replied, "No need to ask us for permission, Sean. We're the ones unexpectedly in your home."

"Good point," he muttered as he retrieved the phone from the front pocket of his backpack and checked to see who had called. He was surprised to see it had indeed been Paul, the bartender from the night before. He shot a quick glance at Breena. How had she known? Sean listened to the message and his brow creased as he did. He hung up and turned to the others. "It was Paul, the bartender from last night. He found Ken's backpack down the block last night after closing. No phone in it, but Ken's not answering. He's trying to track him down. Seems odd. He usually lights up a hit on his way home, but this seems out of the ordinary, even for him." Sean tried to call Ken himself, but it went straight to voicemail.

The others shared a look between themselves, and Kallan told Sean to try Ken's wife, Anne. When Sean expressed surprise that they knew his wife's name, Kallan said, "Ken was another candidate that we observed. His late-night proclivities made him a bit too risky in our eyes. He shares many of the qualities that attracted us to you."

"In fact," continued Breena, "it was more than just his late-night habits that led us away from him and toward you. You, Sean, despite putting on a seemingly stoic business-as-usual attitude, feel things more keenly. Even more so with the closing of your show. Your emotions, and those of your friends but especially yours, are raw right now. More exposed. The veils that conceal them are thinner. Walls that you have constructed are slipping. Some would see that as something to exploit. We think it brings you closer in alignment to us. Empathy is powerful, when controlled."

"Yes," Kallan interjected. "It's no coincidence that something is stirring now when this work of yours has completed. Emotions are high, true, but you are also out of the public eye, at least temporarily. It could be days before you were missed. Other than amongst your friends."

"And," Alara spoke, "the time of year is no coincidence. We are near Samhain. A time when the physical and spiritual worlds are nearest. We are entering what many call the dark half of the year. Someone is trying to take advantage of these things."

Shaking his head at even more new and confusing information, Sean called Anne at the O'Carroll's home number. She answered before the second ring. "Hi, it's Sean. Paul at Beer Culture found Ken's bag last night but hasn't gotten through to him to let him know. Can you just let him know they have it at the bar?"

There was a lengthy pause as he listened to her response. The color drained from his face and he replied, "OK, I'll check with the guys. Maybe he just had one too many and crashed with one of them. I left first, so I wouldn't know."

Another silence as he listened, and the remaining color drained from his face. "Oh. OK, I'll call Paul and let him know. I'll get the guys to meet there as soon as we can manage. I'm sure there's a logical explanation..." He sounded unconvincing even to himself and rang off with a promise to call back soon.

He put the phone down and looked at his visitors. "Ken never came home last night. Anne can't get in touch with him. His phone must be turned off because she tried the Find Your Phone App and it didn't work. You all know what that is, right? Find Your Phone?" They all but rolled their eyes in response and Breena said, "Yes, Sean, we know. We're not stuck four thousand years in the past. We're well up on your technology and how best to make use of it."

"Great," Sean continued. "That makes things easier. Anne has also texted the others and no one has seen him since they left last night..."

Kallan and Odette stood, glanced at each other, and disappeared. Where they had been standing was empty. Sean's mouth opened to say something, but no words came, and he looked in surprise at the others.

"You'll get used to it," Bayard said. "Won't even notice in a few days."

Breena looked to Sean with concern. "Kallan and Odette are the most skilled at tracking and dealing with physical threats. They'll find Ken. It's possible this is just a simple misunderstanding, but my fear is that this is the first sign that our worries were correct. If we've been watching you and Ken, others likely were also. In which case…"

"In which case, this could be very bad news," Sean said. The concern on the faces of the others was all the reply he needed. He picked his phone up, checked his text messages, and started feverishly responding to a thread from his fellow Grumbles. "My friends and I are on our way to see if we can help. Is there anything you can tell me? Anything that will help us? Anything I should look for or look *out* for?"

"We don't know the nature of any threat, as of now, so we don't know what to look for ourselves. But we're not without resources. Meet your friends and know that we'll be nearby working as well."

"Nick was able to trace the missing phone's last movements. Apparently, it was shut off in Central Park. There's no reason Ken would have been in Central Park last night."

With that, Alara and Bayard stood and disappeared as well. Sean shook his head slightly and turned to Breena, who said, "That is not good news, Sean. They are on their way now to look. I will stay close to you. If something has happened to your friend, it could happen to you. Apparently, our work has not gone unnoticed. Just know that I'll be near. Meet your friends, and then let's find Ken."

CHAPTER 7

One hour later, Sean walked toward the front door of Beer Culture. It was hours before they would open, but he could see Paul setting up inside and he knew the bartender was really there to help with Ken. He saw Brandy and Stewart as well, sitting at the bar drinking waters and frenetically checking their phones. Nick was coming back in from New Jersey, so he would be the last to arrive.

Sean tapped on the door and Paul hustled over to let him in. He went to the bar and sent a questioning look to Brandy and Stewart, but their grim faces told him that there was no new information.

"Did anything happen after I left last night?" he asked.

Both the others shook their head and Stewart responded, "It was business as usual. We left just a few minutes after you. All went our own way. The last I saw of Ken he was lighting up and headed home. Absolutely nothing out of the ordinary." Brandy nodded to back him up.

Sean turned to Paul and asked, "Paul where did you find his bag?"

Paul lifted Ken's backpack from behind the bar and placed it by

Sean. There was no mistaking it for Ken's. It was black with a black HBO logo stitched into the side. Noticeable but not garish. Classy. A gift for an episode of a TV show Ken had done for them. "It was about two-thirds of the way to the end of the block headed west," Paul said. "It was at the foot of one of the trees by the curb. Not open or anything. Just looked like it was dropped there."

"Thanks, Paul. Glad you spotted it. Anyone object to me having a look inside?" Sean asked. He unzipped the large front pocket and looked inside. "Nothing unusual. AirPods, charger, pens, pad of paper, script..."

"Over a year into the run and he still didn't know his lines," Brandy quipped.

"True, but his ad libs make us laugh harder than just about anything else that happened onstage," Stewart replied.

"Guys, no phone, no keys, no fake cigarette. But his AirPods are still here, so he probably wasn't robbed," Sean said.

Nick came tapping at the front door and Paul let him in. "Anything?" he asked, but was answered with a somber shaking of heads. "I haven't gotten hold of Trout yet. I'll keep trying. Well, the last hit I got on Ken's phone was from just inside the park. I say we head there."

The Grumbles gathered their things and headed toward the door. Sean turned to Paul before they left. "Paul, we can't thank you enough. Let us know if he shows up here or you hear anything?"

"You know it, guys. I'll be here watching for anything. Let me know what you find," he replied.

They left the bar, turned west, and headed toward Ninth Avenue where they headed north toward Central Park. Seen noticed Breena on the opposite side of the street mirroring them. As quickly as he spotted her, she was gone again. Somehow, though, it made him feel more confident knowing she was there.

As they walked, Stewart spoke up. "I'm sure there's a logical explanation, right? I mean, he could have been going up there to buy some more pot. Or...?" His voice trailed off, trying to find any other possibility.

"Well, anything is possible," said Brandy. "But if that were the case, we'd have heard from him. At least Anne would have. And I think he has his pot delivered to his house now. I just don't know. Getting a bad feeling, gang."

They walked on in silence for the next few blocks. They'd spent the last year experiencing some of the best the city had to offer, and it suddenly felt as if that bubble had burst and the reality of life in a metropolis like NYC was making itself known in a particularly harsh way.

They entered Central Park through the Merchants' Gate on the southwest corner, and immediately the sounds of the city started to slide away. A few yards in and it felt like they were in a different world altogether—lush greens, bird calls, and none of the bustle speeding past just steps away. Nick kept checking his phone to find the last location for Ken. Or at least his phone. He turned and looked from the screen to a copse just off the path as it headed northwest.

"There," he said and pointed. "Somewhere in there."

As they headed in that direction, Sean noticed all the Peripherals nearby. They seemed very alert and were keeping a close eye on the Grumbles as they approached the trees. None of the others seemed to notice their watchers and Sean wondered if they were able to see them at all or just so focused on finding Ken that it escaped them. They spread out as they approached the area, all looking downward hoping to find any trace of Ken. They moved slowly through the trees and if they attracted any odd glances from the park-goers around them, none of them noticed.

Suddenly Brandy gave a small cry and reached down at the foot of some shrubs. She stood up holding a keychain that displayed a picture of a marijuana leaf and the saying *It's Hard to Be Mean When You're Stoned*. "Found Ken's keys!" she shouted, and they all stopped to look. They slowly approached Brandy. A shaky silence settled between them as they all considered the implications.

"Not good, not good," said Nick.

They all looked to each other and agreed saying "Not good" in unison.

The finding of the keys seemed to add a sense of urgency to the searchers. The emergency felt somehow more real even amongst the idyllic setting of the park. As they spread out to continue looking for Ken's wallet or phone—or Ken—Sean drifted off on his own. He was hoping to see something of the Others who were also searching. Within moments, Breena appeared by him as if from nowhere. "We placed the keys where you and your friends would find them," she said. "They were deep in some brush, and it was unlikely you'd have found them on your own. We need your help in coordinating with your authorities. Obviously, we can't do that."

Sean spotted Alara beneath a nearby footbridge, examining the banks of a pond. Bayard was prowling near the entrance to the park, somehow managing to blink in and out as he paced the line of horses and their buggies waiting to take tourists on a ride through the park's highlights. Suddenly, Odette and Kallan materialized nearby and gestured briskly for Breena, and by extension Sean, to hurry to them. Sean quickly glanced behind him, but none of his friends had any idea about the Peripherals, too focused on the grounds near them and their friend who was clearly in danger.

Sean followed, behind a stand of trees and then in amongst the undergrowth. When he arrived, Odette was showing Breena an area where the greenery had been trampled close to the ground. An unnatural deep brown had seeped most of the vibrant life from the plants. It looked to Sean as if a large animal had nested there, but his city boy impressions were quickly dispatched when Odette said, "There was violence here. Violence not brought by humans." She lifted some of the leaves and showed traces of crimson drops scattered throughout from below. "Your friend was brought here and then spirited away. I have some thoughts on what did this but I have to keep looking to be sure. Sean—" she fixed a cold look on him "—this is very bad for your friend. Something of our world is interfering here and his chances diminish with each hour."

Alara appeared next to them suddenly. Sean started, thinking that it would be some time before he got used to this. If he ever did. "Wendigo," she whispered to the others and a chill fell amongst them.

"Wendigo?" Kallan responded. "Here? That makes no sense. In the city?"

Bayard was next to suddenly join them. Another start for Sean. "I have even worse news," he announced. "The horses are terrified. They tell of the Wendigo arriving last night. It brought your friend and met another creature here before they left at speed. They met a Dullahan."

The Peripherals all froze as Sean looked on in confusion. "Wait," he said. "What's a Wendigo? What's a Dullahan? What's happening?" His voice rose in volume and pitch with each question as his fear clashed with his confusion and ignorance. The stern looks on the faces around him set him back. What could possibly be so bad that it made *them* fearful? "What does this mean?"

"It means," Breena said, "that there was violence here that defies the natural order. An order we've been safeguarding for thousands of years. None of these things should be happening. Not here. The creatures who have taken Ken should not be here. Should not be together at all. It means none of us is safe, especially your friends. We must get them someplace else. They don't belong here. And we may have very little power to protect them if what we hear is true..."

"I'll talk to them and come up with a plan that gets them out of the way, but I have questions. Lots of them. We need to find Ken. And fast. I know that. But I need to know what we're dealing with here, and what use I can be..."

Breena nodded. "Of course. I'll answer all of your questions, but we need to move. I'll do it as we go. But we must get your friends to safety."

"Hey, gang!" Sean shouted to the Grumbles as the Peripherals blinked out of sight. They turned and approached him, seeming to sag in despair at having found nothing else to lead them to their missing friend. "Look, we're spinning our wheels here. He was clearly here but isn't now. I think we need to split up and cover more ground. Nick, what do you think about heading out to Jersey to talk with Anne, see if she has anything to add and, well, be there for her? She's tough, but even she could use a friendly face right now, I'm guessing." Nick looked as if he might protest, but nodded reluctantly.

"Brandy," Sean continued, "how about you go back to the bar. Talk to Paul, see if they have any cameras either inside or at the entrance. Maybe we can spot something on them? Maybe some of the other businesses on the block have cameras, also…"

"Good idea," Brandy responded. "I wouldn't have thought to check for cameras."

"I watch a lot of British mysteries. Probably too many," he responded.

"And bold move sending me to a bar. I accept that assignment." Her attempt at banter felt hollow, but the guys mustered a tense chuckle.

"Stewart," Sean said, "you live in Midtown. Head to the precinct and see if you can get the cops to look into it. Ken's a grown man and it's been less than a day, but maybe we can convince them to take an interest given what we've found. Worth a try?"

Stewart nodded. "I actually have a couple of friends there from Margarita Mondays at Arriba Arriba. I'll see if I can get them on board."

"Why am I not surprised at all about that?" Brandy said. "And what are *you* going to do, mastermind?" she asked, turning to Sean.

"I'll stay here. Keep looking and show Ken's picture to people and see if anyone has spotted him. Not likely, I know, but someone might have noticed something out of the ordinary."

"Um… guys," Nick interjected, "Ken's phone just pinged. It's turned on and it's in… Staten Island?"

The group turned to him in confusion.

"I'm absolutely sure that Ken has never stepped foot on Staten Island," Brandy said. "I'd be surprised if any of us has."

"I have," Sean said. "I dated someone from there."

"Ah, yes," Nick said. "The fetching and elusive Jenny Blevins."

"Short-lived in your life, but forever in our hearts," quipped Brandy.

"Yes, ha, ha," said Sean. "She's a nice girl. Sorry it went the way it did. And don't call her Jenny. She hates that."

"Crap," Nick said. "The phone's off again. Only on for a minute or two."

"OK," Sean said. "Change of plans. I'll head to Staten Island and check out where the phone pinged. Probably someone just found and took the phone, but it's a lead. If I can't find the phone, maybe I can find someone who knows about it."

"Best-case scenario is you find Ken in a blissful pot-induced haze trying to figure out how he got there," Brandy said.

The group agreed. The reappearance of a signal from the phone had given them some energy. Something to act on and they were rallying.

"Nick, can you send me the coordinates that you just got? Actually, just send me the Find Your Phone info directly so if it turns on again, I can react faster."

"You got it," Nick said. "Oh, and say hi to Jenny for us."

"Very funny. Let's keep each other posted?" Sean asked.

All in agreement, they headed out of the park with a renewed sense of purpose. Sean headed toward the Columbus Circle station to catch the 1 train and none of his friends seemed to notice as the Peripherals joined him silently one by one as he walked. In fact, no one seemed to notice the group moving together with grim determination. Sean held his questions, although they were fairly bursting out of him. Time enough for that on the train, but he had to get to Staten Island as quickly as possible. One thing was clear to him. Something beyond his understanding was threatening one of his friends. He was damned sure he was going to do anything he could to get him back.

CHAPTER 8

The cacophony of the city struck them viscerally as they emerged from the park. Car horns, the rush of traffic, the constant hum of voices, and the occasional wail of a siren settled onto them. The Peripherals flinched in reaction. As they walked, Kallan and Alara not so much blinked out of sight as slid. One second, they were there, the next their absence was enough to make you doubt your own senses.

Sean glanced a question at Breena who said, "They are going ahead. They will arrive much faster on their own. The rest of us will ride with you. We won't leave you alone. Not now."

"But if you can get there faster, you should go," Sean pleaded. "You may be able to help Ken if you all are there."

Breena shook her head. "We don't yet fully know what to expect. This could be a feint to get us to rush off, leaving you vulnerable. That phone alert from Staten Island makes me suspicious. It's either a ruse or a trap. That was no accident."

Sean nodded. "It struck me as odd, too. What about my friends? Are they safe on their own?" he asked.

Odette, from Sean's other side, responded, "They should be fine.

We never considered approaching them, so once they're out of your orbit, and Ken's I suppose, they should be safe. I'll be monitoring their situations just to be safe, but our resources need to be focused on protecting you and finding your friend." With that, she slid farther back, leaving Breena next to him. Bayard took a position on his other side, thrumming with energy and eyes alert to anyone who passed close by.

"When we reach the train, I'll answer your questions. Until then, keep alert. Even though you may not always see the others, they're with us," Breena said as she picked up their pace.

The crowd in Columbus Circle kept a New York pace, meaning keep up or get out of the way. They wove their way to the top of the station's stairs and headed down. Immediately, they were hit with a burst of hot, stale air, moist with subterranean steam and filled with odors that were best left unidentified. Sean couldn't help but see the Peripherals falter at the unnaturalness that assailed them. For the first time, he saw them out of their element and felt, somehow, deep inside that the cement and steel city around them demanded a painful price from them. This was not their place and it showed.

The train arrived not long after, and Sean led them to the first car, explaining that it would let them out nearest the ferry exit. "I assume we'll take the ferry?" he asked. Breena said that they would and led him to one of the two seat benches at the front of the subway car, as far from the other riders as they could get. Bayard and Odette drifted to other seats on the train, keeping an eye both on the other riders and through the window in the front of the train. They were on edge, and even with them seeming uncomfortable and out of place in the confined space, Sean felt completely safe under their protection. He just needed to know what they were protecting him *from*.

"OK," Sean began. "Talk to me. "What's a Wendigo? What's a… Dullahan? What have they done to Ken and why are you all so surprised and on edge?"

"Sean, this has been a day full of shocks for you. I'm afraid you need to prepare for some more. A lot more, actually," she responded.

Sean's chin fell to his chest, he took a deep breath, then raised his face to her and said, "Tell me everything."

The lights of the subway tunnel flashed by as the train made its way south. Sean always thought of the boat ride in the Willy Wonka movie when he was on the train like this. This time, the crazed manic scene from the film hit a little too close to home as Breena sat next to him and began to speak.

"Sean, you've done remarkably well in adjusting to what we've told you, so far," she began and earned a dubious look from him in response. "No, you have. Your openness is one of the things that drew us to you and you're proving our trust to be well placed. I've told you of our people, the Tuatha, and how we retreated from contact with your kind so long ago. While we're spread across the earth, we are predominantly known in the Celtic histories and to some extent in Western Europe. But cultures around the world have their own unique what you would call mythologies. Some creatures are specific to a place or region while others appear in similar forms across numerous histories. The Sasquatch, Yeti, and Bigfoot are the same creatures but seen through the lens of different human cultures. Does that make sense to you?"

"I mean... if I can get past the part where you're telling me that Bigfoot is real? Yes, I can understand how different cultures would have different names and stories of similar creatures... Wait. So, you're saying Bigfoot is real?" Sean repeated.

"Nearly all such creatures, where seen across multiple histories and geographies, are rooted in some kind of truth. Don't worry about the Sasquatch. Basically, peaceful and shy. They rarely come into contact with any of us, let alone you. Now, if they ever ran afoul of lycanthropy or were zombified, that would be a problem. Not likely, though."

Sean was trying so hard to keep his face neutral, but inside he was excited and dumbfounded. "OK," he said softly. "What else? Say... Loch Ness Monster?"

Breena laughed and it sounded like water burbling down a stream. "Of course, she's real. We often wonder how your people ignore signs all around you. Nessie, Champ, Chessie, Ogopogo, Mokele-mbembe... the stories of similar creatures come from all corners of the earth, but you choose to disbelieve. Many of these creatures, like my own people, have simply chosen to retreat from you and your kind. As you now know, there can be elements to the world that you know very little about."

"Yes, today has made that very, very clear. Pretty humbling, actually," Sean said.

"Ah! Your ability to feel humility is another reason we came to you, Sean. A rarer and rarer quality these days."

"OK," he replied, "you have me open to an entirely new worldview. As unbelievable as it seems. But what is happening now? With Ken? With me? With all of you coming here now?"

"Well, we're still trying to figure out the why of it. Something is upsetting the order of things, something we have monitored and protected for so very long. What we do know is two creatures are here doing evil. Creatures who should not be here. And who should absolutely not be together..."

"This Wendigo, you mentioned?" he asked.

"Yes," she replied. "A very unpleasant creature and one specific to the indigenous people of this continent. They are known to dwell in this part of your country, the north, and the east, but they are notorious forest dwellers. They shun crowds, cities. This behavior is unheard of. They are without a doubt malevolent. They are insatiable, greedy... cannibalistic. They kill and consume at will and prey on anyone who enters their sphere. Tall, lanky, pale, they carry the stench of decay and death with them. Anyone who falls under their sway is likely doomed. Doomed to lose self-will, doomed to become either victim or minion."

"Ken," he whispered.

"Yes, your friend is in grave danger. At best. He may already be lost."

"Shit."

Breena looked at Sean with concern in her eyes.

"Indeed. This is a danger we had never foreseen. It's never occurred before. This behavior is wildly out of character. Which brings us to the second creature. The Dullahan."

"Why do I feel this is about to get even worse?" he asked.

"Because it is. I'm sorry. The arrival of a Dullahan is even more perplexing than a Wendigo. Dullahans are creatures of Celtic origin. They live, and belong, in Ireland. So, we have two creatures, behaving in ways never before seen in their history. They shouldn't be here. They shouldn't be cooperating. It's... wrong."

"And what exactly is a Dullahan?" Sean queried.

"Very bad news, I'm afraid," she responded. "Evil. They are an ancient evil. A Dullahan, many believe, was the inspiration for your legend of the headless horseman. They ride an enormous grey horse and carry their own severed head in their arms. The head is animated, with a leering smile that stretches across the entire face. Their black eyes are constantly darting back and forth. They are reputed to bring death to anyone who they name, but they spread terror and fear wherever they go, wielding a whip made from an enemy's spine. Until now, they have solely been creatures of our land, what you call Ireland. How and why one would be here... we cannot fathom."

"Thanks for not sugarcoating that," he quipped. Desperate to lighten the tone as the Willy Wonka lights flashed faster and faster as the train picked up speed.

"We must find your friend. It may already be too late to save him, but we must try. If the Wendigo has turned him, we may be facing even greater odds."

"I'm sorry," Sean started, his voice straining to hold his rising panic inside, "but what the hell can I do to help with any of this?

Why would they want Ken? I... just don't get it. And what do any of you want with me? I'm a tenor, for God's sake!"

"Sean, I understand. This is a lot. None of this is simple. We just don't know everything. Yet. We fear that these creatures are being manipulated by something, or someone, greater. To what end we haven't discovered, but nothing good for either your people or mine. As for you... I explained earlier what attracted us to you. I imagine it attracted these creatures, also. You are, by genetics, personal history, and certain ancient standards, a foil for them and a natural ally to us, even though it's been millennia since our peoples allied together... And don't underestimate the power of a tenor," she said with a grin.

And despite the circumstances of the ride, and the threat of imminent danger they faced, he found himself liking her. Trusting her. And curious to tap into whatever she believed lay inside of him, even though he could not imagine what it could possibly be.

The rest of the train ride passed uneventfully. Only once, when a stranger boarded at Rector Street and took a seat directly across from Sean and Breena, did Odette even make herself known, as she stepped protectively toward them from mid-car. But the person exited two stops later and Odette slipped out of sight. He never caught sight of Bayard throughout, though he was assured that he was close by.

The train came to a grinding halt at the South Ferry station, and they exited through the forward doors. Again, the burst of moist, stale air, and again Sean was aware of the personal cost to the Peripherals to be here. Bayard took the escalator a few paces in front of them. Odette was a few paces behind, carefully watching everyone who came near. They eventually emerged into the bustling space in front of the ferry terminal. The afternoon press of people surged in and up the stairs, most heading over to the island after their workday, along with a healthy sprinkling of tourists taking advantage of the free rides and view of the Statue of Liberty. Sean couldn't help but notice the bomb-sniffing dogs perk up as the group passed by at the top of the stairs. Odette was all business and scanned the large room for threats, but Sean grinned to see Bayard unobtrusively pet one of the dogs, a German Shepherd, on the head as he slipped past. The dog responded with a hearty tail wag and looked as if he wanted to follow along. They had just missed the ferry, which meant they had fifteen minutes until the next departure, so the group found a corner of the large hall, well away from the fast-food stands and gift shops and tried to stay out of the way and draw no attention.

Sean checked his phone to see if any of the Grumbles had called or texted. He had a text from Nick letting them all know that he had gotten to Ken's house in Maplewood in New Jersey and was with Anne trying to think of anything that could help.

Brandy had also texted a photo of her with Paul and a short message saying she was reviewing CCTV footage of the front of Beer Culture from the night before. "So far nothing of note," she had written.

Stewart had been the last to text, simply sending a photo of a margarita and the caption, "Checking in with the boys in blue," and an emoji of a police car.

Sean responded to all, letting them know where he was, with a rolling eye emoji in response to Stewart. By the time he was finished, the ferry was announced for Gate 2 and the mass of people shuffled forward as one to board. Sean and the others held back until the hall was nearly empty and made their way onto the ship last.

The ferry was massive, with three decks, a snack bar, and outside benches for anyone who wanted to get a breath of the fresh-ish air. Row upon row of benches were already almost full on the first two decks they passed through. Weary commuters collapsed onto them. Some had bought a snack or a beer. Most were seeking outlets to charge their phones. Almost all had their faces buried in their screens and headphones or earbuds in, completely shutting out the world around them. The tourists headed to the starboard side of the boat, knowing that they would get the best views of Lady Liberty there. In response, Sean and the Peripherals headed to the port side which was much emptier. They took a bench toward the back, again to stay as isolated as possible. The enormous orange craft eased out of its berth for the roughly twenty-minute crossing. The harbor was full of smaller ferries buzzing back and forth, tourists' helicopters taking off and landing nearby, and a few sailboats taking tourists on a more leisurely trip around lower Manhattan. The high-rises slid silently away, and Sean took a moment to admire the view, one rarely taken in by New Yorkers. The ferry really was one of the most underappreciated New York experiences, Sean thought, as he vowed to acknowledge things like this more when he got through with finding Ken. If he found Ken, he corrected himself. If he got through it himself, he corrected yet again.

The call came from the other side of the harbor. Whispering malevolently on the wind with a voice like rushing water. It called others to heed it. To enter the fray. It seeped through the harbor, unheard by human ears. But others heard. And answered.

CHAPTER 9

Brandy sat in the cramped office in the back of Beer Culture, her face just a few inches from Paul's laptop watching and rewatching footage from the night before. One camera was above and behind the bar, catching all the seats and the cash register at one end. Brandy had watched and relived their celebration of just last night. It felt a lifetime ago already. And the sight of Ken, laughing, full of life in all his ridiculousness made her breath catch. He had to be all right. At one point she saw the woman who had bought drinks for Sean. She was petite, blond, and beautiful. Strangely, she never saw the two of them interact, and at one point, the woman simply... disappeared. Brandy chalked it up to a glitch or skip in the recording. Other than that, everything had played exactly as she remembered. Fun, bittersweet, jovial.

The second camera was placed inside above the front door and aimed in a way to capture anyone coming or going. A small part of the sidewalk behind was visible in the background, but distant and out of focus. Brandy had been through most of the night, starting before the group had even arrived, but nothing had stood out to her.

She watched again on fast-forward. Nothing. She had gotten to the friends leaving and Ken wandering off on his own, pot at the ready, but nothing had grabbed her attention. She decided to give it one last look before leaving to canvas the other businesses on the block to see if they also had cameras. This time a movement caught her eye. Something had shifted in the shadows of one of the doorways as Ken ambled past. It was faint. Barely noticeable. She paused the video and nearly pressed her nose onto the screen. Still too hard to see. She took her phone and snapped a picture of the frozen image and enlarged it.

There was something there. Something tall. Thin. Darker than the darkness around it. She transferred the photo to an editing app she had and began sharpening the image. It was still difficult to make out, but slowly something began to take shape. Her eyes finally made sense of what they were seeing, and her hand fell to the desktop with the phone still in it. A gangly figure had moved along after Ken. It was tall. Too tall, seeming to be over nine feet in height. What she could make out of it looked pallid, grotesque, and clearly unhealthy. Its flesh was pale, and even in the poor photo, looked fetid. And what was on top of its head? It looked like some sort of crown, or... could it be antlers? That made no sense. She replayed the video. At one point, the figure turned and seemed to look straight unto the camera as if it knew it would be seen. As it did so, its hideous face broke into a vicious grin. Then it turned and with a quickening pace, leapt after Ken, as if it knew whoever saw this would be too late.

She stared into the distance, seeing nothing. Concentrating. She called to Paul, barely whispering his name. Adrenaline kicked in, and the next time she called him, her voice was full-throated and tinged with fear. "Paul!" she shouted. "Get in here!"

A moment later, the door opened and he looked a question at her, trying to simultaneously finish a comment to one of the patrons behind him at the bar. Brandy turned the screen of her phone toward him. The picture was now expanded and as focused as it could be. She thrust it toward him. "Paul, what the hell is THAT?" she nearly shouted. He looked and his mouth dropped open. He rubbed his eyes, looked again, and still had no answer for her.

CHAPTER 10

The air had a hint of salt, a hint of city, and a hint of fog as the ferry moved forward. The day was bright and sunny, with barely a breeze, making for a smooth crossing, and Sean felt himself relax ever so slightly for the first time in hours. It felt like so much longer. He leaned forward on the bench and put his head in his hands and found himself pondering his sneakers. They had spent the last year shuttling him to and from his Broadway job and now were coated in mud and dust from the most bizarre and unlikely morning. This couldn't be real, and yet...

He peeked through his fingers at Breena sitting next to him. There was a protective air to her, but more than that, he felt some sort of connection between them. All of the Peripherals were incredible, but Breena somehow seemed... more in tune with him. He seemed to vibrate at the same pitch as her, which made no sense to him, and yet somehow did. He watched as she sat, looking out toward Governors Island and its ant farm of tourists tracking back and forth across its paths and hills. The sun caught her eyes and they lit up with the most otherworldly blue he had ever seen. She felt him looking and turned to him. He blushed involuntarily, and looked away quickly, although he wasn't sure why. She smiled at him in the most openhearted way, which he missed as he pretended to look elsewhere.

Odette stood not far to their right, closer to the front of the ferry, while Bayard stood slightly to the left and leaned on the railing, staring absentmindedly into the water rushing past. It was the most still Sean had seen him yet, but even now his left foot scraped back and forth on the deck like a bull about to charge. All three of the Peripherals seemed weary, pensive. As if they were saving their strength for what they knew would be a difficult day ahead. Sean, with no idea what to expect, felt useless, as if he were bobbing along in their wake.

Sean noticed that the sky had become a darker grey. It seemed sudden. Hadn't he just been watching the sun glint off of Breena? As the grey clouds rushed across the harbor toward them, he noticed a sudden drop in temperature. On another day, he would think nothing of it, but this was anything but a normal day.

He lifted his head from his hands and the question he was about to ask his companions died on his lips. All three had changed their stances and looked on high alert. Bayard had risen from the rail and had his face thrust into the wind. Odette scanned the deck, and seeing nothing new, trained her gaze on the oncoming storm. Breena had leaned to the front of the bench and her eyes were closed tight and she seemed to be listening for something.

"Hey, is something happen—" Sean began when Breena rose quickly to her feet.

"There... Do you hear?" she asked the others. They nodded and took on a wary stance. Sean could hear nothing unusual but the steadily increasing wind. The harbor was growing turbulent. White-caps began to buffet the ferry from a harbor that had been calm mere moments ago. The ship began to lurch under the battering and the captain came over the intercom telling passengers to take their seats.

Odette pointed over the railing and cursed. Sean rose to see what she was pointing toward. He caught a quick glimpse of raging water, pounding the side of the ferry, pushing it violently. And somehow, the water was behaving in a way that made no sense. Sean was no sailor, but he'd been on plenty of boats, including this one, and had never seen such a confusion in the currents. It was as if the harbor was launching itself again the ship, whether to push it in a direction or overwhelm it he couldn't tell. All he knew was that nothing made sense.

And then suddenly, it made even less sense as his eyes caught glimpses of horselike heads rushing through the water. Their manes were green as seaweed, and they flung themselves at the ship violently. Over and over. Sean felt Breena pull him back toward the bench. She shouted over the winds, "Kelpies!" and the three shared a confused look before jumping into action. Breena placed herself in front of Sean. Odette flung her arm out to her side and suddenly it held a spear. It was scaled precisely for her; short, lethal, compact. It had a blade made of iron at its head. It looked deadly, tapering to a three-sided point. The tip was held in place by large sturdy rivets. The wood looked ancient, almost iron in appearance. Petrified. Like Sean, come to think of it. The spear seemed to merely be an extension of her arm and began weaving a deadly web in the air in front of her. Sean saw that Bayard was suddenly holding two long daggers, one in each hand. As with Odette, they seemed to appear from nowhere and instantly become part of him.

Sean saw one of the horselike figures—did Breena call them Kelpies?—leap from the water, aiming for the deck. The spear flashed toward it, raking across its shoulder, and with a terrifying screech, it fell back to the water. Another threw itself in its wake and met the same fate. Sean saw Bayard dealing thrusts in the same way on the other side.

"Oh, no, wait... What the hell is happening?! I can't... I don't..." Sean stammered. Backing as far away from the rails as he could, his back pressed against the wall behind him. If the window behind him had been open, he would have tried to crawl through it as terror overwhelmed all other thought. Eyes wide with fear, he felt as if he was on the verge of complete panic.

Breena placed her hands on either side of his face and pressed her forehead to his, soothing him through her touch and words. "I know. I know, Sean," she whispered. "This is beyond anything you could have imagined. I understand. But we are here. With you. Holding you close. Trust."

Something in her words, her tone, her touch, connected with him. He was still afraid, overwhelmed, but her presence, and that of the other Peripherals, soothed him somewhat. He took a deep breath but stayed as far away from the water as he could. It was all he could do to control his breathing.

It was then he sensed something shift. He felt a change, even though he hadn't seen or heard anything. He glanced at Breena and her hands were now at her sides. Her lips were moving, and he could barely hear a sound from her, but she almost glowed with... what? Exertion? Something from within? The more he focused, the more he perceived. It was a language he had never heard, but it was oddly familiar. As if it echoed somewhere within him. Her chant became louder as did the light shining forth from her. Suddenly, he heard other voices joining. Not from on board. It sounded as they were coming from the water, and he risked a quick glance over the railing. The Kelpies were still throwing themselves at the ship and continuing to meet an impenetrable wall of blades and spear. As he looked into the waters, he saw them being joined by other creatures. His initial fear lessened as he saw these new arrivals start to surround the ferry, placing themselves between it and the Kelpies. They were female in form, and though their eyes were vacant, they sang in the language Breena was using and added their voices to hers. The Kelpies wheeled away from the newcomers and light broke through the clouds above. Ripping the storm apart and sending the grey skies shattering into the distance.

As quickly as it began, it was over. The Kelpies galloped away into the depths leaving no trace of themselves behind. The latest arrivals turned as one and raised their blank stares to the ship's deck and Breena. They each placed a hand upon their chest and slid silently into the harbor's depths. And suddenly, the waters were calm, the sun shone brightly, and the ferry fell into a comfortable and gentle chug across the water.

The captain came over the loudspeaker, "Thanks for your cooperation, folks. Quite a squall there. Never seen one like that, but all is well now, and we hope to have you safely in Staten Island only a minute or two late."

Sean turned to his companions. "I seem to be saying this a lot today, but I have questions..."

CHAPTER 11

Brandy stared at Paul in open-mouthed amazement, holding the photo out for him to take another look. He shook his head. No explanation. They watched the video again, and now knowing where to look and what to expect, they saw a very tall—well over eight feet—lanky figure practically ooze out of the shadows. What was on its head? They just couldn't be sure. One thing was clear: it was laser-focused on Ken and closing on him rapidly.

Brandy looked at Paul. "I think we call the police now," she said. "We can't wait for Stewart to finish his margarita with the precinct 'connection.' And we definitely need to tell Sean. He could be headed straight toward that thing.'"

"Um… yeah," Paul agreed. "That thing, whatever it is, is freaking me out."

"Imagine how Ken feels."

The ferry was chugging along as if nothing had happened, but Sean knew better. They all did. He turned his very alarmed eyes to the

Peripherals and raised his eyebrows. "Any time you care to fill me in, I'd be grateful."

It was Odette who spoke first, surprising him.

"Sean, I know Breena has explained somewhat to you about who and what we are, but there is so much more for you to understand," she began. "When our peoples decided to remove ourselves from your space in the world, we did so not out of fear, but out of respect for our planet and each other. Your people had started down a destructive path, where you saw the earth as yours. You saw it as a possession. Something you could take. All that lay upon and within it, you believed, was yours to use however you chose."

When Sean began to respond, she raised a hand to stop him. He noticed that the spear she'd held just moments ago was nowhere to be seen. "I don't say that to insult. Your kind were young and knew little of balance. You became carried away with what you *could* do and lost sight of what you *should* do. Thousands of years of advancement continued to propel you down that path until you find yourself today so removed from the planet below you, you barely pay it heed. Your screens occupy most of your time. Your cities pay no homage to the natural world around you. Your petty disagreements destroy not only each other, but the land beneath your feet, the innocent creatures that share your space..."

Bayard took over. "Through it all, we've watched. And advanced along with you, but differently. We are not frozen in time. Your fairy tales and legends leave us as we were centuries ago, ancient, and unchanged, but that is far from what we have become. Our advancements, though, were made with an eye toward preserving and protecting as much of what you would call 'nature' as we could."

He twitched his arms and suddenly the two long daggers appeared in his hands. "You would call much of what we do 'magic,' and some of it is rooted in beliefs and practices you've long forgotten, but at the heart of it, our peoples just chose different paths.

"And when we chose to remove ourselves, we did not do so alone. Many of the creatures in your myths simply chose to enter the shadows with us. Not all were friendly toward you. Not all were friendly toward us, for that matter, but collectively we made a decision that we thought was best for us, our world, and ultimately for you. Our paths could not have continued together without conflict. One people or another would have had to perish.

"What you saw just now in the water were two of the creatures that came with us. The Kelpies that attacked the ferry..."

"I've heard of Kelpies," Sean said.

"Yes," Breena responded, "they have appeared often in your stories and popular culture. In this case, they appeared to have answered a call from someone, or something, to try to stop us from reaching the island. I suspect it was more a testing of us, getting us to show our strength. Or lack thereof."

"And the others? The ones who came to help?" he asked.

"Undines. A sort of water elemental. There is great power in their song, as you just saw. In our shadow world, there is still much strength in music, in poetry, and the spoken word," Breena answered. "Your people have moved away from that, relegating it to simply entertainment. Yes, from time to time a song or poem may touch something deeper for you, but that's become rarer and rarer. To us, these things still carry great weight. They are still very much a force for good and ill, depending on whose voice it is."

"And that's why they answered you?" he looked at Breena.

"Yes. I am considered a seanchaí by my people. My voice, my song, is my particular gift. You may have noticed that Bayard connects with animals in your world. That is his gift. Odette is a fierce warrior, as you've just witnessed. She is a protector."

"A thing to note, as your people drop creatures into extinction, we've often had to step in to preserve them, if possible," Bayard said. "If you're ever fortunate enough to visit with us, you'll see some incredible things. Dodos, Tasmanian tigers, passenger pigeons... we took them in when you drove them out in the hopes that one day they could return to where they belonged. To be perfectly honest with you, Sean, it's getting pretty crowded on our side of things."

"I have no idea why you are here helping us," Sean answered. "From what you've told me, we've destroyed so much of what you believe in. So much of what you hold important. Why risk... anything for us? Why are you here?"

"Many reasons, Sean. Not least of which is that we've never given up on you. Yes, you've been destructive and lost sight of what we all shared at our beginnings, but you've also made wonderful discoveries. In medicine, space exploration, mechanics, technology. On and on. If we ever found a way for our people to coexist... what we could learn from each other would be astounding," Breena said. "And we always knew there could come a day when we needed each other. It seems that day has come. We need you—you specifically, Sean—to face this current threat. And you seem to have a very particular set of gifts that may be what we need. At least, we're hoping."

"I still think you're wrong," he said. "I'm nothing special. Just... a guy."

"By our standards, we disagree."

"Come on, Sean! You could end up paying a visit to our side of things after this. Don't you want to see a dodo?" Bayard asked, chuckling. "If you're good, I may even let you pet a Sicilian wolf. Well, actually, that would more be up to the wolves, but I may be willing to let you try."

"I have no idea what a Sicilian wolf is," Sean responded.

"Exactly," Bayard answered with a grin.

Before Sean could process the idea, the captain announced their imminent arrival. With an ever faster spinning head, Sean gathered himself for what lay ahead, even though he knew full well that he had no idea what that would be.

CHAPTER 12

They disembarked the ferry and made their way through the terminal, weaving through the crowd. Odette and Bayard took up their unobtrusive positions keeping watch on Sean. Breena stayed close. As they passed through the great hall, Bayard noticed large aquariums filled with species of fish reflecting the ecosystem just outside the doorways in the harbor. He let his fingers trace along the nearest tank as he passed, and the fish inside trailed along in his wake. "Brutal," he muttered. "Sorry, friends. Don't worry. I won't forget." As he left the hall, they hovered in their tank watching him. If fish could look wistful, these did.

The group navigated the food court in the great hall and made their way to the taxi stand outside. Sean checked his phone to pinpoint the last exact location of Ken's phone.

"We need to get to Fort Wadsworth... huh. Never heard of it. It's not far, but it is a ride away. At least for me."

"We'll let you ride with Breena. We'll be nearby. No sense making ourselves more obvious than necessary," Odette said as she and Bayard slowed and dropped a few steps behind.

Sean emerged from the terminal and began scanning for an available cab, when to his surprise he heard a voice call out, "Ginge!"

Sean turned in the direction and sensed Breena tense and slide a few steps to the side. Distancing herself and simultaneously preparing for trouble. Sean was shocked to see Dan Trout leaning against the side of an old and distinctly well-used Ford Bronco with Montana license plates in the middle of the taxi lane, much to the chagrin of the cabbies nearby. Trout obviously did not care one bit.

"Trout!" Sean exclaimed. "What are you doing here? How did you...?"

"Hiya! Nick called me and told me where you were headed. I'm just across the harbor in Bayonne, so thought I'd offer a ride. Not always easy to get around here on Staten Island. They don't call it the forgotten borough for nothing."

"Uh... wow. That's amazing. Thanks, but I think I should probably handle this myself."

"What?" Trout responded. "First of all, no. And second of all, you're already not by yourself. You're with her. Gonna introduce me?" he said with a nod toward Breena.

Sean stopped in his tracks and looked to Breena. Trout was the first of the Grumbles to actually see her. Breena returned the look with a raised eyebrow and a slight shrug, clearly as caught off guard as Sean.

"Oh... yeah, of course," Sean stammered. "Sorry. This is... Breena. She knows Ken and showed up in the park after everyone left. She... wanted to help."

"You've been holding out on us, Ginge!" Trout said in a voice that belonged more in Big Sky country than curbside in New York City. "Well... Breena, is it? Great name. Any friend of Ken's, and Sean's," he said pointedly, "is a friend of mine. Let's get Ken and bring him home, huh?"

"Pleasure to meet you," Breena said, and Trout paused for the briefest of moments at her rich musical voice and her accent which was vaguely Old World with a hint of an Irish lilt.

Trout held the passenger-side door open for Breena, with a wink to Sean, got in and started his truck. Sean clambered into the back seat, sitting in the middle, and sticking his head between the two front seats. He felt very much like a kid trying to be part of the grown-up conversations in front.

"Where to?" Trout asked.

"Fort Wadsworth," Sean answered. "Ever hear of it?"

"Of course!" he responded. "You haven't? Great spot. Beach, old fort, nice walks along the water... hidden treasure."

"Well, the last ping we got from Ken's phone was there."

"OK. Weird. Never pegged Ken for a Staten Island type. Or a walk in the park type, for that matter. Unless it was to buy pot. Or smoke pot. Whatever. Good news is it's only a few minutes away. Let's roll."

Sean glanced out the rear window as the truck pulled away in a cloud of exhaust and saw Odette and Bayard watching closely before blinking out of sight. He turned back to the front, wondering just how to deal with Trout's presence without endangering him.

As they drove north on Bay Street out of the terminal, Sean's phone rang. He saw it was Brandy and answered quickly.

"Anything new?" he asked.

"Yes and no," she answered, and filled him on what they had seen on the CCTV. "But dammit, we went to the cops with it and they said there's still nothing they can do about it. He's an adult and it's been less than twenty-four hours. Since the recording doesn't show anything specific happening... we have to wait."

"What about Stewart's connections at the precinct? Can't they help?" Sean asked.

"Oh, yes," Brandy said. "They've been very helpful. They're off duty and I'm pretty sure they picked up the tab for Stewart's second margarita. And maybe the third."

"Oh... I see. Yes, very helpful. Hey, Trout met me in Staten Island. Apparently, Nick let him know where I was going, and he just headed over."

"Tell him about your new friend!" Trout almost shouted toward the phone.

"What?" Brandy asked. "New friend? What's that about?"

"Oh... nothing. Someone who knows Ken," he responded, thinking that it wasn't a complete lie since Breena said they had been watching Ken, too. "I'll fill you in when I see you. Can you call Nick? See how Anne is and give him the latest? We're about ten minutes from where the phone last appeared."

"You got it," she responded. "Should we head your way?"

Sean glanced at Breena who gave a subtle shake of her head, they already had one extra Grumble along, they didn't need to put more in harm's way until they knew what was happening.

"No. You're good. Stay there, connect with Nick, and I'll let you know what we find as soon as we find... something. Don't think you'd make it here in time, anyway."

"Gotcha," she said. "And Sean, be careful. I'm forwarding a screen shot of whatever that thing is that we saw. It's seriously weird."

"I will," he said. "Gotta go. We're pulling into a gas station now. Wish us luck."

"Yeah, you and Trout. And Ken, wherever he is."

"Have to gas up and probably a good idea to grab a quick bite. You all must be starving," Trout announced pulling into a convenience store/gas station.

"I'll get the gas if you run in and get us a bite," Sean said.

"That's a deal," came the response.

With Trout on his way into the shop and Sean filling the tank, he looked at Breena and asked, "How could he see you? No one else has been able to. I thought you could blink out of their sight..."

Breena paused before answering. "I'm actually not sure. I don't have a lot of firsthand experience dealing with your kind. Something about him seems... different. He's more in tune with his natural surroundings, it seems."

"He's from Montana. We call it Big Sky country. A lot more nature, a lot less city. Actually, no big city. Could that have anything to do with it?"

"Possibly... Has he kept that connection active?"

"Absolutely. His mom is still out there, and he visits pretty often. Just got back actually."

"It could be that simple. That and his also being a storyteller... seanchaí... He sings, yes?" she asked, and Sean nodded. "As I told you, we came to you for a reason. It makes sense that your friends would share some of those traits. Although I will admit, this one was unexpected. If they all share some of these traits, it could get interesting."

"Trout always sends us photos of the wide-open spaces out west. He definitely sees it more often than we do and appreciates it in a way I'm not sure the rest of us could. At least not without more first-hand experience."

"That must be it. I doubt it will be the last time I'm surprised in this. He hasn't noticed Bayard or Odette, though, which is interest-ing. They've been holding back, but..." She nodded across the parking lot to where the two were loitering by an ice machine. They were anything but unobtrusive, at least to anyone who could see them.

Sean finished topping off the tank, shook his head at the price of gas and looked up to see Trout leaving the store with two bags and a tray of soft drinks. He handed them off to Sean as he rounded the Bronco and climbed behind the wheel.

"OK," he announced as they all settled back into their seats. "We've got gas station flautas—the best kind—no idea what's in them. The last two slices of semi-warm pizza. Do NOT form an opinion on New York pizza based on them," he said pointedly to Breena. "And bagel with bacon, egg, and cheese. Same advice goes for New York bagels. These are not our finest. Just grabbed a handful of drinks, should be some diet, some high octane. Even got a bottle of water, I think. Oh, and tell your two friends over there to just get in the truck. Probably better if we get there together... and they might be hungry, too." He shot a glance at Breena and another at Sean. "And then how about you just fill me all the way in so we can tackle this together? Sound good?"

For the first time, Sean saw Breena speechless, so he stepped in. "You got it, Trout. It will all make sense, promise. Well, it might make less sense at first, but eventually..."

Breena motioned to the others to join them in the truck, and they wandered over with very perplexed expressions on their faces. They climbed into the back seat with Sean, who thought it was definitely one of the most surreal things he'd experienced in a very surreal day, finding himself squeezed into the back of a Ford Bronco with two ancient... Peripherals? Tuatha? Faerie folk? Rummaging through bags of bad gas station food.

"So... would you believe we all met on that Ireland trip?" Sean tried.

"Well..." Trout replied, "no. I remember that you and Ken ran into each other the first day you were there, yes?"

"Yes," Sean said. "In a town called Cong."

The Peripherals all perked up at this information.

"OK. That I believe. These folks, though? You need to come clean with me if we're going to have a chance of getting Ken, because something's up. Something weird. I can't help if I don't know."

"Fair enough," Sean responded. So as Odette and Breena passed on the questionable food selections and Bayard discovered a love for pizza, even bad pizza, Sean told him. Everything.

When Sean was done, Trout put his head back on the headrest and closed his eyes. He rubbed his face with his hands, let out a big sigh, and fixed Sean with a look in the rearview mirror.

"OK. I see why you didn't tell me," he said. "Any reason I shouldn't just assume you're all nuts?"

Sean looked around the truck and gave an exaggerated blink to the Peripherals. They took the hint and... disappeared. A moment later they were back.

"Yup. That works," Trout said, not missing a beat. "Let's go get Ken. After that, I have questions."

"I've been saying that all day..." Sean muttered as Trout started the engine.

"Less than ten minutes away by the GPS," Trout announced as they pulled back out into the traffic on Bay Street.

Sean sat in the back seat and stared out the window. How could this all be happening? There was nothing unusual about him or his life up until that point. Sure, he'd followed his dream to New York and had... made it? He worked, sure, but no one outside of a small circle knew his name or even particularly noticed him. He'd been fine with that. He did something he loved, had some of the best friends he could have hoped for. If he wasn't a household name, he'd proven to himself that he could swim with the big fish. Even if he remained a guppy. But this? He stole a glance at Breena sitting in the front seat, listening attentively to Trout going on about the natural beauty of Montana. He really should work for the tourist board, Sean thought. He looked again at her. So bright, in tune with everything around her. Intelligence glimmered in her eyes, and something more. Wisdom. He just knew that she had seen and done things that he could never imagine. The world, his world, seemed so different from mere hours before. Things he had been sure were true had been shattered into pieces and the new world that he now saw was full of possibilities and bigger, more beautiful, more dangerous, than he had ever dared to imagine. And these wonderful creatures—these Peripherals—believed in him. In some value within him that he found hard to accept. He looked at her again and realized that he was having a hard time looking away. And he wondered about that, too. So much to process, but no time for it. The weathered Bronco pulled up to the gate of the park. There was no more time for staring out the window. Or at Breena.

Trout's green and white old-school Bronco slowed as it approached a guard house at the front of Fort Wadsworth, which it turned out, was both a park and an active base for the Coast Guard, Army Reserve, and Park Police. The park was enormous, 226 acres, and its paths and beachfront left many places to get away from the city. Or disappear from prying eyes, it seemed. Trout stopped at the gate and glanced into the hut, but it was empty, so he cruised slowly through. Barracks and military housing sat to the left. To the right lay some official, very utilitarian buildings. Basic blocks of pale red brick. They continued on past a parking lot on the left that seemed to lead to more featureless buildings. They crept forward, under the massive Verrazzano-Narrows Bridge, which literally ran above the park. Sean wondered to himself how he had never known about this place. He'd driven that bridge so many times over the years. They came to a dead end and turned left down a short hill following signs for the fort. Trout pulled into a parking lot near the bottom, well-worn brakes squealing as he pulled into a space, parked, and turned to Sean.

"OK, this is it. Where do we start looking?"

"Well," Sean answered as he took out his phone and checked the coordinates of Ken's last ping. "This is about as close as we can narrow it down. The fort and battlements are up that hill. Down the hill to our right looks like another lot and a fairly long beach, believe it or not. Oh, and Brandy's photo just downloaded." He opened it on his screen and his eyes grew large. He turned the screen for the others to see and the Peripherals shared a grim look at each other.

"As we thought. Wendigo. Powerful. Evil. It's crucial we find and deal with this as quickly as possible. We may have to split up to cover more ground," Breena said. "I don't like it, but remember, we're only a breath away when we're needed."

"Well, you are. I'm more than a breath away, but I'll do what I can," Trout answered with a lopsided grin.

Sean pulled Trout aside and spoke quietly to him. "Look, Trout, you're probably about to see some pretty weird stuff. Dangerous stuff. These three"—he gestured toward the Peripherals—"will seem tame in comparison. Just... a word of warning. Make sure you stay alert."

"Ginge, I go hiking in grizzly country with nothing but a stick and some bear spray. I know how to keep an eye out. Honestly, I'm more worried about you than about me."

Sean chuckled and gave him an affectionate clap on the shoulder. "Let's just get this done and all go home."

"Roger, that," Trout responded.

Trout, Odette, and Bayard headed up the hill toward the old battlements. Kallan slid in beside them. Trout looked a question at Bayard who introduced the two. "Alara has moved down by the beach. She wanted to see if any of the local fauna had noticed anything. Haven't heard from her in a bit," Kallan said. When he heard that Breena and Sean had headed in that direction, he nodded, pleased.

There seemed to be more people walking up in this direction, but there were plenty of small, isolated, wooded areas and abandoned buildings where someone, or something, could hide. The path up was steep, and Trout quickly found himself winded, but pushed on determined to hold his own. Children rode their bicycles down the hill past them and couples strolled down stopping to take pictures. As they crested the hill, directly under the bridge, old artillery sat to their right. More photo opportunities for the tourists and a reminder of the more solemn history of the grounds. The thunk-thunk of traffic over their heads drowned out most other sounds, but Trout could see his companions were on high alert. A truck passing overhead backfired, and Trout jumped, startled, but saw the Peripherals were unmoved. They glanced at him and gave a reassuring shake of their heads. He crossed to the edge of the walkway and was rewarded with an expansive view of the entrance to New York Harbor. As container ships moved slowly past and the occasional tugboat appeared to lend a hand, he reminded himself to take more advantage of all the city offered. He needed to spend more time outside.

He turned in time to see Bayard peering in the empty window of one of the abandoned buildings. He moved some vines out of the way to get a better look and slipped silently, and suddenly, over the sill to explore inside. Odette had wandered farther up the path past the view of the harbor and fort itself down below to a large wooded section that was overgrown with tangling vines and scrub. He cast a questioning look her way and she gave a small shrug, then slipped through the fencing that surrounded the area. Kallan had already disappeared farther up the path. Not sure which direction to go and finding himself suddenly on his own, Trout ambled by the open window Bayard had entered, but could see nothing more sinister than discarded trash on the ground and evidence of kids using the building as cover for a party. He also did not see Bayard.

He was sure he could never disappear into the building the way his company had, so he walked ahead to the overgrown stretch where he'd seen Odette disappear. He couldn't imagine anything could be hiding in there. It didn't seem large enough and he could even make out the path on the other side at the bottom of the incline. So the path wound around and down to the fort. He would head down and hope to rendezvous with Odette below. He trusted that Bayard would catch up when able.

"In the fall, they bring in goats from a local farm to eat all that vegetation," an old man wandering past said to him. "They do a great job, let me tell you. No gas fumes or nasty machinery, either. I come every year to watch them. They're not here yet. No idea why."

"Really?" Trout responded. "I'll make a point of coming back. I'd like to see that myself."

The man wandered back in the direction from which Trout had just come. They both cast a curious look back at each other as they walked. Trout was on edge, he realized, and felt very vulnerable on his own. He didn't really know what he was looking for and had no idea what he could do if he actually found anything. But he had a friend in trouble and Montanans don't run. He picked up his pace and, looking into the brush in the center enclosure, hustled down and around to find Odette. Or Bayard. Or Kallan. Or some sign of Ken.

Meanwhile, Breena and Sean headed in the opposite direction, down toward the beach. Breena paused for a moment and a faraway look crossed her face. When she looked again at Sean, she told him that Kallan had rejoined the others and they should keep an eye out for Alara. "She does best near water, so we're likely to find her somewhere on the beach. Or in the harbor. You never know," she said.

There was a small roadway leading to a gravel lot of a dozen or so spaces. To their right, a wide paved path led toward Staten Island's south beach, something most New Yorkers didn't even know existed. Pedestrians walked slowly along toward the boardwalk that lay around a bend, many with thick Russian accents, and bicyclists and skateboarders weaved their way among them. On either side of the path were thick bushes and tangled vines. The sound of the ocean rose over the dense greenery, but it remained out of sight. To the left, a gate was pulled across the path to stop cars from passing, but the lane itself stretched on toward below the bridge. It looked to be some sort of service area. There was a seemingly abandoned park service truck, quite a bit of debris, and a large pile of lumber incongruously stacked near the path.

Sean had a moment of nerves. Why had Odette and Bayard both gone the other way? They both were armed and clearly capable. He was here with Breena, and while he was growing to enjoy any time spent in her presence, he wondered what they would do if they ran into any sort of danger.

"Sean," she said, sensing his concern. "We'll be fine. I'm not without my resources. Trust me."

"I do. Of course, I do," he protested. "I just really don't know what to expect. And frankly, I have no idea what use I will be to *you*."

"You'll know when you know," she responded. She nodded to the wider path to the right. "I think we should head that way, cut over to the beach and double back into the abandoned space under the bridge. I think we're more likely to find something there, but marching directly in seems... unwise."

"Sounds like a plan to me. Which is good because I definitely didn't have one," he said.

About a third of the way down the pavement, they saw a sandy path cutting through the brush. Turning left, they headed in that direction and the sound of the waves. They emerged onto a surprisingly wide beach. Looking in both directions, there were very few people here. Late October was hardly peak beach season in the city. They took stock of where they were, surrounded by the remnants of bonfires and the occasional discarded piece of fishing equipment. Farther down the beach, they could just make out the beginning of the boardwalk and a much larger crowd of beachcombers.

Breena turned to Sean. "Give me your hand," she said. "I want you to see something."

On the other side of the park, Trout turned a bend in the path to find Odette and Bayard close to the central fence. Bayard silently slipped over the fence and crept through the brush while Odette scanned in the opposite direction. She nodded as she noticed Trout and motioned him over.

"Nothing so far," she said. "Bayard noticed something inside there that he wanted to investigate."

"Nothing on my end, either. An old man told me about some lawn-mowing goats, but that was about it."

"Goats?" she asked.

"Apparently, they bring them in every autumn to clear out this brush. Eco-friendly, I'm told."

"Surprisingly civilized," Odette quipped, "for your kind."

"Surprisingly civilized for Staten Island. Even more impressive."

Bayard emerged from the enclosure and brushed some stray leaves from his shoulder. "Some deer in there. Unexpected. They haven't seen anything strange on this side of the park, but there were some disturbances on the other side near the bridge. Less traffic over there."

"Wait. He talks to deer?" Trout asked.

"And a lot more than just deer. You'll get used to it. Like everything else. Let's take a quick look through these other buildings and work our way over in that direction. No word from Breena yet. If they're hiding, they're doing a good job of it. If it's a trap, it's well disguised."

The three continued down the path, examining the outbuildings as they approached the fort itself. More tangled bushes and vines, but not much else, greeted them. As they turned the last corner, the fort rose up above them. Impressive in its day, no doubt, but now a shell. Trout considered it for a moment. Not for the first time in the last hour or two, he felt like a stranger in his own city. He'd heard of the fort, but never taken the time to hike it himself.

The fort was surrounded by tourists, pedestrians, and on the water side some fishermen who had ignored the "No Entrance" signs. But there was no sign of trouble. No sign of anything out of the ordinary. Nothing other than "No Trespassing" and "Don't Feed the

Goats" signs placed on the fencing. The three Peripherals blinked out to look at the fort's interior, which was off limits to Trout. He stood outside, noticed a lighthouse perched on one side of the fort, and thought about how many lives had passed by that light. How many had it saved? He couldn't help but wonder if anything like what he was involved in had ever happened here. Whatever it was he was actually involved in...

CHAPTER 13

Sean hesitated, but only for a fraction of a second before placing his hand in Breena's. At first, he noticed nothing other than the cool, soft feel of her hand. And he felt a blush rise up his neck. The curse of the fair skinned. But after a breath, Breena began to not so much hum as vibrate. With her voice, but also from somewhere deeper within. It was a resonance the likes of which Sean had never experienced, or even imagined. As it grew, seemingly only in her, and as it reached deep into him, the air around them crackled and Sean's vision began to clear, even though he'd had no idea it had been clouded. Her strength now emerged audibly as a note, clear and crystal. And then more notes, until from deep within her a chord came flowing that seemed to contain nothing but goodness and optimism and light. The air around them shifted and something inside of Sean split apart. Split open. Soared. Around them, the muted colors of a grey day, where the harbor swells had melted into the gunmetal clouds above, suddenly exploded with color. Blues. So many different blues. The water emerged a beautiful deep cerulean and all evidence of mankind's negligence—trash, refuse, ships belching smoke and leaving streaks of oily residue behind them—vanished.

The sky opened up in its own hue. A brilliant azure, with no contrails from passing airplanes. No smog hovering over the city skyline. The sand beneath their feet suddenly appeared golden and untouched. The discarded beer cans, fishing gear, cigarette butts—all of it was gone. Sean turned his head and saw the brush appeared a shockingly verdant green. Lush and bursting with life, there were flowers where he'd seen none a moment before. The birdsong reached him next, and it carried such unrelenting joy that his eyes filled with tears. Joy at being alive, at the beauty of all that surrounded them. Joy at being able to be what they were meant to be. Free of unnatural fear and danger.

Sean's breath was taken away. He kept a firm hold of Breena's hand as he turned, finding a new marvel everywhere he glanced. He looked at her in astonishment, questions in his eyes, but unable to find his voice, so moved was he.

"This, Sean, is a glimpse into the world that we see. The world as it is meant to be, free of pollution, violence, malevolence. It's a dream world, really. It's been millennia since this was reality anywhere other than our homeland. It's what we fight to preserve in any small way we can. This is what our space looks like and what we wish we could convince your people to aspire to..."

"I never... I can't..." he stammered. "How can you ever bear to leave your space. How can you see our world and not break into a million pieces?"

"Because without us, this vision, this ideal... the memory that this is how things once were and can be again, would be lost. We go on because we must."

An osprey flew over them, gliding on unseen air currents. It was so beautiful, so perfect in its being, that Sean wept again. It was exactly as it should be, as it had been created. Its piercing yellow eyes took them in as it sailed over, and it watched them, wheeling around, and gliding over again. Its sharp beak and fierce talons clearly visible. It continued to circle them, seemingly answering some call that Sean could not hear. His heart felt as if it would burst with the sudden beauty of... everything. Nothing was as he'd always believed, and nothing could ever be the same again. He knew. Felt. Believed. He thought of all the lives who had passed never seeing this, never knowing. He felt the history of the place they stood and was filled with both sadness for all that had been lost and hope for what could be reclaimed. Restored.

He suddenly gripped Breena's hand tighter and something within him answered her wordless song, adding to her resonance, and suddenly the world around them exploded into even more vibrance. A chord of sound, music, poured from him. Wordless but universal. He let it out, as taken aback by it as Breena seemed to be. He heard her gasp and turned to her. She stared at him mouth agape, and he saw that her eyes were filled with tears as she looked at the world around them, seeing it magnified unexpectedly. For a moment, there was nothing in the world but the two of them and the song they created together.

"I never... I've never felt anything like that. Never seen anything like that," she whispered. "I knew you were the one."

"I don't know what that was," he responded. "I don't know what happened."

Something over her shoulder caught his eye and his heart sank. "But I think I know where we need to be."

She turned to look, and in the midst of the explosion of life and color around them, one spot below the bridge remained shrouded in darkness. A blackness neither could fully describe, as if the most angry and violent storm was holding its breath ready to wreak destruction on anyone in its path.

"I think you're right," she said. "We're needed there. Later, I have questions..."

She released his hand and the world slipped back to the colors and grit Sean was used to seeing. They each took a deep breath, turned, and started toward what they did not know.

CHAPTER 14

Breena and Sean backtracked along the beach toward the abandoned space under the bridge. Sean was struck by how drab the area seemed after what he had just seen, the colors washed away and a weightiness over everything. His sneakers, not made for walking in sand, felt heavy on his feet, and the more he walked the more it felt as if the sand itself were grabbing him and trying to pull him down. Whether it was pulling him away from the danger he sensed he was approaching or pulling him into some unknown depth, he had no idea. The beach eventually gave way to a rockier terrain, and he was able to pick up his pace. Breena, of course, seemed to feel nothing similar and glided across both sand and rocks, focused on the mysterious grey gloom ahead of them. They passed a solitary fisherman off to their right who took no notice of them as they pushed ahead.

As they neared the spot, Sean heard something disturbing, a mewling sound. He couldn't tell if it was human or not, but it was definitely the sound of something in distress. He sensed that Breena had heard it too, and they both picked up their pace. Where they were headed looked as if a pitch-black rain cloud had perched itself above and stayed in place. Sheets of dark grey rain fell in front of them. Before they stepped into the grey, they paused and looked at each other. Breena reached out and placed her hand in Sean's. Her face took on a faraway look for a breath, and when she was back, she looked at Sean and said, "The others know. They are ready to be here as soon as we know what we are facing. Keep your hand in mine."

With that they stepped into the gloom and the unknown. Two steps forward and it was as if someone had pulled a black curtain around them. The rocky beach they'd just crossed looked distant and filmy. The fisherman on the shore was nowhere to be seen. The black clouds above weren't actually raining, but the air was humid and unhealthy, making it difficult to catch a proper breath. They somehow felt damp, even without the rain falling, and it was a damp that felt malignant. Something you wanted to wash from your skin any way you could. But they walked on.

The cries of distress grew louder as the shade behind them pushed them farther from the safety they had left and closer to the center of whatever evil lay ahead. On the ground, it was as if every piece of trash and neglect had accumulated here over years. Sickness and danger lay all around them and they had to pick their way through it, wary of jagged edges of metal, discarded needles, and the rotting corpses of both fish and fowl. It was a landscape filled with decay. It was trap after trap waiting for the unwary. The vines and brush that fringed the rocky beach were a putrid shade of green. The green of illness and disease. They stretched across the ground toward Sean and Breena and seemed to writhe in an attempt to ensnare them.

Ahead, there was a clearing amidst the refuse. A sandy circle ringed with stones. The sounds were coming from there and as they rounded an outcrop of dull grey stones, the source of the sound became clear. A wrought iron post had been planted in the center, thick, sturdy, unnatural. Up its length ran a series of symbols. Sean could not make them out. They were of no language he knew, but they glowed with malice. Next to it sat Ken, tied to the post with a length of thick hemp rope. The strands of the rope were rough and seemed made to cut into flesh and inflict pain. And that's exactly what they were doing to Ken's wrists. His eyes were unfocused, staring into a distance that lay beyond Sean's or even Breena's sight. His whimpers were empty, wordless. His eyes seemed almost inhuman. Dark, nearly black, as if what they had been subjected to had stripped away all color and humanity. Sean was reminded of stories he'd heard of goats being tethered to stakes to lure tigers, and the hair on his neck stood up as he realized that's exactly what Ken was. Bait.

And then the bait, Ken, turned seemingly sightless eyes toward Sean and whispered his name. Barely audible, it sounded both plaintive and menacing. And that was when the beach around them exploded into motion and violence.

The tangle of vines to their left burst outward, sinuously reaching toward them with barbed tendrils thrashing. In the middle of it all strode a massive creature. Well over seven feet tall, it was emaciated almost to the point of being skeletal. Its long, corded muscles lay close to the surface and shook with rage and barely contained pulsing. Its skin was a deadly pallor, the grey of things long dead. Atop its head, it wore a set of brown, viciously knotted antlers. Whether it was a crown or a physical attribute, Sean couldn't tell. The face was hollow, filled with rage, the mouth snapped open and shut, flashing angry pointed teeth. The eyes were deep set, black, bottomless, but not unintelligent, and it took in Breena and Sean coldly before letting out a roar that echoed off the rocks that lined the water behind them. Just behind the creature, two smaller creatures of similar looks, emerged. More timid, but no less angry, they were clearly under the thrall of the first entity.

Breena gripped Sean's hand tighter, and he heard her whisper the word "Wendigo," but whether it was in his mind or in his ear, he couldn't say. "Do not allow it to grasp you. If it does, you will be lost like its minions."

The Wendigo took two large strides into the clearing. Ken, seeing it moving closer to him, strained even harder at his ropes, but they held firm and his desperation rose along with his cries for mercy and help. The stake to which he was tied started to glow a vicious red and Ken found himself caught between the searing heat of the stake and the approaching Wendigo. His eyes widened and he began to cry loudly, caught between certain death on either side.

Breena began her song, deep within her, and a pure light blossomed outward, enveloping Breena and Sean. She moved forward, closer to Ken, who was still beyond her light. Sean felt his song, his chord, his music, rising and answering, although he still had no idea how it happened or how to control it. For now, he was happy to simply contribute. And he did. With the addition of his power, Breena's circle expanded and nearly reached Ken, whose wits had deserted him as he faced evil beyond anything he had ever imagined could exist.

The song gave pause to the Wendigo and its followers. It staggered backward a half step before raising its face to the sky and crying out in a language that no human had heard for millennia. As it did, the water behind them began to swirl and churn a few yards out from the shore. Something was coming, but whatever it was remained hidden beneath the waves for the moment. Ken, however, noticed, and promptly fainted, overwhelmed at the possibility of a new unknown danger approaching him from behind.

Breena's expression took on its faraway look and as soon as it did, the air around them crackled. Kallan, Odette, and Bayard slid onto the beach. As one, they marched on the Wendigo trio. Kallan flexed his arm and suddenly his hand was holding a massive, gleaming sword, that seemed to glow with the purest light Sean had ever seen. He approached the lead Wendigo and it screamed and covered its eyes but gave no ground. Odette with her ancient spear held in front of her, and Bayard with his short swords carving the air in front of him, dashed toward the minions who seemed instantly overwhelmed and began to disappear back into the vines with the two Peripherals close behind.

Breena moved forward, making sure that her light now covered Ken, who lay prone on the ground. Unmoving.

But with all the attention now focused away from the harbor, no one noticed at first the massive head that emerged from the water. Another roar broke through the air, and all turned to see an enormous serpent rising from the depths. It had the head of a horned dragon and rushed through the water at enormous speed. The beach side was entirely exposed, and the serpent sped toward Ken with its jaws opening and shutting reflexively, as if it was already claiming its victim.

Everything was happening too quickly. Sean heard Breena again, but the word she spoke, "Oniare," meant nothing to him. He guessed it referred to the serpent, and his first thought was to somehow protect Ken. He ran forward, dropping Breena's hand and placing himself between the fiend and Ken. As he did, the shower of light that had protected him faltered. It didn't fail entirely, but it became smaller, diminished. When it did, the Oniare and the Wendigo immediately shifted their focus to him, and he found himself the object of their fury.

With Sean exposed, the Wendigo seemed to find a new well of strength. It reared back and struck out at Kallan, who stumbled backward and fell to his knees. When he did, the creature rushed past, heading straight for Sean. Meanwhile, Sean's song faltered, and the serpent closed in on him from the water side. Even though Breena rushed to his side, it seemed that there was no way he could avoid disaster.

And suddenly, Alara appeared. Striding through, almost on top of, the water, she left a wake behind her as she fairly flew toward the Oniare. She was accompanied by a host of Undines, flowing through the water around her and lifting their voices. The great serpent paused, taken aback by this unexpected assault. A handful of Kelpies that had been ringing the serpent heard the Undines' song and turned to disappear into the depths of the harbor. The serpent turned to face the newcomers which was the opening Alara needed.

Her hands made elaborate motions before her and chanted in a language Sean had never heard. A great wave answered her summons and rushed toward the beach. It broke over the Oniare, and with a horrible cry it was upended and went tumbling end over end in the surge as the water crashed and pulled back out into the deeper reaches of the bay. The water left behind flattened instantly and was as still as glass.

The Wendigo saw its ally fall and screamed, renewing its effort to reach Sean, but Kallan had also had time to regroup. He lashed out with his sword, slicing through the back of one of the Wendigo's legs. The creature howled in pain and anger, and hesitated.

Just then, Bayard and Odette emerged from the brush. Odette's spear dripped with gore, and Bayard was wiping his swords on the leaves of nearby bushes and smiling a vicious grin that spoke of recent violence and the hope for more. The lesser Wendigos were nowhere to be seen.

The Wendigo was surrounded, outnumbered, and turned in every direction. Far from being defeated, it seemed to be gearing up for another lunge. At just that moment, when all seemed in hand for the Peripherals, an enormous scream broke from beyond the circle under the bridge. With a thundering of hooves, the Dullahan made its entrance astride an enormous black steed. It carried its own head aloft in one hand, and the head bore a terrifying smile that stretched from ear to ear. Its flesh was dull, waxy, grey, devoid of life. In its other hand, it wielded a whip that it snapped constantly in all directions. Upon further inspection, it became clear that the whip was made from the spine of something long deceased. The length seemed distinctly human, which added to the terrifying effect. The horse was solid muscle and foamed at the mouth, whether from terror at its rider or a desire for blood was impossible to tell.

The Dullahan's appearance gave the Wendigo the breath it needed. It whirled and backhanded the approaching Odette, who flew backward and fell to the ground, motionless. Bayard was a few yards away still, and turned his attention to the Dullahan, launching one of his swords through the air. It was a deadly throw and flew true, looking to pierce its chest, but at the last second a flick of the whip knocked it aside and it fell to the ground. Useless. By now, Breena had reached Sean and joined his song again, but he was distracted, unsure where to focus, and their power was diminished.

The black horse pawed the ground angrily, as it approached the center group of Sean, Breena, and Ken. The Wendigo flanked it to come from the opposite side. Alara was chanting in the shallows, but her water spells did not reach far enough onto the land. She drew a savage looking scimitar and dashed ashore but was still out of reach. Kallan was still rising from his knees and knew he was too far away to stop what would come next.

And then, the air was filled with the sound of a mid-nineties Ford Bronco horn. One that had seen better days but was rising to the occasion. Trout's green and white truck came screaming through the metal security gate that had been closed over the path. The metal tubing went flying and the truck barreled in, catching the Wendigo unawares from behind. It threw the creature through the air and plowed forward, ultimately pinning it against the stacked lumber off to the side. Trout was out of the cab in an instant, and with an enormous cry, launched himself at the creature. With a windup worthy of his home state, he landed an uppercut to the jaw of the Wendigo, who went sailing through the air to land yards away, barely moving.

At almost the same time, Odette had recovered enough to rise and take aim with her ancient spear. But rather than aiming for the Dullahan, she had centered on the massive steed and her aim was true. The spear plunged into the breast of the beast. Instead of crying in pain, it simply vanished in a shower of dust, leaving its rider on its knees, and surrounded.

With the Peripherals closing in, the Dullahan swirled its cloak through the air and reappeared at the side of the wounded Wendigo, which lay injured on the ground. It began to fling its cloak around the two of them. Before the two vanished, the whip snaked out one last time and flicked itself against the nearest foe. Ken, even in his prone state, writhed in pain and cried out. Then the evil disappeared in a black and grey mist and the beach fell silent but for the panting of the combatants and the almost childlike mewling of Ken.

The grey fog that had blanketed the shore disappeared, leaving behind a surprisingly normal day. The sun was trying to break through the cloud cover. Fishermen to their right reappeared, none the wiser to the furious battle that had just taken place. The water lapped lazily at the rocky shore, listlessly rolling in and out. Traffic sounds from the far-overhead bridge resumed and a truck horn blared over the sound of a jackhammer, a symphony of congestion and ever-present construction.

On the beach, Ken lay in a heap on the ground, still bound to the ornate post. The runes on the stake had faded and were slipping away altogether. Ken's eyes were vacant. Lifeless. Bayard used one of his short swords to cut through the ropes that bound him, and his arms fell seemingly lifeless to the ground. Breena knelt next to him and whispered ancient words while placing her hands on his brow. Concern played across her face, but she stayed with him.

Odette retrieved her spear from the ash that had once been the massive black stallion, sifting through the dust left behind. As she lifted it, a breeze swept in behind her and spread the ashes over the mirrorlike waters of the bay. "Rest well," Bayard muttered from behind her. "They can't hurt you now."

"Whoooooooo!" Trout exclaimed. "That was one helluva dustup. Everyone OK? Other than those whatever-they-were whose asses we just completely kicked!" He grinned as he strode over to take a look at his truck. "Hey, folks, I think I have some pieces of that ugly horny guy stuck in my grille."

"Don't touch that," Kallan quickly said, and approached with his sword in hand. He used it to pry pieces of dull, lifeless Wendigo flesh from the front of the truck and launched them high out over the water. Steam hissed from the surface as the flesh bobbed to the surface for a moment and then sank slowly. "Best not to take any chances," he said, looking at Trout.

"You don't have to tell me twice. Hey, we found Ken! What's up, buddy..." His voice tailed off as he noticed Ken lying motionless. "Is he...?"

"No," Breena answered. "He lives, but he has suffered greatly. The Dullahan could easily have killed him with that whip but chose to leave him like this. They're not done with your friend yet, sadly."

"We must move," said Bayard. "For Ken's safety and our own. They could be regrouping to attack again. Gathering forces. No need to make it easier for them."

"I agree," replied Alara, crossing up the beach. "There are still rumors of darkness in this water. The sooner we're away, the better."

"But where can we go?" Sean asked. "My apartment is well over an hour away this time of day. We definitely need to get Ken somewhere quiet and private. And someplace we can defend, if necessary."

"Bayonne, baby!" Trout beamed. "Close by. My apartment is a third-floor walkup with no one above and it's just me living there. Everything we need."

"Trout, that's amazing. Thank you. We should probably check in with the others..." Sean took out and glanced at his phone. "Oh, cripes. Forty-two text messages. Yeah, we need to check in."

So as the others carefully loaded Ken into the back of the Bronco, Sean began to pore over the messages. They amounted to not a lot of information but did descend into worry and then panic as time had passed with no response from Sean.

He texted Brandy. "Sorry for the delay. Things complicated here. Will call when we get someplace quiet. Please let others know." He left it at that, buying them the time to discuss what had just happened and decide how much, if anything, they should share with the Grumbles.

Sean clambered into the back seat of the Bronco with Breena.

Odette sat up front with Trout driving. Bayard excused himself, saying he had a quick errand to run. Kallan and Alara once again left to reconnoiter along the way. One by land, the other over the water. And so, this most improbable group headed off for the most unlikely destination of Bayonne, NJ, a town which most assuredly had never seen their like before.

CHAPTER 15

Forty minutes of bumper-to-bumper traffic later, Trout pulled up outside his apartment in Bayonne. He let out a small whoop when he found a street parking space not far from his front door, pulled in, and the odd assortment of passengers rolled out. Kallan and Alara blinked in by the front door and nodded that they had taken a look around and all seemed clear. Trout and Sean took Ken from the rear hatch and put his arms around their shoulders, supporting him the few yards along the sidewalk. Sean looked nervously around, hoping no one would notice their incapacitated friend. Trout noted his anxious glance and said, "Don't worry about anyone seeing. This is par for the course. Happens on a regular basis around here. Big party 'hood."

Sean gave an awkward half-smile and continued toward the front door that Trout was holding open. Three flights of stairs later, Trout again held a door for them, this time the front door to his apartment. As they were entering, Bayard blinked in next to them with a pleased look on his face.

"Perfect timing," said Trout.

Safely inside, Sean took a look around and let out a low whistle.

The apartment was significantly bigger than he'd expected and surprisingly well appointed. It occupied the entire top floor of a brownstone. The living room was enormous with two L-shaped sectional couches taking up opposite corners. One wall held the biggest flat-screen television Sean had ever seen. The kitchen was to the right, and the facing wall had been cut out, creating a countertop with three tall stools and a view through to the kitchen proper. The appliances were all top of the line and gleaming stainless steel. An island in the middle of the kitchen floor was filled with chef accoutrements, and a wine refrigerator filled to capacity hummed quietly beneath it. Everything was sleek, contemporary. Except for a retro fridge in the far corner with scratches that could only come from wear, and magnets spelling out "Grandpa's Fridge." Obviously, an homage to Beer Culture and possibly a sign that they all spent too much time there. The apartment had two bedrooms, one significantly larger than the other and with three of four windows looking out over a park. The large bedroom also had its own bathroom which had been upgraded and included a large, jetted tub and a separate rain shower. The second bedroom was less elegant, but included wall-to-wall bookshelves full to overflowing, with books sitting in and on every available bit of space. Another bathroom sat across the living room. In short, Trout was living pretty large in Bayonne.

"What?" replied Trout to the unasked question. "I've done over twenty Broadway shows. You never asked yourself why I still live in Bayonne?"

"Actually, right now I'm asking why you ever leave town at all with an apartment like this," Sean answered, still gawping at each new luxury he noticed.

"Well, you can fix up a city apartment all you like, but it will never take the place of a good Montana hike along the river and a sunset over the mountains."

"I'll take your word for that. Just let me know if you ever need to sublet," Sean quipped.

The Peripherals had settled Ken onto one of the sofas, where he lay twitching slightly and occasionally mewling like a small child. The others took up places around the room and considered each other, wondering what would come next.

Breena began. "Our first order of business needs to be finding a cure for your friend, Ken."

"I'll have to defer to you on this one," Sean responded. "I'm way out of my depth here. All we could do is bring him to an emergency room where they would have no idea what the problem is or how to fix it. And there's no way I could possibly explain what happened to him without being admitted myself."

Odette spoke up next. "Is that really our first priority, though? He seems damaged but stable. Couldn't we leave him here, maybe with some of your friends, Sean, and track down the Dullahan first? The greatest threat lies there."

"But what if his condition is temporary?" Kallan responded. "We don't know exactly what's been done to him. If he turns, as most Wendigo victims do, he would be free to wreak havoc while we're off tracking. And before anyone suggests that we divide ourselves, we barely made it out that last encounter intact. They will be better prepared the next time now that they know who we are and that we have... terrestrial help."

"We absolutely cannot expose the humans again," Breena broke in. "They are completely out of their depth, and we have no idea what will be used against us the next time. We should leave them behind or somewhere safe."

"Now, wait a minute, here," Trout exclaimed. "I'm not sitting anything out. In case you forgot, I saved your bacon just now, my friend is drooling in the corner in need of help, and, well, I don't sit out when things get dangerous."

Bayard looked to Sean and mouthed the word "bacon?"

Sean motioned that he'd explain to him later before saying, "I have to agree with Trout on this one. You came to me specifically because you thought I had something to contribute that could only come from me. Breena, we clearly have some sort of... symmetry or connection? Something that works here. And how could you leave us behind anyway? Wouldn't we just be exposed on our own? How do we know that's not exactly what they want? Us on our own."

He looked meaningfully at Breena and saw her accept the logic of what was being said. He also saw concern in her eyes, and he held her gaze a moment longer than needed. Something was there, between them, but he felt himself flush and glanced at the floor.

"I think the answers to both problems, our foes, and our stricken friend, lie in the same direction," Alara said softly. "The Undines spoke to me of a powerful place. To the east. At the far end of the eastward island is a place of immense importance. A confluence of old and new powers. The old ways have been practiced there for as long as they can remember, but more recently, terrestrials tried to exploit a portal in the area. A window into other times or... dimensions? It was foolish, and exposed many to dangers they could not understand." She paused and looked pointedly around the room. "It's a place of ancient native power, but it flows in both directions, both good and evil. If he is to be cured, the answer can be found there."

"I suspect our adversaries have laid another trap for us," Kallan interjected. "There are, of course, other places of power around the globe, however, this is the only one close enough to be of use in saving your friend. We have no time to waste, and they are aware of that. Much as they drew us to the last scene, I'm guessing they knew we would have to head to this farther island if we are to heal their victim. Which is exactly why they left him hurt but alive. No need of even a cellular device to draw us in."

"They're pulling us out," Trout said. "Exposing us. Getting us away from crowds... distractions. Wolves do it. I've seen it back home. Choose their prey and then cut it from the herd. Easier to take down. Lions do it, too. Guess they've chosen their prey." He looked at Sean and, trying to lighten what he'd just said, snarled like a wolf in his direction. Sean shook his head but couldn't hide his chuckle in response.

"This powerful area. What is the name of this place?" Breena asked.

Alara and Sean both answered at the same time, "Montauk."

From the far side of the room, Ken cooed like a baby.

Trout grabbed a blanket from a closet hidden behind a bookshelf in the spare bedroom and placed it over Ken. He then crossed the room to sit by Sean. The Peripherals had scattered about and outside the apartment, keeping watch and letting the two friends have some time to process all that happened in the past few hours.

"Sean, please tell me I'm not insane. This is actually happening, right?"

Sean looked at Trout and opened and closed his mouth before finally saying, "If you weren't here with me, seeing and hearing and experiencing all of this, I might think I was crazy, myself. But he," he said gesturing to Ken, "is definitely not a figment of our imaginations. And these... people, who can blink in and out at will are really here. And these things definitely tried to hurt me. Us. Them. So... hard as it seems to accept, it must be real."

"Yeah, yeah, I guess so. I mean, I was picking evil monster skin out of my grille, so... what do we do about the others? They will be needing some sort of answer soon. Brandy will be expecting something from us. Hell, Nick may be triangulating our locations right now from our phones."

"True. And even Stewart can't still be sipping margaritas with his cop friends."

"So, what do we tell them? I don't know if giving them all of this information is a good idea. Or if they'd even believe us."

Sean considered. "Maybe we give them an excuse? We found Ken and... he had an accident? We're at the ER with him and will... let them know when he can have guests?"

"Possibly..." Trout responded. "But what about Anne? She

deserves to know something. Hell, if I know her, she'll *demand* to know something."

"Yeah. I don't feel good about keeping things from her, from any of them, but how do we explain this?"

"I know. Maybe we just tell them we've tracked Ken to somewhere on Long Island? Stall them for a bit?" Trout suggested. "The last thing we need is them showing up unexpectedly and placing everyone in danger."

"Honestly, I can't think straight right now. I need something to eat and to close my eyes for a few minutes."

"OK. There's a great Thai place on the block. Or there's always pizza," Trout responded.

Bayard blinked in next to Trout with wide eyes and a wider grin. "I vote for pizza," he said.

Trout laughed. "Pizza it is."

An hour later, Sean had sent a text to the Grumbles saying, "We'll have news soon."

The living room held three empty pizza boxes, a very sated Trout and Bayard, and the TV tuned to the Red Sox game. They were losing, but no one seemed to mind. In fact, only Trout and Bayard were watching. Sean was sitting on the other couch, his eyes half closed in exhaustion. Odette and Kallan stood off a bit, looking at Bayard with shades of disbelief and disapproval, while Alara and Breena seemed almost amused.

Bayard turned to Trout and asked, "So what exactly is this pepperoni? It's delicious."

"Probably better if I don't tell you. Same reason I never ask too many questions about black pudding, when I'm overseas. Best if you just enjoy it. And, now that you ask, I'm not entirely sure I know myself," Trout chuckled.

"I see. All right, I'll take your advice. Now, about this game we are watching. I have no idea what is happening." Bayard said, eyes intense with curiosity.

"Again, best if you keep it that way. Last thing you want is to get hooked and become a Sox fan," Trout quipped.

Bayard looked at him from the corner of his eye and nodded as if Trout had offered sage advice. Trout retreated to the kitchen and returned with two cans of Moose Drool beer.

"A treat from my home state. Can't get it here and you strike me as a guy who enjoys a beer." He held one out to Bayard, who sat up and brightened.

"And you would be correct, sir! Beer is one of our greatest gifts from the gods!" As he reached out for the bottle, he noticed shaking heads from each of his fellow Peripherals and withdrew his hand. "But maybe now is not the time. We'll save that until we have completed our task, yes?"

"Suit yourself," said Trout as he popped the can and took a gulp. "More for me."

Across the bottom of the screen ran a breaking news alert. All the fish from the displays in the Staten Island Ferry terminal had disappeared. They were nowhere to be found. Anyone with information should call a phone number that crawled past. Trout, the only one really watching the television, shot a look toward Bayard and raised an eyebrow. Bayard grinned in response and motioned for Trout to keep quiet. Trout guffawed and nodded approvingly.

"Speaking of our task," Kallan said, "how long will it take us to reach this Montauk? Or I should say, how long will it take you in your vehicle?"

Trout took out his phone and punched some information into his maps app. "Just under three hours, if traffic is friendly. And traffic here is never friendly. Even longer during rush hour."

"Rush hour?" Odette asked.

"Times when more people are on the roads. When they're coming or going from work. So, morning and late afternoon. More traffic. Longer waits," Trout explained.

She shook her head. "There is so much I will never understand about your lifestyle."

"In that case," Kallan said, "we should leave early in the morning. Darkness will only give aid to our foes, and I can see our two new friends are weary," he said with a glance to the sagging Sean. "Just before first light, Alara and I will travel there. You can catch up later and we'll have had a chance to survey the area."

"Sounds to me like we have a night off!" Trout exclaimed, as he grabbed the other can of beer and threw it toward Bayard. This time, Bayard did not hesitate and popped the can, taking a huge swig with glee. The other Peripherals shook their heads, but Breena was grinning as she turned away and crossed to where Sean was struggling vainly to keep his eyes open.

"Sean," she said gently, "You really should let your friends know something. We cannot have them surprising us here for some reason. And you need rest, so best to do it now."

Sean stirred slowly, his eyes slowly coming into focus, his hair matted to one side of his head, and his clothes askew.

"I know," he said. "Pizza made me sleepy. Couldn't fight it. What do you think I should say?" he asked. "I don't know how to keep them away."

"I think it best if you follow your earlier idea. Tell them we will travel to the eastern island."

"Long Island," he said. "It's called Long Island."

"All right. Tell them we travel to the Long Island tomorrow, and we will alert them when we have more news."

"Yeah, OK," he said. "But this isn't going to work much longer. They'll take things into their own hands soon. Like Trout did."

"I understand, Sean. Right now, it's best to keep them safe. But circumstances may change. For now, though..."

"No, you're right. I don't know what I'd do if anything happened to any of them. Bad enough that Trout is involved now."

"I heard that," Trout said from across the room. "Don't you dare

try to lose me. Besides, you need my ride." he said, without taking his eyes off the television.

"Don't worry. I know we can't get rid of you at this point," Sean replied.

He sent a group text to the Grumbles asking them to be patient and that they had information Ken was on Long Island and they'd collect him in the morning, that for now they should take care of Anne and keep checking in with the police. When he was done, he turned his phone to silent to avoid the inevitable texts full of questions and slid back onto the sofa.

Across the room, Trout roused himself to cross to Ken and put a washcloth under his face.

"Can't have you drooling on my expensive sofa, buddy," he muttered as he grabbed two more beers from the kitchen and sat down next to Bayard for what was sure to be another disappointing finish by the Sox.

Two innings later, they had pulled off an improbable win and Trout and Bayard celebrated appropriately long into the night.

CHAPTER 16

The sun rose the next morning, crisp and clear with a hint of real autumn in the air. Sweater weather was here, and as a heat-hating ginger, Sean was thrilled. He rolled out of bed and emerged into the living room to find he was the last to rise. Trout was in the kitchen making eggs, bacon, and a pot full of hot coffee. Bayard sat on one of the breakfast bar stools watching and discussing which of the morning's offerings would go well on pizza. Kallan and Alara were nowhere to be seen, presumably already in Montauk sleuthing about. Breena and Odette were at the window, looking out over the park and seeming to breathe deeply the cooler air that had arrived.

"Well, well, look who finally decided to join us," Trout teased as he slid a full plate down the countertop.

"It's six o'clock in the morning. What are *you* doing up? Theatre folk don't do mornings." Sean replied.

"Montana time kicked in. This is late on the farm. We've got things to do, miles to drive, evil monsters to vanquish. You know, a normal Tuesday."

"Well, I'm glad you're excited about it," said Sean as he tucked into his breakfast. It was good. Really good. And he toasted Trout with a raised fork and a full mouth.

Breena approached, touched Sean on the arm and said, "We should leave as soon as possible. The earlier we get there, the better. Daylight will be our friend, so best to make the most of it."

"Got it. Totally understand. I'll get a move on," Sean said between bites.

"Any word from the others?" asked Trout as he began cleaning the breakfast dishes.

"Oh, wow. Haven't even checked my phone yet. Just a sec... Oh. Yeah. Lots of angry messages. Our friends want information."

"I thought as much," Trout responded. "We have to give them something. Not really fair to keep them in the dark like this."

"I know, I know. I just don't know what to say. Hard to explain... all this... in a text."

Ken let out a small yelp from the corner of the room as if in response. Clearly, he'd not improved overnight.

"All I can do is text them that we'll let them know as soon as we have a location. That will buy us a few hours. Hopefully, they're not up yet."

Sean sent the text and turned back to his breakfast but any hope of a few hours head start was dashed by the almost immediate dings of three different very worried and angry Grumbles. Sean responded that he understood but didn't have any more information just yet and turned his phone to silent.

Trout gave him a skeptical sidewise glance and went on about his business in the kitchen. Sean gave a shrug, finished his food, and brought his plate into the kitchen.

"I really just don't know what to do," he said to Trout. "We can't drag them into this. It's dangerous, and inexplicable, and... I mean, look at your living room. Can you imagine trying to explain the Peripherals to Brandy?"

"No, but Nick would think they were awesome!" he quipped. "I get it. I do. I just feel bad. Ken's their friend, too. They must be out of their minds. And Anne…"

"You're right. I mean, we must keep Anne far away, she's got to be there to watch out for the kids, but the gang… Let's get there and see what we're up against. I think our new friends can handle themselves, but if we need more hands…?"

"I'm right here and can hear every word you're saying, you know. Without even really trying," said Bayard from the counter. "Trust me, we're up to the task ahead, and your friends would probably just distract us, to be honest. But I take it upon myself to keep them in mind and if there is a point where we need their help, I'll take care of it. And them. But for now, we need to take your rusty automobile and begin."

"Easy to forget they're around, even when they're not trying to hide," muttered Trout to Sean as he finished up the kitchen.

"Heard that!" came Bayard's response.

Sean and Trout grinned to each other as they grabbed their things and headed downstairs to the Bronco. Bayard and Odette half-carried, half-dragged Ken to the street and hoisted him into the Bronco's hatch. Trout gave a last look at his apartment as he closed the door behind him. Sean noticed him pause and silently wished that his friend would be safely back in his apartment at the conclusion of everything.

They climbed into the truck, Trout revved the engine and off they went. Sean checked his GPS for a route and time to Montauk. Traffic was light this early heading east and it would take under three hours. He checked on Ken, nestled in a blanket in the back, and hoped that Montauk's nickname, The End, was a good omen and not a bad one.

They rolled out of Bayonne, back across Staten Island, took the Verrazzano-Narrows Bridge, with Fort Wadsworth, the sight of yesterday's violence, sitting peacefully below, and onto the Belt Parkway headed east. Coney Island lay off to the right and at one point they could see some of the rides rearing above the nearby buildings, symbols of a simpler, more carefree time that seemed so far away to Sean right now. On they went, past the exits for JFK airport, with planes flying low overhead.

The miles slipped by—the Belt Parkway, then the Southern State Parkway, then Sunrise Highway with its small strip malls, one after the other until they became fewer and farther between and the road opened up ahead of them. Each of them had withdrawn into their own thoughts. Trout drove, eyes ahead but only semi-focused, trying to make sense of all he'd seen in less than a day. Bayard stared out the passenger-side window, wide-eyed at common sights that he'd never seen before. As a Peripheral, he slipped or blinked to move about, so the small things—fast food restaurants, auto body shops, health clubs, cars—all of it was new, marvelous, and strange and he tried to soak it in. In the back seat, Breena had closed her eyes and seemed far away. She was clearly awake though, and from time to time she reached next to her to reassure herself that Sean was still there, nestled safely in the middle seat between herself and Odette. Sean rode in the suicide seat, so named because an accident, or even a sudden stop, could send him through the windshield. The 1996 Broncos were safe... for 1996. Odette sat behind Bayard and stared at the passing scenery, taking little in. She was focused on the battle ahead and from time to time flicked her compact spear out to sharpen it with a grinding stone that also mysteriously appeared. The weapon sat nicely on the floor of the large SUV, not even reaching above the headrests on the seats. She preferred to use a wet grind wheel, but when in the field, one must use what is at hand. She was not afraid of the violence in front of them. She embraced it. Defeat never crossed her mind.

On they rolled, the wump-wump of the tires on the concrete a steady drumbeat in each of their private soundtracks.

CHAPTER 17

Declan Gormley was groggy, the result of a two-day bender hangover, red-eye flight, lack of sleep, and coming down from an adrenaline rush after the best trip home to Ireland in years. His plane had landed early for him, 9:00 a.m., and he'd jumped into his rental car. The coffee he'd grabbed on his way out of the JFK terminal was wearing off fast, as was his euphoria from the visit. Had it just been the night before last that he'd been in Dan Murphy's Bar in Sneem singing along with the musicians, great craic flowing along with the Guinness? Ah, his "Fields of Athenry" had left not a dry eye in the house, and his rendition of "God Save Ireland" had set every foot in the place thumping out a rhythm along with him. He'd even hit it off well with a young lady, Maureen, who thought his stories of America to be the most exciting things she'd ever heard. Little matter that most of them weren't true. She'd given him her number and email, told him to call her Mo, and made him promise to let him know when he was back. And he'd somehow managed to avoid her boyfriend Roger, who had the look of a jealous man. And so what if he'd embellished the truth a bit? Sure, didn't he deserve an escape from his dreary job as an insurance telemarketer out in Riverhead?

Not the glamorous life he'd imagined when he first came over, but he paid his bills and met his pals for drinks on the weekend. And sometimes midweek. He steered away from that thought. He earned his nights out. Nothing to worry about there. He did feel a bit sorry for the couple who'd sat next to him, one on either side, for the flight back. He'd been on the sauce for twelve hours before he boarded, and the flight crew had continued to ply him with cheap wine. The curse of a clever tongue and a quick wit. Hardly his fault. Had the couple said they were taking their honeymoon in NYC? Ah, he was sure they bore him no ill will, even if he couldn't remember half the flight and came to with his shirt, shoes, and socks on the floor in front of him. He was loads of fun and now they had a story for their friends about how the honeymoon started with a larger-than-life Kerryman amusing them all the way across the Atlantic. They'd probably write a story about him. As well they should. One of many he was sure he'd inspired.

He continued on his way, choosing the smaller highways to ease himself back into the pace of America. He'd have to find a way to spend more time back home. Long Island was feeling more and more like a dead end, and at the age of forty-four, it must be time to settle down a bit. Right?

His head started to have the dropsies as he fought the urge to sleep. He realized he was driving slower than he should and gave himself a pinch on the neck to wake up. He saw a truck coming up quickly behind him and moved over to the right to let them pass. In his side view mirror, he noticed that it looked to be some antique SUV, green and white and in great shape. He let out a slow whistle of appreciation as it neared, and then passed him. His eyes grew wider as he noticed the woman in the back seat. She was blond, beautiful, fair, and... was she sharpening a blade? Was that a spear? She noticed him noticing her, cocked her head to the side as if in mild surprise, and gave him an eager, almost feral, grin. He shook his head, sure that the hangover was playing with him more than he'd realized. When he looked back, she maintained eye contact, winked, and...

was gone. He sped up to drive next to the truck and stared into the backseat. Nothing. Just a middle-aged ginger sitting alone in the middle seat and a mustachioed driver in front.

He took the next exit and pulled into a Dunkin' Donuts. He needed coffee. And a quick lie back in the parking lot. He was definitely not feeling himself.

The Bronco rumbled on. They passed one of Sean's favorite pumpkin patches on their right. He stared wistfully as they passed, thinking of easier times, and hoping they would return. Somehow, he knew nothing would ever be quite that simple again. Then they passed a winery on the left. More bittersweet memories. He'd come here on a date once, long ago. Jennifer Blevins. More farm stands flashed by as they rolled ahead. So many landmarks Sean had always meant to visit. Why had he put them off for so long?

Into the Hamptons they drove, passing stores that were obviously overpriced because most of them bore the designation "boutique." The lifestyle out here had never been appealing to Sean. It had also never been an option, which made turning one's nose up at it a lot easier.

Trout caught Sean's eye in the rearview mirror. "I worked a catering gig out here when I first got to the city. Long time ago now. It was at Billy Joel's... house? Let's say compound. Had a great time. Spent most of the night sitting out by the pool with the man himself drinking beer and harmonizing to some of his music. Surreal."

"Are you kidding me?" Sean responded. "That should be in every interview you ever give. That's... Mr. New York."

"Yeah, I know. He even talked about bringing me in as a background singer. I think we both knew it would never happen, but, man, it made for a fun night."

Kallan turned in his seat and asked, "Who is this Billy Joel? Why is he Mr. New York? I listen to our own singers more than yours, although I know others feel differently." He shot a look at Breena and Alara.

"I like what I like," Alara said. "Makes no difference to me if they are ours or theirs. Music is universal."

"Oh, come on!" Trout nearly shouted to Kallan. "I figured even you all must have heard of the greatest singer-songwriter of our time!"

"Well, let's not get too carried away. Dylan, Springsteen, Dolly Parton, Joni Mitchell, Prince, John Prine (may they rest in peace) and a few dozen others might have something to say about that. I mean, c'mon, you live in Jersey! Where's your love for The Boss?" retorted Sean.

"Well, I live in Jersey, but my heart is in… well, Montana, but The Big Apple next. So, how about Billy Joel as the greatest New York singer-songwriter? Can we at least agree on that?" Trout responded.

"I'm pretty sure Carole King and Lou Reed (also rest in peace) are New Yorkers, too, you know…" answered Sean.

Surprisingly, Odette joined the conversation and said simply, "Play me this Billy person. So, we can make up our own minds on this."

Trout switched on the radio and turned to the satellite station for Billy Joel.

"Wait," said Sean, "You have satellite? Why have we been driving in silence?"

"I just figured it was early, everyone had things on their mind, and we should focus, but yes, of course I have satellite. You did see my apartment, right? I like modern amenities wrapped in unassuming packages."

"Fair point," came Sean's response. "Turn that volume up!"

"Movin' Out" came on and Trout and Sean immediately began singing along, unable to control themselves. The Peripherals all shared a glance and a smile. Clearly, the two friends were lost in the sheer enjoyment of making music together. The tension of the drive had broken, and they all sat back a little easier in their seats as they rolled through Eastport, Westhampton, Quogue, Shinnecock Hills, Water Mill, and on toward the villages of East Hampton. One Billy Joel song ran into another, and the two actors kept happily singing along, almost in defiance of what might lay ahead of them. When "Only the Good Die Young" came on they shared a glance, paused, and Sean said, "We're not that young anymore."

"Very true," came Trout's response and they launched into the song at full volume.

A few heads turned as the rickety truck passed through the narrow streets of the very chic Hamptons. Two loud voices rang forth as it traveled on, and even though the voices were quite good, they were met with varying degrees of enjoyment and annoyance. One of the heads that perked up belonged to a certain New York musical icon who recognized the strains of his own music. He grinned and went back to his crossword, never knowing one of the voices had almost been a backup singer for him years ago. At a nearby table, a national anchorman and celebrity started tapping his toe and began singing along without even realizing it. Socialites and titans of industry took note, never realizing that some of them had paid hundreds of dollars to hear those voices on Broadway. The singers could still be heard as the truck lumbered along, the Hamptons receding into the distance and the Pine Barrens rising up ahead of them. They were getting closer, but they sang on, letting their voices carry them along on a sense of optimism and freedom and sheer joy. The fear would come later. Not now.

The Peripherals listened intently to all of this and smiled. For a people who valued music, this was the first time they'd heard their new companions sing offstage and it resonated with them. Somehow it gave them a confidence, as they realized there was more to their new friends than had so far met the eyes. Bayard even joined in a chorus of "Piano Man," after catching on to the lyrics. All three of them agreed that Billy Joel was indeed a fine songwriter.

Trout changed the station to Springsteen and as "Born to Run" began, Sean and Trout increased their volume and the song echoed across the lonely trees on either side of the road. They all silently sensed that the song was appropriate. The road trip to likely end all road trips was picking up speed and hope. The music carried them forward and they all sensed possibilities that had seemed impossible not so long ago.

CHAPTER 18

Meanwhile, the other Grumbles had reconvened at Beer Culture. They had seen Anne back in New Jersey and assured her that they were doing everything that could be done. It was important, they told her, that she stayed home for the kids and on the off chance that Ken made his way back there. The police were on it, and they would be in touch. But the Grumbles felt helpless to actually do anything until they had found out where their friends were on Long Island. The bar was closed, but Paul had opened up for them and sat with them. This was the last place any of them had seen Ken and a sense of dread was seeping through the group as the hours crept by. Even Stewart, usually optimism personified, seemed down, although that could be due to the fact that it was too early for a margarita, and Beer Culture didn't serve them anyway. Nick was constantly checking to see if there had been any pings on Ken's phone but the look of frustration on his face told the group all they needed to know.

Brandy was about ready to suggest getting a train to Riverhead so they could be closer if a call came through and Sean needed them to help when a loud knock came on the door. Their heads turned in unison, surprised that anyone would be here so early. A large shadow filled the front window, but the tinted glass prevented them from seeing who was there. Paul shrugged and Nick stood up to answer the door. Collectively, they felt something was about to happen. Whether good or bad, none of them knew.

The Bronco cruised through the parklands outside of Montauk. Windows were down to catch the brisk breezes off the ocean that lay just over the dunes. They had turned the radio down and switched to the more sedate Simon and Garfunkel station. The passengers seemed to tense as Montauk grew closer. Breena took it upon herself to cut the anxiety and said, "It's unlikely we'll have any issues until after dark. I suggest we find a place to gather ourselves. Take the lay of the town. Prepare."

Sean replied, "I know exactly where we should set our stuff. This is one of my favorite places anywhere, so I can show us all around. And I happen to know someone who might be of some help to us..."

Trout half turned to him. "Are you thinking who I'm thinking?"

"I'm pretty sure I am," Sean answered. "Do you have a number for her? I don't think she'll open for a little bit yet."

"Pretty sure I do. Let's settle in and then give her a call."

"Sounds like a plan."

Odette spoke up, "I'm not sure we should be involving anyone else..."

"Trust us," Sean said. "She knows Montauk and then some. She'll be a valuable resource."

The Peripherals let it drop for now as Sean gave Trout directions and they pulled into the parking lot of an oceanfront hotel. Sean jumped out and walked into the office while the rest waited in the truck.

The Royal Atlantic called itself a beach resort, but it was more of a beachside motel at this time of year. The pool was closed. The bar was closed. It was really just a very affordable option with efficiencies. Some faced the road, some faced up or down the beach with partial water views. Some faced the beach and the wild Atlantic. Montauk lay at the easternmost tip of Long Island, jutting far out into the sea. As a result, it often was the victim of high winds and raging seas. This made it an exceedingly popular destination for surfers who tested their mettle against sometimes towering waves. It also made it a roll of the dice at certain times of year for vacationers. This time of year, the throngs of tourists that showed up in the summer months had moved on, leaving the town feeling more like Cabot Cove than Daytona Beach. And that was exactly how Sean liked it.

He returned to the truck announcing, "Early check-in achieved!" and found a lively discussion in progress. Bayard had come out in favor of Billy Joel. It seemed unsurprising that Odette had gone for the grittier, driving beats of Springsteen. Breena was the lone holdout, insisting that while they were both wonderful, she saved her top marks for the Waterboys.

"Never heard of them," Trout responded.

"Well, trust me. When you hear them, you'll understand," she responded and looked questioningly at Sean.

"Well, I can't say I know them, but if you think so highly of them, they must be worth a listen." Breena shot him a grin that would have weakened his knees if he weren't focused on other, more life-threatening, issues at the moment.

"I got us two double queen rooms, both facing the beach," Sean announced. "I thought it might be helpful to Alara to have that access. And I guess if anything comes at us from that direction, it would be good to see it coming."

Trout drove around to the far side of the gravel parking lot, and they all tumbled out of the Bronco. No one had any luggage, as such, so they headed up the outdoor stairs to the last two rooms on the second floor. They let themselves in and found perfectly comfortable, functional, if not luxurious, rooms. Each had a small balcony that opened onto the ocean side and the sound of the surf filled the rooms. Bayard, Odette, and Trout (who admitted a grudging respect for Springsteen), were still debating the musical merits of each artist as they closed the doors behind them and sat down to take a deep breath and consider what their next moves would be.

Ten minutes later, one of the doors whipped open and Trout and Sean came scurrying down the stairs into the parking lot.

"Sorry! Sorry!" Sean shout-whispered as they walk-ran to the truck. "Coming, Ken!"

"He won't remember this! He never needs to know," Trout said, as they pulled their listless, unseeing friend from the hatch and carried him up and into the rooms.

"Well, I'm definitely not going to be telling him," Sean said as they closed the door behind them.

Curious eyes followed them up the stairs from the hotel office window. As the door closed behind them, the curtains were briskly closed, and the manager offered a muttered wish that the new arrivals weren't going to be trouble.

The group dropped their few belongings in the rooms and gathered on the balconies, which sat immediately next to each other with only a small divider between. The day was brisk and clear, the ocean calm. A smattering of beach walkers wandered past, the last remnants of the tourist season that was now past. They likely saw nothing more than two middle-aged guys on neighboring balconies watching the ocean swells. On the balconies themselves, it was another story as there was barely enough room for everyone.

"Kallan knows we're here," Odette stated. "He's finishing around the northeast beaches of the island and should be along soon. I haven't heard from Alara yet, but when she gets here... well, we'll probably see her coming from here."

Sean nodded toward the water and all eyes drifted beyond the surf line where a pod of dolphins was lazily working its way east, fishing and playing.

"Good omen," Bayard said. "No way they'd be here unless things were safe. Quiet."

"Well, let's take that as a good sign, but prepare for trouble," Odette responded brusquely.

"I know you have qualms, but I'd like to pay a visit to my friend in town. Even if it's just to touch base and get the lay of the land, I think she could give some good local info," Trout began, ready to argue his point if needed.

Sean nodded in support. He knew who Trout meant and thought she could be helpful.

"Sandy," Trout answered the unspoken question.

"Sandy Dale," Sean affirmed. "Wow. Haven't seen her in... I don't know how long. I had forgotten she was here permanently now. How long has she been out here? I should have paid her a visit last year when I was here but didn't think of it."

"Got disillusioned with show biz, chucked it all and headed to the beach. She's had some sort of holistic shop out here for a while. She always leaned into things like that, so... makes sense. She seems really happy."

"Didn't she put little fairy houses all around her neighborhood once? Just because?" asked Sean.

"Yeah, I remember that," Trout said as all of the Peripherals suddenly became very interested in their discussion.

Bayard jumped into the conversation. "You know, maybe it is worth a visit. But, new rule, no one goes anywhere alone. So, I'll go with you."

"Well, OK. That's a deal," Trout beamed. "Let's get moving. If you're good, I'll buy you a treat."

As the two headed out the door, Kallan blinked into the room. His eyes followed the two as they left, and he turned to the others with an upturned eyebrow.

Breena spoke. "Trout has a friend here who may be of some help. As big a surprise to us as it is to you."

"I see. Good," he responded. "Odette, there is one more area I'd like to examine, but I thought it best if I did not go alone. Interested?"

"Absolutely," she responded. "This town is already intriguing me. I want to see more."

"Oh, you will be surprised. Many times, I'm guessing. Do the two of you mind staying here in case Alara returns?" he asked Sean and Breena.

"Not at all. Shall we agree to meet back here? Assuming all goes well on your task?"

They agreed and blinked out of the room. Sean was surprised at how quickly he'd become accustomed to it. He was, however, grateful when Breena suggested a quiet walk down to the beach. Might as well enjoy the morning before whatever lay in front of them. Down the outside stairs and directly onto the beach they went. They found a perch on a large piece of driftwood and sat, contemplating the ocean, listening to the gulls and the waves. They each had many questions for the other, but sat in silence for long minutes, neither wanting to ruin the calm. Likely one of the last peaceful moments they would know for a while.

CHAPTER 19

The Bronco rattled through the streets of Montauk. During the summer, it may have stood out among the wealthy vacationers, but in the off-season the town returned to its roots with a collection of locals: fisherman, surfers, aging hippies, new age types, and general misfits who came to the farthest reaches of Long Island not to be seen, but to disappear. And so, the Bronco fit in all too well. In fact, both Bayard and Trout felt at home, too, wishing they had arrived here under different circumstances.

Montauk Highway became the town's main street and they cruised along, getting a sense of the town before backtracking and taking the first right off of the roundabout onto Edgemere. They drove past Blade & Salt, which advertised pizza and good food. Bayard almost pressed his nose to the window when he saw the sign. Just past that and a few doors down to the right they saw the sign for the Montauk Brewing Company. At this, both sets of eyes in the Bronco followed longingly. For better or worse, they were closed now, but Trout turned to Bayard and said, "If we make it out of this, we are visiting both of those spots and not leaving until we've had our fill. Deal?"

"I think that is the best idea I've heard in quite some time," Bayard said.

"So... this connection you have with animals... What's up with that? How did that happen?" Trout asked.

"Ah. Long answer or short?"

"Let's split the difference? We probably have five minutes or so until I have to really concentrate on where I'm going."

"Middle ground answer it is, then. And I'm afraid it won't be as interesting as you may hope. In human mythology, or history, I suppose, depending on your point of view, Bayard was a noble and quite magical horse given to the Knight Renaud during what you would call the first Crusade. Through various events, that horse eventually ended up with no less a figure than Charlemagne. Humans being what they are, some attempted to destroy the horse, but he escaped and is said to live forevermore in the wild forests of France. How much of this is true? I'm not sure. But... the horse did exist and was given to Renaud by my family in thanks for his aid to us. What he did for us has been lost to time... yes, even we can forget some things... but Renaud and Bayard were real. Bayard was named after me. If you have ever heard of a 'Bay Horse,' it came from Bayard, who had an auburn coat and a black mane." He gestured to his own auburn hair. "You can see why. As for the communing with nature, wildlife specifically, it was simply always my family's... role... gift. In the Tuatha, we tended to the welfare of the wild creatures of the world. I am simply one in a long line. And there you have it."

Trout sat silent as they drove on, contemplating. And finally, "That is so COOL!" he almost shouted. "Man, I have got a lot of questions for you when this is all done. So. Many. Questions! Oops, but right now I just missed our turn," he said, turning around at the next opportunity. "You have got to come to Montana with me. I need you to talk to a grizzly. 'Cause I have questions for them, too!"

Bayard chuckled and turned an amused eye to Trout. Maybe there was something to the youthful exuberance and almost naive curiosity of these humans, after all.

Sean turned to Breena finally, and asked, "Are you afraid?"

"Afraid? I am not even sure what that feels like, to be honest. We have been living in our own space for so long and anger there is… different. Rare, to begin with, and more… existential. We rarely fear for our lives. We fear for our way of being. The world we have created. Rarely do we feel in peril ourselves."

"Then why risk being here? Why even bother to get involved with this? We play no role in your world. We don't even know or acknowledge you exist. Why are you here?" he continued.

She paused, looking at his profile while he watched the waves, then turned to the sea herself.

"Interesting questions. We did have that debate amongst ourselves. I cannot say that we were all in agreement with the final solution, either. Some of my people argued to let the evil play itself out. Watch and wait, let it reveal its goals and react when we had more knowledge."

"Sounds reasonable," Sean interjected.

"Reasonable, maybe. Kind? No. Wise? Almost certainly not. You call us Peripherals. I find that name amusing on many levels. In a practical sense, yes, we chose to exist peripherally to your kind. But it was more a choice of survival, of preserving ourselves and our ways," she said eyeing him closely. "In fact, it was your kind who moved away from the natural order. You isolated yourselves. Serving advancement, power, control, domination. All those things drove you farther away from the things we valued. But you also pursued science, medicine, exploration, technology. Your kind are the most baffling combination of avarice and nobility. Cruelty and kindness. Our world is more often clearly defined. You have always frightened and intrigued us. We can't imagine the world without you almost as much as we can't imagine sharing it with you more intimately."

"So, the voices that spoke in favor of intervening carried the day, obviously. You're here," he answered.

"Yes and no. There was strong sentiment to let your kind bear the brunt. Ultimately, though, we were too concerned that the destruction would be too great, potentially greater than we could repair or reverse."

"That's more than a little terrifying to hear."

"It was a sobering moment for many of us, too. But as we told you earlier, we are hardly the best of our best. The five of us are misfits. We were deemed expendable and least likely to be missed," she spoke quietly. Almost sounding ashamed.

"You're the canaries in the coal mine, so to speak?" Sean asked.

"I'm not familiar with that phrase."

"In the past, coal miners…"

"That's a topic for discussion all by itself," Breena bristled.

"I'm aware," Sean said. "At any rate, they would bring canaries in cages with them into the mines. The birds are more sensitive to poisonous gases, so if they died, the miners knew to get out as quickly as possible and address the issue."

"That's… horrific," Breena said. "Barbaric."

"And it didn't stop until the mid-1980s, which really wasn't all that long ago, I'm embarrassed to say."

"Please, never tell Bayard of that. He's amusing and quick-witted but has little patience for cruelty to helpless creatures."

"I definitely got that impression."

"And you think we've been sent here under similar circumstances? To gauge the danger?" she asked.

"Well, yeah. You basically said so yourself. If it's too tough for you to handle, others will step in, but overall, they seem willing to risk you to find out. Seems pretty similar to me," he said quietly.

Breena fell silent and watched the waves some more. Her brow furrowed as she thought about what he'd said. He was worried he'd been too blunt, and said, "Tell me how anyone could ever see the five of you as anything less than miraculous? You all are so strong, wise... capable. How could you ever be dispensable?"

"I should let the others speak for themselves. But for me... as you can sense, I am an empath. From a family of empaths. Our place is to sense pain, trouble, imbalance. As well as positive emotions, of course. There have been times when I became overwhelmed by the emotions I sensed. I was paralyzed more than once by my own reactions. It is a delicate balance to strike. My family decided I was less successful at that balance than was needed... I am sorry. I'm probably saying far too much."

"No," Sean responded. "Not at all. I need to know these things. We are about to face something I don't understand. It helps me if I know more about the people on my side. About you."

"One thing that has surprised me, though," Breena began tentatively, "is you. I do not understand why you and I... complement each other. There are comparable stories of symmetry between one of you and one of us, but it's been so long I think most of us believed they were just stories. Or impossible after all the time that has passed." She changed topics, suddenly. "What drew you to music?" she asked.

"Me? Well, I'm not sure I remember, exactly. It was just always a part of me. I think one of my earliest memories is of my father playing the piano for me as I fell asleep. I could hear him, down the hall from my bedroom." Sean paused to think, then continued, "I loved his playing, but I'd always whisper down the hallway for him to sing something. Even then, I felt something... powerful... organic? The piano was lovely, but the thought of him singing, the breath in him creating something and sending it floating down to me—a piece of him, sent out into the world, meant for me, but also for anyone who could hear. It was literally a part of him. I loved that thought. I wanted to do that. I don't know, but *something* about music, especially the human voice. It just resonated. And never stopped."

"The way you describe it... it sounds almost spiritual. Maybe there is still magic in your world," she said quietly.

"Maybe so," he answered. "Maybe we've just forgotten how

magical it can be. He was gone not long after, so I always felt some of the magic had been taken away. Or never really existed."

"I'm sorry. That must have been very confusing at such a young age. And yet, you chose to make it your life's work. To use your voice to create something and send it out into the world to touch all those who sat in your audience. Listening. To a part of you," she said.

"Oh, but it's not the same," Sean answered. "Not at all. It became my job. There was nothing special about it, by then."

"Was it really so different? There was surely something magical about it for those who heard you. Even if you had become numb to the magic, it was still there, yes?"

He sat silent. Unsure how to answer. Maybe she was right. Just because he had lost his sense of wonder didn't mean it wasn't there.

"So, what I'm hearing is music has always been there for you?" she asked, sensing his hesitation.

"Yes. I suppose it has, although I'd never thought of it like that. It's just always been in me, I guess. And all those things you said... about storytelling, and music, and poetry? How your people value them?"

"All true," she answered. "All of them. And they were what drew us to you. Hearing you speak about it now, like that... I know we were correct. I just do not think any of us thought the results would be so immediate. Or so powerful. I certainly have never experienced anything close to it," she said, allowing her gaze to return to the water. "Or maybe I have. My history with music is similar. And different. I remember when our peoples first decided to withdraw from your world. There were so many of us. From different cultures. Regions. We were... immigrants. Refugees from everything we had ever known." Her eyes remained fixed on the water. "The first thing we experienced together... amidst all the fear and confusion and grief at leaving everything we had ever known, was a song. A simple song. One we all knew, although the words were different in each language. That simple melody brought us all together. Told us we would be all right. That we were related."

"I've heard of similar stories. Where displaced people turn to music to remind them of where they came from. Where they belong. Where they can go."

"As have I. A reminder of the power of song. A language that knows no language. Music. Somehow, I feel it knits us together. Our groups, yes. But also, all of us."

"Is that... a good thing?" he asked.

"I honestly don't know, Sean. After we withdrew from your kind, we committed ourselves to maintaining a connection to all the others in our 'world.' We knew that, to survive, we would need each other. We knew one another. Good, evil, all existed and had struck a balance," she explained. "Our differences were superficial, and we decided to celebrate them and exist together. Although we come from different lands, and in many places look different from one another, we did not let that affect us. Your kind, though, we have watched as you war with each other over... so many things. The color of your skins, what you choose to believe in, over money, land, resources. All things that we decided long ago to share. There were infrequent incidents when something would fall out of the order, but it was quickly restored. We've never seen a concerted effort to bring down what we created. Both in our own world and in yours. You were off limits to us. We thought we all were safer apart. But the attack we're seeing and also my connection to you call many of these ideas into question. Maybe we were wrong all those millennia ago when we gave up on you. And maybe we were wrong to trust ourselves to be able to preserve the order on our own."

"I've seen questions in Kallan's eyes, although I haven't really seen much of him," Sean said. "Odette seems more straightforward, eyes on the task at hand. Bayard... well, he's himself, isn't he? I like him. And Alara... she's a mystery to me. So far."

"I'd say that's all correct. You are perceptive, Sean. More than any of us believed your kind could be. It could be we were wrong to believe that you were incapable of empathy. It seems we still have much to learn. Or relearn... about you."

"Well, I hope we get the chance," he answered. "Also, I think we have company."

Breena looked to the sea and saw Alara emerging from the surf. Her face was set and determined, and Sean had a feeling he was about to get to know her better.

CHAPTER 20

Trout turned right at Kenny's Tipperary Inn and continued along West Lake Road, scanning both sides of the street.

"You kind of have to know it's there from what I'm told," Trout said, slowing to look from side to side.

He let out a small whoop, hit the brakes, and took a sharp left into a dirt and gravel parking lot. A small tiki bar, shut up tight for the off-season, lay to the right and he parked next to it. Emerging from the truck, he walked the full circumference of the bar and came back to the front looking confused. He turned around and retraced his path and eventually stopped and stared at a very faint break in the bushes in the small patch of trees behind the building. He moved a few branches out of the way and turned, beaming, at Bayard.

"Never had a doubt. Follow me, horse whisperer. You're about to meet the force of nature that is Sandy Dale!"

They followed the trail for a few yards, barely far enough to lose sight of the parking lot, but the trees blanketed the area and almost no sound found its way in. Eventually, they saw a... what was it? Too big to be a shed, but too small to be a hut, it was a tiny structure. Obviously, no parking lot, but there was a bike rack out front and an elaborately colored and seemingly hand-painted sign that simply said "The Realm." Another path led in the opposite direction to another parking lot through trees behind it. There were no signs of activity and Trout turned to Bayard and said, "Huh. I sure hope she's open."

"Shut up and get in here, you big fool!" boomed a voice from inside.

"She's open!" Trout said with a huge grin. "Hey, let me go in first, sort of prepare her for you and... well... everything. She's about to get some big surprises. Probably best to ease her into it. Cool?"

"Cool," answered Bayard, amused.

Trout opened the door and strode into another world. Bells on the door didn't just jangle when he opened it. They gently found a melody of their own and gave the impression that, rather than warn the occupants, they were more to relax any newcomers. The small room was filled top to bottom with splashes of color. The sound of birdsong filled the space. One wall was filled with books of all shapes and sizes. Another area was filled from the floor to the ceiling with herbs and homeopathic remedies. Trout saw gemstones, a Tibetan singing bowl (although he had zero idea what it was), crystals, clothing, tapestries, incense, figurines of mythical creatures (and some not so mythical), totems, there was a reiki section, and everywhere he looked were reminders to be kind, to care, to love, to be gentle, to stay aware. It was exactly the kind of place Trout would be hard pressed to find back home in Montana.

"And what the hell brings your sorry ass to my door?" came a large voice from behind the counter, but the enormous grin and open arms contradicted the volume and the words, and Trout found himself engulfed in a hug that was big enough for a Big Sky prairie and then some.

Sandy Dale wore a flowing purple skirt and an elaborately

embroidered shirt, reminiscent of something Trout had once seen in a Mexican street fair. Her feet were bare. Her blond hair was tied back in a braid and her bright blue eyes shone with amusement, intelligence, and flat-out life. She was one of Trout's favorite people, and he instantly regretted losing touch with her when she moved out of the city for her new life.

"Sand, how are you?" Trout asked earnestly. "I'm sorry I haven't visited sooner. I should have. I suck."

"Well, yes, you do suck, but I forgive you. Some two-hour trips are longer than others, and Montauk is a lot farther than just two hours in most senses. Especially in the off-season, it's kind of the polar opposite of the city. I get that."

"Still, that's no excuse for me to..."

"No, it's not an excuse. But it's true. Your excess energy leads you to Montana. I get that. Plus, no one really wants to hang out with their friends who leave the biz. It's awkward. Seems like I gave up, makes you question things, feel sorry for me. None of which you should do, by the way. I'm happier than I've been in a long time."

"Why *did* you leave? Is it OK for me to ask that?" Trout said tentatively.

"Trout, you can ask me anything, you know that. I... just had it. You know the business is tough at the best of times. Unfair, full of lies, untalented people who get ahead, good people who get left behind. Producers who do it for the money and don't care who gets hurt. No actual artistry in most of the things happening commercially... I mean, should I go on?" she asked staring out the window. "It's nothing we haven't talked about over beers after a show. Especially women. It's infinitely harder for women. Toss in that I crossed the dreaded forty-year-old line and... I mean, no one 'discovers' a middle-aged actor. At this point we are what we are. Our industry worships the young. I just got tired of it."

"I get it. I do. It's just so hard to see a friend—you, *this* friend—go. Especially someone as talented as you. I guess I always thought we'd be in it to the end. We were lifers," he said.

"I know. I thought I was a lifer, too. I did. But I'm happy now. Genuinely happy in a way I'd forgotten existed. It's a big, beautiful world out here, at least for me... and leaving taught me how to appreciate that again. Best thing I've done in a long time."

"I'm happy for you. I am. Sad for me to have you so far away, but happy for you."

"Thanks. OK, now that's out of the way. Seriously. Why the hell are you here? You didn't travel to The End to apologize to me," she said. And he could tell from the look on her face that she already suspected that it was no casual weekend at the beach.

"Well, I'm not sure really where to start... It's complicated," he answered.

"All right, well let's start with you telling your friend to stop skulking around out front and get in here," she said, giving him a pointed look.

"You... Wait, how did you know he was out there?"

"I have a motion sensing camera over the front door. You can take the city out of the girl, but..."

"Yeah, OK. Got it. I just thought..." He looked at the video monitor she held up from behind the counter. There was Bayard, looking up at the camera with his head cocked, apparently aware of what was being said. He had a curious look on his face, shook his head, and started into the shop. The door chimes sang as he entered and he stopped, taking in the singing of the birds, and smiled.

"I think he likes your soundtrack," Trout explained.

"Oh, that's no soundtrack. That's the real thing," Sandy said as she swept back the curtain from a window behind her and revealed a collection of bird feeders scattered among the trees behind the store. Dozens of them, all filled with the happy fluttering and singing of well-fed birds. "Much better than a sound effect station, yeah?"

Bayard's grin grew even bigger, and he crossed to the window, staring happily.

"OK, now. Tell me who he is, why the two of you are here, and what you need from me. Let's get on with it."

"Long story," Trout began.
"I'll do this," Bayard said, and turned bright eyes to Sandy.

CHAPTER 21

Montauk had been considered a strategic location from the earliest days of the American Revolution. It was remote enough to be a tempting target, yet offered access to two important major cities, New York to the west and Boston to the north. Because of this, from 1792 on, there were defenses put in place to warn of danger. The first was the Montauk Lighthouse, still standing today at the easternmost point. Various battlements were installed during World War I, with a Naval Air Station coming online in 1917. Dirigibles, airplanes, and troops occupied the area.

Camp Hero toward the easternmost end of Montauk was commissioned by the US Army in 1942 to protect New York from a sea invasion. Originally, it was disguised as a fishing village, so deception and mystery were woven into the site from the very start. Three-gun batteries were built and covered with earth as camouflage. New York was never attacked. However, the area was still seen as important strategically, and armaments continued to accumulate. Seaplanes, more barracks, and an enormous torpedo testing facility were added. Artillery continued to be added and more barracks and recreational buildings appeared as the camp swelled. The fishing village ruse, however, persisted. Bunkers were given false painted windows. The gymnasium was given a steeple to lend it the appearance of a church. The deception continued to grow.

During the Cold War, amidst the fear of a Soviet air attack on the mainland US, the camp incorporated significant radar facilities which continued to be upgraded over the following decade. Eventually, the camp was incorporated into the NORAD defense system. Security grew tighter.

In 1960, a high-powered, very sophisticated radar facility was put in place. It was so strong that local television and radio signals were disrupted, and the facility had to be shut down numerous times for recalibration.

In 1981, the base was closed. The radar installation was finally considered obsolete and too large to move, so it was simply abandoned. Left to decay over time, yet still guarded and observed. Over the ensuing years, the site was proposed to become both a subdivision and a golf course. Both plans were abandoned for environmental reasons.

In 2002, most of the area was opened to the public as Camp Hero State Park, although the radar installation remained off limits. It was in the intervening "quiet" decades that the camp earned its reputation as the site of unusual, perhaps illegal, and definitely extranormal programs.

In the 1980s and '90s, rumors surfaced that the base was the site of highly secretive mind-control experiments. Some claim that the government experimented with placing ideas in people's brains. Others believe that the tests included weather control. One scientist believes that he was sent backward in time to the late 1960s. Further, there have persisted dark rumors that a labyrinth of tunnels below the camp were used for even more nefarious purposes, using mind control to train kidnapped children to become the Montauk Boys, super soldiers whose young minds were easily tapped into and controlled.

In fact, so rife with rumor and innuendo is the area, that it became the inspiration for the popular television series *Stranger Things,* which tapped into even darker rumors of a portal below the ground that led to... someplace else. Perhaps another dimension.

Whether some, none, or all of the rumors about Camp Hero are true, it remains a genuinely curious and potentially sinister location, visited by the curious and macabre traveler alike. They mingle with unsuspecting families, who visit the park for a hike along the trails or the view from the bluffs looking out over the ocean.

This is where Kallan brought Odette to explore. He believed they were the only two of their group that could safely navigate the potential dangers there. He was wrong.

Alara strode up the beach toward Breena and Sean, who rose to greet her. Sean had never actually seen her come from the water like this and was surprised but concealed it and filed it away with the few hundred other surprises he'd had in the last day and a half. Her hair was wet and slick to her head but not dripping. She seemed less like she'd just emerged from the ocean and more like she'd walked through a quick rain shower.

When she reached them, Breena gave her a quick rundown of where everyone had gone and that they'd been waiting for her. When she finished, Alara asked, "Where is your friend, Ken? The one injured?"

"Oh, dammit," Sean exclaimed, scrambling up the beach back to the hotel. "We all forgot him *again!*"

The two women moved quickly behind him. Breena shot a knowing glance at Alara. Both were fully aware that even from the beach, Breena would have sensed any danger, either to Ken or themselves, but they let Sean run ahead. A healthy degree of mindfulness could be a good thing with what they faced in the hours ahead.

Back in the room where they'd left Ken, the women entered to a very relieved Sean, who was securing a blanket around his still incoherent friend. Sean checked him over, made sure he was tucked in, and examined the rest of the room to make sure it was empty. This consisted of opening the bathroom door and then looking on the balcony, but it reassured Sean. His mind at ease, he turned to Alara.

"I am so sorry," he said. "I didn't mean to run off like that. We just keep forgetting him and it makes me feel horrible. It's not like he can take care of himself, right?"

"No apology necessary," she responded. "We are all under a lot of stress at the moment. You, I would imagine, even more so than the rest of us. This is all very new and strange to you."

"Well, yes, it is. Thanks for understanding. Just trying to keep my head on straight at this point."

"You're doing a wonderful job of it, Sean," said Breena. She added, "Really," when he gave her a dubious look.

"It is true, Sean," Alara said. "You are doing better than anyone could have, or should have, expected."

"What news do you have for us?" Breena asked her.

"The sea is alive. Calls have gone out and I'm hearing reports of creatures from all over answering. It's likely most will arrive here too late to affect tonight, for good or ill, but it does point out that what-ever is happening is important. Spanning all of our peoples. I've never seen anything like it."

"Nor have I," responded Breena. "Who, or what, can we expect?"

"The easternmost points of the island are ringed with Undines. They have put aside their usual indifference to continue aiding us. I think the attack on the ferry woke them to the very real danger we all face. While appreciated, their help will likely only serve to warn us. They are of little practical help. Their song may deter some lesser creatures, but anything of real strength will eventually find its way through."

"That's not encouraging," said Sean.

"On the contrary," said Breena. "Undines normally remain neutral and stay to themselves. The fact that they are joining us is very encouraging, indeed. But also indicative of the peril we face."

"Exactly," Alara chimed in. "It seems we'll need every help we can find, so they are most welcome. Interestingly, there are numerous families of Selkies at the very end of the island. They are also warned and should be of help when and if things happen. It seems this town and its environs are full of conflicting power gateways, with good and evil. It is no coincidence that we were led here, but it may not be the advantage our adversaries expect."

"Selkies?" Sean asked. "I thought they were part of the attack on the ferry, no?"

"Ah," Alara answered, "easy mistake. Those were Kelpies, a variety of Scottish water creature. Decidedly unpleasant. Selkies, while also water creatures, are gentler. Kinder. They shapeshift, from human to seal. More prone to friendly, sometimes even romantic relations with humans. They will certainly be a help."

"OK," he responded, "I may need help keeping the good guys from the bad guys."

"Trust me, Sean," Breena said. "You won't."

"On the negative side of things, the Kelpies are in the area. This is not good. Obviously." Alara added, "Oh, and our friend the Oniare is rumored to be in the area. Perhaps more than one."

"Is this as bad as it seems?" Sean asked.

"Yes. And no," Alara answered. "These are all foes to fear, but the natural order of the sea is pitted against them. Our enemies defy the order of things and nature does not abide that. The dolphins you saw earlier were no accident. They will keep watch. Along with all the other creatures who belong here."

"All of them?" he asked.

"Yes," was her response. "All of them. Even the most fearsome creatures of the ocean know their place. And ours. They respect the balance. They will come to our aid."

"Huh. So much for Jaws," Sean muttered.

On the far bed, Ken snuffled like a puppy.

Kallan and Odette blinked into the area surrounding the massive and deteriorating radar installation at Camp Hero. The blocklike building was topped by an enormous radar dish. It had been considered state of the art during the Cold War, but eventually abandoned decades earlier and was falling apart. The dish itself appeared almost skeletal, the membrane between the ribs nearly entirely flaked away. What was left had become a perch for dozens and dozens of crows. Their cries echoed through the compound. Eerie, as they were the only sound in a forest that should be teeming with life. The silence was unhealthy. A warning. However, the two Peripherals were focused on the cement building and paid no mind to the crows. Or the absence of other noises. The station itself had long been sealed off, the only entry was through a vent that continued to attract teenage thrill-seekers from the area. A sealed door, however, was no obstacle to the two and they simply blinked inside.

The interior was what one would expect. Stairs, walls, ceilings, had all collapsed. Asbestos fell from exposed openings. What little furniture remained was disintegrating. Any wire or metal had long since been looted by vandals. Even the normally silent tread of the two Peripherals sent faint echoes skittering throughout the facility. The building felt hollow, empty, dead, but somewhere underneath all of that was something disturbing. Off. Evil. Not so much active as the memory of wrongdoing. Something that defied the laws of nature had happened here, and whether it had been abandoned in haste or fear, or deliberately when that work had completed, it had left the building corrupted to its core. The fabric of the place had been altered.

A brief look around the ground floor revealed nothing more than an entrance foyer and some offices. Papers lay where they had fallen, gathering dust as the years passed. There was nothing of value here. There was also nothing of any danger here.

They returned to the entrance way, and a glance toward the upper levels gave neither of them any sense of... anything. As one, they turned to a set of stairs descending below ground and into complete blackness. Below ground was where the rumors always placed the most nefarious of the activities here, and below ground was where Kallan and Odette sensed there was danger. Not the echoes of a long-gone wrong but living, breathing evil. Something alive and active. Something they needed to know more about.

They took the stairs downward. As the darkness enveloped them, Kallan's sword appeared in his hand. It glowed an icy blue and gave enough light for them to make their way. Odette followed, her spear at hand, closely matching where Kallan set foot. One level, two levels, three levels. They continued down. The sense of malignancy grew the deeper they went. After four flights down, the stairs ended, and they emerged into a warren of what seemed to be offices and laboratories. Farther in, they came to what seemed to be cells. Empty square rooms with only one door that bore a barred window. Some had padded walls. Some had what looked to be chains attached to the walls. All were open, their prisoners long freed and presumably gone. Or dead.

A scratching noise behind them echoed and the two whirled in unison but the blackness was complete, and they saw nothing. Kallan's light was faint and exposed only a few feet in front of him. Silence fell again. The scratching was gone, but with a silent glance to each other they both acknowledged what they had heard. They were not alone down here, which is exactly why they had come.

CHAPTER 22

As bright as Bayard's eyes had been at the sight of the singing menagerie outside the window, Sandy's eyes seemed twice as bright and twice as large when he finished explaining everything to her. Who he was, how he had come to be here, what they faced. All of it, and she looked thrilled.

"This is amazing. I'd say it's unbelievable, but I *really* want to believe all of it. I mean," she added sheepishly, "I'm sorry about Ken, but that seems to be in hand now, yes?"

Trout and Bayard responded with a so-so hand gesture, but she plowed on.

"I mean, look around you. Look at this store. This store that I've built. Me. To help people. To heal people. All because I've always hoped—no, believed—that there was something more to... everything. More than just us, daily slogging through this weird nine-to-five world we've created. Where we work the best years of our lives and then retire to enjoy life when we're too old to enjoy it and then probably die soon after anyway. I was right! There is more!"

Bayard chuckled. Surprised once again by one of these unpredictable creatures. "Yes, you were, apparently, right. There is more.

And what you have created here is remarkable. You are, and have been, on the right path. A path of your own making."

"So... make this clearer for me. You are... from the Tuatha? Does that make you fairies? Help me understand," she nearly pleaded, as she showed him a book from one of her shelves called *Gods and Fighting Men.* "This is by Lady Gregory and was written over a century ago! How have we lost you so completely?"

"It was necessary," answered Bayard, "and it happened much longer ago than a century. There have always been a few of your people who believed we still existed. Or had ever existed. I actually knew Isabella, or Lady Gregory as you call her. She was incredibly gifted. She almost belonged more with us than with you, but she chose to stay with you. That's a story for another time..."

Sandy stood, stunned, as if rooted to the floor before erupting again with, "So... you've been here all along? Watching? Avoiding? Who else is out there that we don't know about? What else?"

"The simplest way I can tell you is to say: Think of all the myths, the legends, the fairy tales you've heard that have passed from one generation to the next. Think of all the cultures and peoples who share comparable stories and yet also make them distinctly their own. All of this, every one, is rooted in some truth. All of them. We simply left you to yourself because... well, you left little room for any of the rest of us."

"All of it," she whispered. "Everything. Real. Big Foot?"

"Real. And under many names."

"Loch Ness Monster?"

"Real. Very shy. Keeps swimming into the loch and getting stuck. Not the brightest."

"Leprechauns?"

"Real. Highly amusing until they aren't. Some of my best friends."

"Mermaids?"

"Real, but too many varieties to even begin to recount right now."

"Sirens?"

"Real. Complicated."

"Chupacabra?"

"Real. Horrible temper."

"Vampires?"

"Real. Also complicated."

"Ghosts?"

"Not my area of expertise, but real."

"UFOs?"

"Not my department. Requires a *much* longer conversation. Let us keep it to this planet for now. You have a lot to grasp as it is."

"Yes, of course. This planet... but not necessarily this dimension?"

"Yes, true, and as I mentioned, we happen to be here on a matter of some urgency, so if you have any suggestions on how we can proceed, it would be very much appreciated."

"Yeah," added Trout, "I thought you may be able to give us some information on the island... something to point us in the right direction?"

"Right, yes, of course, I'm sorry," Sandy muttered. "What's the date?" she asked and looked at her phone. "Just past the autumnal equinox... you may just be in luck. He may be here."

"There is no such thing as luck and there are no coincidences. Not with this. Everything is happening for a reason. Who are you referring to?" Bayard urged.

"Kelphit. An indigenous healer, called The Father of Medicine. He's a master of herbalism. A good, kind spirit. Ancient beyond our knowing. He travels with the seasons. If he is here, I know where you may find him. I'll give you directions. If you do find him, that would be... huge. I know of him, but that's about it. To meet him would be the thrill of a lifetime. Maybe a few lifetimes. I'll stay here and prepare this as a haven. A safe place for you... or whoever may need it. I'm not good with the violence end of things, but I am very good with the healing and protection parts. Find Kelphit if you can. Then bring Ken here. I'll keep him safe."

"My thanks," Bayard said as he took her hand in his. "I promise, if I survive this, and I have every intention of doing so, I will sit with you and answer your questions until you have none left."

"That could take quite a while. I have a lot of them," she answered, eyes still wide.

"No worries. I have time. And I enjoy your birds... I'll need some rest when this is done."

Minutes later, Trout and Bayard found themselves racing down Montauk Highway. They turned right onto Camp Hero Road and parked on the shoulder, never knowing how close they were to Kallan and Odette. They walked back along the highway about a hundred yards until they saw a small sign marking the beginning of the Seal Haul Out Trail. There was no one nearby, tourists having mostly abandoned the trails this time of year. The way looked still wet from a recent rain, and heavy brush was trying to reclaim the path with the slowing of foot traffic. They looked at each other and then up and down the highway. Not a soul in sight, they turned to the forest.

"Stay as loud as you can. Hunting season, so we'd best keep an eye out for hunters. Don't want to end up one the wrong end of an arrow. Or a shotgun," said Trout.

Bayard paused to take that in, then turned to Trout and said with steel in his voice, "I think they'd best look out for me."

And with that, they plunged into the trees.

Kallan and Odette turned a corner and the pale blue light that was showing the way revealed a long corridor, angled downward, and disappearing into blackness with no end in sight. They nodded to each other and moved cautiously ahead. The angle wasn't severe, but steep enough to feel as if they were being gently pushed downhill. The concrete walls of the upper levels had been replaced by a sheer, black, smooth surface. It reflected no light, not even the ice blue of Kallan's blade. On they went, a lonely blue wink of light in a sea of darkness. As they continued, something caught their eyes ahead. A glow. A rectangle of dark orange seemingly suspended in the air far ahead. They each took a better grip of their weapon and walked on, determined.

As they got nearer, they realized the light was not suspended in midair. It was the outline of a large steel door. Easily twelve feet in height, the light seeped from the edges and occasionally pulsed ever so slightly. They approached cautiously, Kallan still in the lead. As they reached the door, he reached a hand out to test the surface. There was no heat, as he had expected. In fact, the opposite was true. The door was ice cold to the touch. There was no visible handle to the door, merely a plate roughly waist high that seemed to indicate a push would swing the door inward. He placed his hand on the plate and instantly the light around the edges vanished, leaving them with only the faint blue that was swallowed by every surface around them.

The door gave. It began to swing open. Beyond was total blackness. There was no sign of the orange light from before. There was no sign of anything. The two cautiously moved inside, but they were blind. A noise, that same scratching sound, came from the hallway behind them. As Kallan turned to it, the room they were in erupted in blinding, fiery light. They went from blinded in darkness to blinded by flames. The hallway outside the door swallowed the firelight and remained black. Kallan saw nothing there that could have made the sound. As he took that in, and just as quickly as it appeared, the fireball of light extinguished, leaving the two seeing bright lights in front of their eyes. They reached their arms out to each other, taking a defensive position, weapons at the ready. Back-to-back.

In the sudden blackness, a snake of red slithered into view, a sinuous, undulating scar in the blackness. And then it flicked. Not a snake at all. It was a whip. A whip made of the spine of a humanlike creature. A whip they had seen on the beach at Fort Wadsworth. It flashed out, wrapping itself around Odette's arm. Had she been human, the whip's touch would have sealed her fate, but she was a Peripheral, and her ancient strength kept her upright, but just barely. She cried out and Kallan felt her snatched from his side. He heard her being dragged across the floor and, his eye on the line of flame in front of him, he dove to where he thought she should be, but his arms closed on nothing. Another cry, this time farther away, drew him forward and he threw himself at it, but ran headlong into a wall. The crimson whip extinguished and was gone. The room plunged into darkness once more. He heard one more cry from Odette, tinged with a fear he had never heard from another Peripheral, and then it was cut short. The only sound left was a metallic clatter. He reached out and his hand closed on Odette's spear, left on the floor. She was gone and defenseless. Whatever had taken her, had left him alone in the darkness and he shouted in frustration as he sank to the floor.

CHAPTER 23

Trout and Bayard followed the faint path. Small markers placed on trees from time to time helped Trout find his way. Bayard moved confidently ahead, never slowing or hesitating. The leaves had begun to turn but had not fallen, so their steps were muffled by the dirt track and the various ground growth through which they had to pass. The oranges, reds, and yellows of the canopy lent a kaleidoscope effect to the dappled forest. Trout's boots left deep impressions as he passed through the occasional muddy spot, but he noticed that Bayard left nothing in his wake. In fact, he didn't make a sound as he marched ahead, stopping from time to time to listen, before plowing on again. They passed no one and they seemed to be the only souls on the way to or from the Seal Haul Out, an area of rocky beach known as a favorite resting spot for the local seal population.

Nearly a half mile into the woods, Bayard stopped and stared intently off to the right. There was no discernible track leaving the main path, but Bayard sensed something and left the marked trail, weaving between trees and under fallen boughs. Trout, seeing little option, paused briefly before following. They continued for nearly ten minutes in that direction before coming upon a small clearing. Nothing man-made, simply a break in the trees. In the center by a fallen tree was a simple lean-to made of branches, some large enough to be called logs. It had three sides with an opening facing away from them. There were no sounds or smells of anyone being there, but the construction was clearly recent, though ancient in design. It was startling to see it here, in the midst of nothing. Someone had wanted solitude, and Trout felt very much a trespasser.

They approached quietly, well, silently on Bayard's part, and as quietly as possible on Trout's. As they got nearer, they could see symbols drawn on some of the branches on the lean-to. The ground around it was untouched, scattered with twigs, leaves, and not a footprint in sight. Just before they reached the hut, a voice broke the silence, "You've taken quite some time. I've been listening to your approach since you left the path. Please, come in. There is much to be done…"

From the far side, a compact figure emerged and approached them. He was no more than five and a half feet tall, with long black hair tied back in elaborate plaits. His clothes were timeless, neither modern nor antiquated. He was dressed entirely in earth tones— deep brown pants, a dark green shirt with tortoise-shell buttons, heavy well-worn leather boots, topped with a light brown leather duster coat that fell nearly to his ankles. What Trout noticed imme- diately were his eyes. A deep, gentle, knowing brown that conveyed great strength, depth, compassion, joy, and sadness. His skin was lined, as if he had seen many, many years, but he radiated a youthful energy. Both joyful and somber. Airy and rooted. Trout felt both humbled and protected immediately in the man's presence and glanced at Bayard and saw that even the Peripheral was impressed by the individual now before them.

"I am Kelphit, as you well know. I have been preparing for your arrival. In, in. There is much to do..." And with that he turned and entered the lean-to.

When the two ducked into the wooden structure, they were surprised to find it much larger than they expected. Trout stopped in his tracks, taking it in. "It's so much..." he began.

"Larger on the inside. Yes, visitors are often surprised. The few I have," Kelphit answered and motioned for the two to be seated on some blankets that had been strewn about the floor. A small fire crackled off to one side, though no smoke had been visible when they approached.

"I am Bayard, of the Tuatha. Thank you for your welcome. We are humbled."

"I doubt that very much," Kelphit answered with a smirk, "but you are, indeed, most welcome. I have not seen any of your tribe in many, many years."

"Hi. I'm Trout. Dan Trout. No tribe, no ancient anything. Just a guy from Montana who's probably in over his head. But thank you for seeing us."

"You are quite tall. I doubt many things are over your head. Believe me, you are much needed here."

Trout bowed his head, thankful for the kind words, given his incredible sense of not belonging at this moment.

Kelphit approached Bayard with his hands outstretched and asked, "May I?"

Bayard assented and Kelphit placed his hands on either side of his head and leaned his forehead against Bayard's. They stayed that way for a few moments, and when Kelphit withdrew, his eyes were clouded and worried.

"Thank you," he said to Bayard.

"The honor is mine. Truly," Bayard responded, and this time his words were heartfelt. Brash, carefree Bayard was indeed awed by this wise man.

"I understand you are preparing for violence," Kelphit spoke.

"While I believe violence should be avoided when possible, there are times and places that it is not. This is most certainly one of those times. I am afraid I can be of little direct help. But I can offer some totems and symbols as protection. I draw my strength, my medicine if you will, from the earth and the natural world. As such, it is more a body/spirit method of life and avoidance, rather than the techniques of modern medicine, which treat the body as a machine to be repaired when it breaks down. But I am not without resources, and in trying times good folk must work together."

"Thank you," said Trout. "We need all the help we can get."

"You do indeed. However, where I can be of more service is in the protection and healing of your friend... Kenneth?"

"Yes, Ken, that's right. That would be incredible. Thank you!" responded Trout.

"Bring him to Ms. Dale's store. Between her and me, he will be very safe there while you and your friends... deal with what must be done. Before that, though, I will offer you both what little I can."

He went to the fire and removed a clay pot that had lain nearby. Carrying it back to the two, he dipped his fingers in and when he removed them, they were covered in a grey-black ash. He went to Bayard and Trout and drew something on the back of each of their necks.

"A simple protective ward. Alone it would be of little use, but it may tip the balance if you find yourself in dire need."

He placed the pot back where it had been and returned with a leather pouch. "Bayard, you need no totem from me. In some ways, you are your own totem. You know yourself and what you can and must do. Daniel, you are filled with great strength, willpower, and courage. But this knowledge is new to you. I give to you this totem now, not because you are weaker, but to remind you of that strength should your belief falter. It is made not from stone, but from a fossil taken from the lands of your home. Montana. A place of great beauty and power. Do not look at it until you are clear of here, but keep it close in a pocket, where you can hold it if needed. I have carried it for many years. Not until now did I know I was carrying it for you."

Kelphit took Trout's hand and placed a small carving in it. His hands were calloused, ancient, strong, but somehow gentle. Trout felt the touch echo throughout him. It was profound, as if he had glimpsed a piece of the earth's creation. He felt honored. And small. The carving was smooth with age, but heavy and solid. He immediately placed it in a pocket of his jeans, tucking it as far down as he could to keep it safely in place.

"I... don't know what to say..." he began.

"Best to be silent then," Kelphit responded grinning. "It speaks louder than your words ever could."

He placed his bag back near the clay pot and turned to them purposefully. "I must prepare," he said. "Bring your stricken friend to me at Ms. Dale's. I go."

With that, he stepped outside with a flourish of his duster. By the time Trout and Bayard reached the entrance, he was nowhere to be seen, but they could faintly see a swirling of dust and leaves as he sped away through the trees.

***

Back at the hotel, Sean and Breena were getting anxious. Alara could be seen nearby on the beach, scanning the waves and the skies. All seemed calm outside. Ken remained wrapped in a blanket on the bed farthest from the balcony. Safer, in theory, tucked into the deepest part of the room. From time to time, he murmured or let out a small cry, but he had moved little and spoken not at all. Once his eyes opened and they had hoped he was coming around, but he had stared ahead, unseeing, before slowly drifting away again.

The two sat on chairs by a table near the sliding door to the balcony. The screen door was pulled across to allow the ocean breeze to fill the room. It was cool and fresh, and they both closed their eyes to enjoy the moment. When Sean opened his eyes, he looked at

Breena, whose eyes remained closed, but she sensed his gaze and said lightly, "Staring is considered impolite in many cultures."

He chuckled and turned again to the beach and Alara, watching, vigilant. "True. I'm sorry. I'm still just... processing everything. It's a lot. You're a lot. I mean, not just you, all of your group." Motioning to the beach, he continued, "I know nothing about her. We've barely spoken. You trust her, so I trust her, but why is she risking herself, everything, to be here? To help me... him,"—he tossed a look back at Ken—"our friends. I understand that you retreated from us millennia ago. But what I don't really understand is why any of you are here to help. Alara seems... different from the rest of you. Her hair is dark, her manner is more restrained. So... what's her story?"

Breena paused, considering. "You're right, of course. Alara is different. Her family, culture, homeland. All different from the rest of us. Most of the rest of us are from what you would call Ireland or the United Kingdom or the West of Europe. Bayard and his family, for example, come from the lands you would now call France. Kallan from the north of what you consider Scotland. Odette from your Germany. I, as you know, from Ireland. Alara came to us late. We thought it important to include others of our kind from different regions, but as I mentioned, the task was not exactly seen as high priority. They sent those of us they deemed least valuable. You call us Peripherals... we are that in many ways. Even to our families. All of us have something to prove..."

"And Alara? What does she have to prove?"

"I hesitate to tell another's story, but given the circumstances, I think it's important you know all you can. Alara and her kind are from what you now call Siberia. You would call them water fairies, sprites," she explained. "Their connection to the water, all bodies of water, is primal. Profound. Her gift is to answer the call of the brokenhearted. She can remove hate and greed from the hearts of those who need it. If they're open to it. She can also ease the path of true love. Sadly, a young girl came to her for help, asking for guidance with her lover. Alara, trusting too well and too quickly, helped the girl, but the man the girl loved was faithless. He betrayed her and she took her own life. It was not true love, but Alara had misunderstood the situation. She had never seen deception like that before. This was a very long time ago. Ever since, her family has... not quite shunned her, but removed their faith in her. She is solitary. Morose. Which is not in her or her people's nature. Even though I've known her the least, I think I worry most about her. This feels like a last chance for her, somehow."

"Well, I would think she speaks to your empathic nature, yes? If I can feel her sadness, what is it like for you?"

"At times, it's overwhelming. She has been this way for centuries. It is a horrible burden for anyone to carry, to be turned aside by your own family. It is something each of us can understand. I hope, through being with us and going through this, she will see that there can be more to her world than what she has been living for so long. Maybe an important part of all this will be to show us that even we can be more connected. More helpful to each other. To those in need."

"I think that's a lesson we all could learn," Sean answered and held Breena's gaze for a moment. And then another moment that was possibly too long. He felt his face flush.

The very polyester blanket around Ken swished unnaturally as he turned in the bed. He cried out, quietly. Sean crossed to him, but nothing else had changed. He remained as he'd been, senseless to his surroundings.

Breena sat up straighter in her chair as she saw Alara whirl around on the beach and fix the hotel room with a stare. The air pressure seemed to change, became charged. Loudly, the door sounded to the pounding of a fist. Repeatedly, the door seemed to shake on its hinges. Breena and Sean looked to each other as Alara blinked onto the balcony.

A cry of rage came through the door. A deep voice boomed from outside. And then Kallan blinked through the door. Quietly, he almost whispered, "Something has happened."

Kallan stood still, his face a mask of pain. Breena drew him farther into the room, keenly aware of his distress. He settled on the empty bed as she looked out onto the breezeway beyond the door.

"Don't bother looking. She is not there. Odette is gone. They took her. I have failed. Again."

CHAPTER 24

As Kelphit disappeared, Bayard turned to Trout with a plea in his eyes. "Can you make it back to the truck on your own? I need to visit the beach up ahead. I think there is valuable information to be had, but I know we can't waste time."

"Sorry, pal. We were told to stay together, and I plan to do just that. We found one ancient being in this forest, no telling if we find another whether it will be as friendly. You might need me to protect you," Trout answered.

Bayard laughed out loud at this, but gave in to the logic of staying together, so the two plunged farther into the woods and toward the water. Another half mile of trudging along the marked path, over a few barely trickling creek beds, and at last the dust and mud began to turn to sand. The trees eventually gave way to tall shrubs and vines, and as they continued, the silence of the forest was broken by the approaching sound of the surf. Finally, the path branched off to their right. Turning, they walked a very short way and suddenly the bushes gave way to the broad expanse of Block Island Sound with the larger Long Island Sound filling their view.

They continued to a small shelter that had been built for hikers to rest. The walls were filled with graphics detailing the wildlife that one could hope to see here. Shore birds and the various species of seals that frequented the spot. Bayard took one look at them and gave a "humph" and they both turned to the water.

The sound was relatively calm, with gentle waves lapping at larger rocks that jutted above the incoming tide. The largest boulders were covered with dozens of seals, basking in the sunshine. Many curled up in a banana shape, as awkward out of water as they were graceful and wildly quick in it. As Bayard stepped out the far side of the shelter, a ripple seemed to pass through the seals present, and their heads turned, one by one and then all together, to stare at the newcomers above the beach.

"Well, that's not creepy, at all," Trout muttered, feeling as if the seals were looking at and straight through him. It was unsettling, but not alarming. In fact, he felt rather moved by it. Their faces, eyes, were clearly intelligent.

"Wait here," Bayard said as he strode down to the beach and stood near the waterline. Two of the seals immediately slid from their rocks and flashed through the water toward where he stood. He walked knee deep into the water as they approached. The seals bobbed not far in front of him, and it seemed to Trout that they had some sort of discussion, although he heard no words spoken. Bayard bent over, dipping his hands into the water and the seals inched closer, brushing past him, almost as if he were petting them. Suddenly, both the seals and Bayard froze, turning left, to the west, where a commotion had begun. Birds took flight, panicked and crying out. The seals gave a bark and shot back out beyond the rocks. The other seals that had stayed sunbathing also took note of something in that direction and nearly all of them slipped quickly into the water and farther out into the sound.

Trout heard a thundering of hooves before he saw a thing, then suddenly a massive black stallion appeared down the beach, galloping full speed toward the east and the very tip of the island. A young seal that had lain hidden on the beach behind some shore boulders, barked in fear and began an ungainly retreat toward the water.

The horse grew nearer, and Trout could see that something was hideously wrong with it. Its face was misshapen, its lower jaw jutting far off to one side. Its mane and tail were sparse, unhealthy, and literally falling away as it powered along the sand. Its eyes, though—its eyes were yellow, unnatural. The horse did not seem evil, rather it seemed diseased. Corrupted.

Both Trout and Bayard could see that the young seal would never make the safety of the water in time. Its huge dark eyes widened in fear as it threw itself even more into what was sure to be a fruitless effort. Trout was closer and started toward the beach. He had absolutely no idea what he could do, but he knew he couldn't stand by and watch. Bayard rushed back toward the shore but would clearly not reach the seal in time, slowed by the water. Trout grabbed a large piece of driftwood and angled himself to intercept the horse before it could reach the seal. At least, that's what he hoped he was doing. It would be close. Too close.

The seals bobbing in the water had all stopped to watch the tragedy unfolding. They floated, only their heads visible above the waterline. Many of them barked alarms, helpless to do anything more. Trout's driftwood was a good six feet long and stout, solid. As he and the horse neared each other, he saw that he would make it and fell into a kneel, thrusting the branch into the path of the mindlessly streaking beast, planting it in the sand. The horse's eyes never looked from side to side. It remained focused solely on whatever eastward point it was racing toward, plumes of sand flying behind each hoofbeat. As a result, it never saw Trout or the driftwood he had shoved into its path. It ran headlong into it and the branch caught its pistoning legs and sent it flailing, skidding horribly and uncontrollably. It screamed, a horrible earsplitting scream, a sound Trout, who had spent so much of his life around ranches, had never imagined could come from a horse. The horse cartwheeled along the beach and missed the young seal by mere feet. It thrashed on the sand, desperate to regain its feet and the manic dash that had been interrupted. But it was broken, unable to right itself. It continued to scream, but the sounds were not of pain but of anger and it turned its unhealthy gaze to Trout, and he could almost physically feel the hate it directed at him.

And suddenly, Bayard was there. Approaching from the waves, he flicked his hands and the two long daggers appeared. He did not slow, he didn't hesitate. He walked directly to the horse struggling on the sand and dispatched it with two quick and deadly strokes, one from each hand.

The horse fell still, silent. Trout watched as it practically deflated, collapsing into itself, nothing but bones and flesh now that the mad anger had been stilled.

The young seal, at last, slid into the waves and was greeted by two older seals. All three stopped, heads above water, and turned to look in the direction of Trout and Bayard, and Trout had never *felt* an animal, any animal, look into him the way these seals did. He felt shaken. And his shoulder ached, twisted from the violent impact with the horse. He rubbed it with his good hand and turned to Bayard.

"I hate to do that," Bayard spoke quietly. "All creatures, especially horses, are dear to me, but this creature was not truly alive. Someone, or something, had changed it into this monstrosity. This was the best possible outcome. For all involved. But someone will pay for what they did."

Trout had never heard Bayard speak like this. Determined with a seething anger barely below the surface. He was reminded that there was much more to these Peripherals than he had seen so far.

"There were two Selkies amongst the seals. They have spoken to me about a gathering of evil farther to the east. This poor creature," Bayard said, gesturing toward the remains of the disfigured horse, "was answering some sort of call, clearly mindless with pain and rage. The incoming tide will carry it away. I hope it is, at last, at peace. We need to get back to the others as quickly as possible. The

Selkies also told me that this creature comes from an island to the north that is home to many such abominations. It seems your kind is as capable of horrors as we have seen from those of my realm. Apparently, this is a place of 'science' where experiments are inflicted on innocent creatures. They say your kind call it Plum Island."

"I've heard of it," Trout answered, "but not much else."

"It seems the Dullahan has called the broken victims of that island to its side. The forces against us are growing."

"Well, that's just great. Let's get the hell out of here and find the others, then."

With that, they turned from the water and plunged back into the forest and eventually to the Bronco that waited at the end of the mile-long trail. The seals remained where they were, bobbing and watching them disappear from sight. As soon as they were gone, two seals, larger than the others, dove deep below the waves and raced to the east and the end of Long Island. Toward Montauk Point.

Kallan sat on one of the beds and held his head in his hands. He was inconsolable and Sean, Breena, and Alara stood awkwardly unsure of what to say or do. Kallan had always been their leader, their strength. To see him like this was jarring for all of them, especially Sean, who realized that he had come to see all the Peripherals as infallible. Wise and powerful, here to save him and his friends from an otherworldly threat he could barely comprehend. And yet, here was Kallan, the most steadfast of them all, reduced nearly to tears and admitting failure. The absolute protection he had come to assume was there for him seemed to puncture and deflate.

"Tell us what happened," Breena said. Her face reflected the pain Kallan was feeling, her empathy causing her to experience his anguish personally. "Odette is a fierce fighter and keenly intelligent, she knew what the risks were, and she chose to be here."

"I know," Kallan responded. "I do. But I led her there. I pushed us farther than we should have gone. I just never could have imagined that anyone... anything... could take her. Her voice... I'll never forget the sound of her being ripped away."

He reached behind his back and pulled out Odette's spear. Much as his sword remained hidden until needed, he seemed able to do the same with her spear. "She dropped this. She and this spear are bonded. I never even thought it was possible to separate them..."

"Did you see who took her?" asked Alara.

"No. There was some sort of portal... gateway... It was black, impenetrable. As we discovered it, a bright red whip came flashing out, gripped her, and she was... gone. So, while I did not actually see the Dullahan, I think it's safe to assume that's who has her now."

Seeing Odette's spear brought a pall over the room. Sean broke the stunned silence after a moment. "It sounds as if the Dullahan was lying in wait for you. Or knew of your presence near the gateway," he said. "Could this all just be part of the greater trap you thought was being set out here?"

"It likely is," said Breena. "They know their best chance is to separate us. I just did not think anything would happen so soon. Daylight hours are usually safe, but of course you were deep underground, so daylight played no part."

"We must—I must—get her back. If they harm her, I do not know what I will do. Her family... it will mean war. I just don't know exactly who will be fighting who..."

Kallan placed the spear behind his back, and it vanished. "I will be returning that to her," he announced.

Breena gestured for Sean to follow her out onto the balcony. When he joined her, she pulled him to the side, out of sight from the others in the room.

"There are some things I think you need to know. Things that will help you to understand exactly what is at stake. For both Kallan and Odette. As you know," she began, "we were all deemed expendable, which is why we were sent here. Kallan, if you can believe it, is considered the smallest of a very large, very male, and very fierce warrior family. They have essentially lorded over the highlands for as long as anyone can remember."

"I find it very hard to believe that he is considered small," Sean responded.

"And yet, it is true. All his life he has been belittled and bullied by his brothers. Even to some extent by his father, who always found him to be disappointing. Given that, the taking of Odette while she was with him, even though we know it was not his fault, will be held against him as proof of his inadequacy."

"But he did nothing wrong. It was completely out of his control," Sean protested.

"And yet, family politics will paint a different picture."

"Well, no wonder he's devastated. His friend has been taken and he knows he'll be blamed," he said.

"Yes, he will live with the shame and the guilt for an exceedingly long time if we don't bring her back. Ironically, Odette's situation is similar, yet quite different. Her family, also a lengthy line of warriors, was bitterly disappointed that she was a woman," Breena explained with a resigned weariness in her voice. "She's been trying to prove herself worthy of a place in the family all her life. This... will not help. Even if she is rescued, the fact that she required rescuing will be held against her. The current situation plays into the complicated situations that made them, that made all of us, meaningless enough to be sent here."

"Unbelievable," Sean muttered. "I can't believe anyone, anywhere, could find a single thing lacking in any of you. Seems family is family, no matter where you go."

"Yes," she replied. "Yet more similarities between us. I know I said that I would let them tell their own stories, but I wanted you to understand just what the personal cost is for both of them in this."

"Thank you. I appreciate you trusting me. I'll keep it in mind and to myself," he promised.

As they entered the room again, Sean's phone rang, and seeing that it was Trout he answered. "Trout, are you OK? What's happening?"

"Lots. We've added some help. And found out that our enemies have, also. We found Sandy. In fact, we're headed back there now. We'll swing by to pick you up. And bring Ken. We need to make a plan."

Putting away his phone, Sean turned to the others. "Looks like we should get ready. They'll be here soon. And we need to bring Ken."

In the corner, Ken shifted under the polyester bedspread and made a quiet clucking sound.

Trout pulled over to the shoulder outside of town, opened the browser on his iPhone and searched for Plum Island. An article came up and he handed the phone to Bayard. "Here. Read that. Let's find out about this Plum Island and what we're up against."

Bayard took the phone and began to read. Like much of this area, the island was shrouded in mystery and conjecture. And a healthy serving of conspiracy theories. Plum Island lay in Gardiner's Bay, east of Orient Point on Long Island's north fork. It's the site of the Plum Island Animal Disease Center, which the government began in 1954. The US government owns the entire island (purchased in 1899 for the royal sum of ninety thousand dollars) and access is determined, interestingly, by the Department of Homeland Security. There is a military base on the island that has passed through many hands, including, at one time, the Army Chemical Corps. The island, since 1954, conducts studies on animal pathogens, which is the reason given for such strict access being in place. The current status of the island is in a legislative limbo. It had originally been earmarked for sale as a way to fund other government initiatives, but after a wave of lawsuits, territorial disputes between New York State and the federal government, and shifting political winds, it was designated to be turned over to another federal agency for preservation. The one sticking point in all of this seemed to be that no one knew how sixty years of animal disease experimentation had affected the island and its wildlife.

As would be expected, conspiracy theories arose calling the true nature of the experiments into doubt. Popular culture took note and Plum Island appears in everything from books to television and film, to popular music. It is depicted as everything from a secret bio-terror lab to a government installation housing high-risk prisoners, to a haven for vampires. The truth, seemingly, is that little is known and as long as it is shrouded in mystery, rumors and theories will continue to proliferate.

Bayard had been reading the most pertinent facts to Trout as they drove. When he finished Trout turned to him and said, "There is a lot of weirdness going on around this supposedly sleepy little town."

"Indeed. I see why our adversaries would want to lead us in this direction. Chaos works to their advantage. And that certainly explains the horse we encountered on the beach. The question is, how many such creatures will answer the call of the Dullahan. Strange goings-on, most—" Bayard trailed off mid-sentence as a glance out the window revealed a sign for Sausages, a local pizza joint. He whirled to Trout with a pleading look, and Trout laughed as he pulled over.

"Well, we do need to eat something. We'll get enough for everyone. Justify making the stop. Who knows when we'll have another chance to eat?"

"I wholeheartedly support this course of action!" Bayard crowed as he leapt from the Bronco and headed for the door.

"Hold on there, pal!" Trout shouted as he jogged to catch up. "I'm the one with the money, remember?"

Twenty minutes later, there was knock on the hotel room's door. Sean answered and stood, incredulous, as Bayard and Trout entered, loaded down with pizza boxes. There was enough for everyone. More than enough. Sean shot a questioning glance at Trout who said simply, "He couldn't make up his mind, so we ended getting some of everything. Except the Hawaiian. We both agree that pineapple doesn't belong on a pizza."

Bayard proudly spread his pizza bounty out on the bed not taken up by Ken. He opened the lid to each box with a flourish and announced each pizza as it was revealed. "Pepperoni, Grandma slice (a personal favorite, I mean it's like Sicilian, but not. Thick, but crispier... heaven!), sausage, vegetable lovers, all the meats, this one has some sort of salad on it, thought it was worth a try, taco pizza, and the crowning achievement, this is called the Mama Mia. It has sausage, pepperoni, mushroom, green pepper, and bacon... bacon! Plenty for all."

"I let him go overboard. We've been forgetting to eat, and who knows when we'll get the chance again the way things are going," Trout explained.

They noticed a heavy mood in the room. As they took stock of everything, they both noted that Odette was nowhere to be seen. It was Trout's turn to send a questioning look to Sean.

"I think we need to catch each other up. There have been a lot of developments," Sean answered.

And so, as they worked their way through the plentiful pizza choices, the groups caught up on what had been discovered. Less than fifteen minutes later, they loaded Ken into the Bronco, piled in themselves, and headed in the direction of Sandy's store where they hoped they would find some sanctuary and the opportunity to come up with a plan.

CHAPTER 25

As they pulled into the parking lot by The Realm, Trout turned to Bayard and said, "Something is different." Bayard, still happily drowsy from his feast, roused himself and looked out the window in the direction of the shop. A sharp intake of breath followed, and he replied, "Much has changed. Our friends have been busy." They left the Bronco, with Kallan and Bayard supporting Ken between them. Sean was simply relieved that they hadn't forgotten him again.

As they rounded the tiki bar and the store came into sight, it had undergone a transformation. The walls were adorned in a variety of symbols. Many featured arrows, pointing left or right. Some were circles with arrows facing inward. There were turtles at various places. These were clearly indigenous drawings, and the group assumed it was the work of Kelphit. But along with them were symbols from throughout history and cultures—the Eye of Horus from ancient Egypt could be seen, as could the Hamsa from ancient Mesopotamia. On one wall Sean saw an odd drawing of what looked like eight tridents radiating outward from a central point. Bayard explained to him it was The Helm of Awe, an enormously powerful Norse invocation of power and protection.

As they approached the door, they saw that a line of salt had been drawn around the building. The door had a sign that said "Closed," but it opened as they approached, and Sandy ushered them in with a slightly dazed expression.

Sandy and Sean hugged and agreed that, while they needed to have a proper catch-up, now was not the time. Sean introduced her to Kallan, Breena, and Alara. Kelphit appeared from the small storeroom behind the counter.

"Bring your friend in here. We have prepared a place for him. He will be well protected while you are away."

The carried Ken into the back room and found a cot piled high with blankets. More salt was spread at the doorway, and there were additional symbols drawn on the interior walls. Many were duplicates of what they had seen outside. There was a dreamcatcher above the cot. As they gently lowered Ken, Kelphit turned to a small bowl and lit some twigs on fire, placing some stones amongst the flames to heat.

"Wait outside," he said. "I will finish his preparation and be out shortly."

As the group filed into the main room, Sandy stepped forward. "Your friend is remarkable. I've always heard he could be found here at certain times of the year, but never had the honor of meeting him in person. I've never met anyone like him. What he's done here is... well, more than I could have ever imagined."

"There's probably no one else like him on earth, so consider yourself fortunate for the time spent with him. He is older than all of us. And much, much wiser," said Bayard.

The other Peripherals cast surprised glances his way. It was a rare day when Bayard set aside his light heart and gave earnest praise. They were impressed.

"You've seen what we've done outside," Sandy began. "Everything placed out there is at Kelphit's direction. Many of them are from his own personal history, but I'm sure you noticed some from elsewhere. He's an encyclopedia of knowledge. The salt, he said, was to ward off evil and prevent it from crossing the threshold." She gestured around the room to dozens of crystals placed strategically around the room. "Each of those is intended to protect, ward off evil, promote wellbeing. All at his direction, by the way. He recognized things I had that even I didn't understand. And I'm supposed to be an expert!"

"Well," Trout responded, "he does have quite a head start on you. Come back in a few hundred years and see how you match up."

Sandy just shook her head. "Incredible," she muttered.

Kelphit emerged from the back room, wiping his hands and with a weary look on his face. "It is the best we could do given the time constraints. I can feel danger in the air. Tonight, will be perilous for all. If you find yourself separated from the others, try to come here. If you find yourself injured and can move, find your way here. There will be no place as safe as this space tonight. "

Breena stepped forward and gave the medicine man a respectful half bow as did the other Peripherals. "Thank you, elder. We are forever in your debt. If this night proves to be what we fear, it's likely all creatures everywhere will have you to thank."

"Let us not get ahead of ourselves. But I fear you are correct that the forces gathering at the end of the island could put all of us in jeopardy. I am a healer, not a warrior, so I must remain here and do what I can. But know that you can proceed, confident that our friend will be unharmed."

"Can you do anything to actually heal him? He's been like this since we found him. Nothing we do seems to work," Sean said, stepping forward.

Kelphit paused and sent a penetrating look at Sean. "Interesting," he muttered, before continuing. "You have done much to save and protect your friend. I doubt any of you could have done more. From what I've been told, and what I've just seen, the Wendigo must be defeated to give your friend a chance. That was where the evil first entered him. However, though defeating a Wendigo is no small feat, I believe your friends here should be more than up to the task."

Sandy stepped forward. "I thought there was one more with you?" She asked looking at Trout for confirmation. An awkward silence fell on the room before Kallan spoke. "There is. She was taken from us, from me, in the tunnels below Camp Hero. We must find and rescue her. Before anything else."

"Under the fort, you say?" Kelphit asked. "Fascinating. So, they have gained access. Not something any of the creatures you have described could do on their own. I suggest beginning your search for her there. I would expect them to retreat to the Point, but it may lead you there yourselves."

"I was thinking the same," responded Kallan. "Best to get moving before too long."

<hr>

Afternoon was fading into dusk, and Sean made to walk outside. The shop was on the far side of the harbor from the bustle of chartered fishing boats, sunset cruises, and dockside restaurants serving the catch of the day. This side of the harbor was full of working boats and locals and far less busy. A few yards away toward the harbor, the Liar's Saloon, a watering hole peopled by those who liked to keep it local, lay a few feet from the water. The first shift of drinkers, who had gone straight there after fishing since early morning, were making their way back home only to be replaced by the early happy hour patrons arriving after their restaurant lunch shifts, their nine-to-five day jobs, and a few who had just been waiting for the time to be more "drink appropriate." The sign on the road advertised one-dollar beers, and everyone knew they were not exactly the premium beers, but what did you expect for a dollar? Liar's is a Montauk institution and lives up to its t-shirts which proudly proclaim, "Montauk, a quaint drinking village, with a fishing problem."

Sean stood by the parking lot behind the shop, watching the locals straggle past in one direction or the other, to or away from the saloon. He watched the t-shirts come and go and couldn't help but wonder if he would ever again feel as carefree as these people did. Would life ever be so simple that he could just sit in a waterfront saloon and think of nothing but his next beer and the view out the window over the water? He'd always been one to overcomplicate things as it was, more so as he got older. Now, he just wanted some peace. And he knew full well that was impossible. At least for now.

Breena peeked her head around the corner of the building. "Would you mind some company? I think we only have a short while before things start and I could use some fresh air and a stroll. They're burning sage inside, and while I know its value, I do believe there can be too much of a good thing."

"Please, join me," Sean said. "I was just contemplating the simpler lives of the passersby and... hoping for some of my own sometime."

"I understand. I think. Although I suspect that your simplicity and mine may look different, I'm sure the results are the same."

Sean turned to look at her. "I'm not sure if I should stop to take everything in or just keep moving. When I think too much, I start to get overwhelmed by everything that's happened in just two days. How will anything ever be the same again?"

She walked to him and looked, really looked, into his eyes. "Sean, there can be no doubt that your life has changed, and that change will follow you from now on. But change can be a good thing, a necessary thing. Remember how the world looked when we first shared our visions with each other on the beach?"

"Yes, of course. I'll never forget it."

"Well, aren't you better off for having seen it? For experiencing something that most of your kind could not imagine? That vibrance, that color, that—"

"You're right," he answered. "I know you are. Just feeling a bit overwhelmed. I'll get over it."

"No, Sean. Do not get over it. Learn from it. Take from it what you need so you can move forward. And for what it's worth, finding you has changed everything for us, too. For me. You have taught us many things already. About your kind. About kindness. Potential. Surprises. We thought we knew everything about you. We were very wrong. You have taught, not just us, but me. I am changed, too."

"I... I don't know how to say this... Is it possible we've known each other before? Is that a thing? I can't believe I'm saying this—or might believe it. Could I have maybe caught sight of you when you thought I hadn't? Are past lives something? I don't know. I feel ridiculous, but it just seems that I know you. That we understand each other on some level and, well... that's confusing to me, too. I should stop talking."

Breena laughed and then stopped to consider, choosing her words carefully. "Some of those things could very well be true. And I understand. I feel that comfort with you, too. In many ways, more than I have felt with most of my own kind. I very much believe... I hope that we will be able to find answers to those questions."

"After we get through this," he finished for her.

She nodded. "Yes."

They took the short walk to the water and stood by a floating dock watching some fishermen hose down their boat. The sun had begun its late afternoon descent behind them, casting their shadows into the water, where they looked elongated, and the rippling harbor made them seem shimmering and otherworldly. Gulls cried nearby, lamenting the close of the fishing day and the loss of scraps from the boats. They sounded plaintive, lonely. Sean had always loved that sound, and it was oddly comforting to hear it now. A moment to remind him that the things he'd always loved were still around him.

As they stared out over Montauk Harbor, Breena began to hum

quietly to herself. After a moment, Sean turned to her and asked what she was singing. "Oh," she answered shyly, "it's something from The Waterboys. The band I mentioned to you earlier. I didn't even realize I was doing it."

"Appropriate band to be humming, given our current location," Sean replied.

"True, but it's something more than just that. I always think of that song, and the poem that inspired it, when I have a quiet moment, especially by still water. I've never completely understood why..."

She began to quietly recite:
Come away, O human child!
To the waters and the wild
With a faery, hand in hand,
For the world's more full of weeping than you can understand.

Where dips the rocky highland
Of Sleuth Wood in the lake,
There lies a leafy island
Where flapping herons wake
The drowsy water-rats;
There we've hid our faery vats
Full of berries
And of reddest stolen cherries.

"I remember that one. I don't think I ever fully understood it. I have a completely different perspective now, of course," Sean responded.

"It's extraordinary. Especially coming from one of your people. I doubt one of our poets could have done any better," Breena said.

"That's high praise, to say the least," Sean marveled at her words.

"Words that would rarely be uttered," she said, eyes fixed on the water.

Sean brought out his cell phone and turned to her. "The Water-boys, you say?" She nodded and he did a quick search online. "Here it is... Seems extremely popular."

He tapped the screen once. From the speaker, a rolling piano, joined by a guitar, and then a simple flute floated over them as Sean joined her in looking out over the water. The setting sun nearing the golden hour when the world seemed closer to its best self than most any other time. Eventually, a gentle soft voice began to sing, echoing in an almost otherworldly way. Sean recognized the lyrics as nearly identical to the poem Breena had just shared.

Sean was transfixed. Carried away to another time and place, and keenly aware that he was sitting next to someone who many would consider a "faery." He caught his breath, afraid to even look at her, and was completely caught off guard by the next voice that emerged from his phone. The singer was replaced by someone speaking, reciting the next words of the poem in a voice so deep and rich it seemed to reach across the ages and into Sean's self. It was as if the voice of a giant, something otherworldly, was rolling down through time to him, to the listener, to remind and warn and share that the world was full of mystery and poetry and pain and joy... and more.

Where dips the rocky highland

There lies a leafy island

Full of berries

Sean felt tears falling, not entirely aware why, but knowing that the song had reached him in a way he hadn't felt in years. It reminded him of how much pain there was in the world, how much joy, how music and poetry could transform a day, a life, a person. The composer had taken that exquisite poem and somehow elevated it, made it even more than it was. Something new. As clear an example of the power of music as he had ever heard. He had made his life creating "art," but knew, on an instinctual level, that this was something else. Something more.

He turned to Breena and saw tears falling from her eyes, as well. She laughed a quiet, gentle sound, meant only for him. For this moment.

"I can't hear that without crying. The perils of being an empath," she said.

"And what's my excuse, then?" he asked.

"I think we may have more in common even than we've realized. That song, by the way, is one of the examples I used to convince my people that, not only is your kind worth saving, but that we may still have much to learn from you."

"What have I just heard? I mean, who are they? I... like so often these last days, I'm speechless."

"I can't explain it either," she said. "Every once in a very long time, I think, an artist—be it a poet, a singer, a writer—taps into something greater than themselves and finds a way to pierce the curtain between our peoples. To find some sort of universal truth— honesty. They have many other songs that I enjoy, but that do not affect me in that way. Which also makes sense. Remember, at one time we all coexisted. It makes sense that some would find a pathway through. A way to reach across. This—and I only speak for myself—reaches across and seems to speak directly to me."

"If I hadn't heard it, I don't think I would understand. But I do. It speaks to me, too. About things larger than I've thought about in a very long time."

"Welcome, Sean. I think your empathic side just got a wakeup call."

"And my artistic side. And my sensitive side. And... and... and."

"You may want to take it a little slower, but yes. Opening your eyes after a long sleep can be... a lot."

"I can't stop thinking about what you said about us turning our music and art into dollars and cents. Penning it into rooms and keeping it from being readily available to anyone who wants to share it. I'd started to just go through the motions. I think I'd lost touch with what had made me what I am. What I wanted to be."

"We have watched that with sadness. Not you specifically. Your people's withdrawal from a communal existence. Over the centuries until we watch you now with your faces in your screens... shut down... shut out. I'm so happy to think you may be finding something you'd lost. Something important. At least in my view."

"I've always felt—believed—there was something more. Even as I let myself get drawn down into the digital world, the solitude of virtual life, I hoped for—wanted—more. I've always been called a dreamer. Makes sense, I guess."

"I think you sell yourself, and dreamers, horribly short there, Sean," she responded quickly, turning to look onto his eyes. "Remember, artists are creators, making something where there was nothing. There is great power in that. Great strength. Every piece of art, whatever it may be, started with one person. One 'dreamer' as you would call them. The storytellers, the bards, the singers, the writers, the painters... they are our connection. To each other. To our past. To the way forward. It's why my people value them so very much. Words, music, poetry, images, ideas... all matter immensely."

"I know. *We* know. We talk about it every so often and then go right back to what we've been doing... I think I'd better focus on the task at hand. That may be enough big thoughts for the moment," he said.

"Yes. We have work to do. And as you have just demonstrated, there are some things your technology does quite well. Thank you for playing the song. I don't think I realized how much I needed it," she answered.

Trout appeared, coming around the corner from the shop,

scanned the parking lot and saw the two of them by the water and Liar's.

"Don't even think about a pre-fight-for-all-that-is-good drink without me!" he called. "But I suggest we wait until after, because you know, Ginge, that if I get you in there, we will have shots."

Sean grinned as he turned. "Oh, Trout, I know it only too well. Time to get down to business, I'd say."

"Business first, shots later! That's my motto," Trout proclaimed and turned back toward the shop.

"Shall we?" Sean asked Breena as they both started off in that direction.

"We shall," she said. They each put their heads down as they walked back, but both somehow felt much better than when they had first walked outside.

They entered the store and found a flurry of activity. More runes had appeared on the wall. The door to the back room was closed and a golden light spilled around the doorframe. The space smelled of sage. Kelphit's face now bore symbols drawn on in some sort of natural dye. Green, to symbolize healing and harmony, along with blue for wisdom, and black for strength. Kelphit was busily applying the same to Sandy's face as she was explaining the significance of each, and seemed to be enjoying every second of it.

"I know this is deadly serious," she crowed, standing, "but this is one of the very few times I felt like I had people in this with me! Curious tourists can only carry me so far. But this... this is for real!"

Kelphit pulled her gently back into her seat and continued his work as she muttered an apology and tried to sit still.

Alara sat quietly in a corner. Whether she was praying, meditating, or simply... elsewhere, wasn't clear to Sean. Kallan sat in another corner, one eye on the window while he sharpened his sword absentmindedly. Bayard stood to one side of the door, his blades spinning a web of motion in front of him. The air in the room was charged. Nervous. Alert.

Trout was at one of the display cases, intently looking through ceremonial items. He turned to Sean, almost plaintively, and said, "I need something. Look,"—he gestured to the Peripherals—"swords, knives... what have I got? Nothing. No good Montanan goes to a fight empty handed."

Kelphit turned to Trout and said, "Just a moment, friend. I will not send you off unarmed."

Trout turned to Sean with a huge grin and nodded toward Kelphit. "Friends in high places..." he said, incredibly pleased with the turn of events.

After finishing with Sandy, Kelphit asked Breena and Sean to join him in the back room. There, they saw Ken wrapped tightly in one of the medicine man's blankets. Warm stones, the size of fists, had been laid down his torso. Kelphit explained, "Ideally, I'd create a sweat lodge to help drive out whatever toxins have been placed in him. This is an old custom and the next best thing."

Trout stuck his head around the doorway. "Sweat lodge, huh? I like the sound of that. If we get out of this, maybe you can help me with one in Montana. You ever get out that way?"

Kelphit turned to him, and with barely concealed mirth answered, "I do. And it would be a pleasure."

"Excellent! I have a spot down by the river I've been eyeing for something like that. Perfect!" and he disappeared back into the main room.

Sean looked around the room and noticed that the walls were nearly covered with symbols and the air was thick with sage and incense.

"Your friend," Kelphit said, indicating Ken, "is very vulnerable. Very weak. We have done everything we can here to shield him. With Ms. Dale and myself here, he will be as safe as can be."

"Thank you, so much," Sean responded. "This isn't your fight. I know that. And you don't even know us. 'Thank you' seems like not enough under the circumstances."

"Ah, but this is my fight. This fight, I fear, will be everyone's before it is done. And how well you know someone is not measured by how long you have known them. I am exactly where I am most needed."

Sean didn't know how to respond, so asked a question he'd been holding onto for a while. "I thought they were after me. Why did they do this to Ken? And... when will they come for me?"

It was Breena who answered from a half step behind him. "Ken was an easy target, and certainly got our attention. There is power in him, but it is flawed. Buried beneath worldly distractions. They likely thought he would be easier to corrupt. To manipulate. He was an opportunity to draw you out. Draw us out. Test us. You offer a cleaner target and more potential. More power, more focus. I fully expect them to come for you tonight. My guess is they will try to cause as much confusion as possible and use that to get close to you. I will not leave your side. They will not take you."

"And I will make sure you are well protected before you leave. Somehow, you are the key to all of this. We will not fail you," said Kelphit.

"Never doubted it for a second," said Sean. And he almost really believed it.

Bayard and Trout appeared abruptly in the doorway. Trout was noticeably out of breath. "Guys, looks like we had less time than we expected. We have company," he blurted out. "And I don't even have my Kelphit special yet..."

Bayard, more even-keeled, said, "It appears to be at least three that we can see. They pulled up in the parking lot beside the bar in back and have shone their automobile's lights this way. They are approaching slowly, but deliberately."

"Well, this is something new. Or someone. The Wendigo definitely won't be driving a car," Sean replied.

"Very true," Bayard answered. "This is something altogether

different. I don't like surprises. That's a lie. I love them. Just not this one."

Sean and Breena rushed into the next room, while Sandy hurried into the room where Ken lay. She and Kelphit closed the door behind them, and a quiet chant could be heard beginning. In the store's showroom, Alara and Kallan had taken up positions near the front door. Bayard was close behind. All had their weapons drawn. Behind them, Breena had taken up a protective stance near Sean and Trout, who was busily trying to find something to use as a weapon with little success.

"I thought they'd wait until we were out of town to attack," Sean whispered.

"So did we," Breena responded. "This could be someone new entering the fray on their behalf. This feels off. Nothing about any of this has made sense. No reason to expect it to now."

Kallan turned to them. "I'm turning the lights out. We are too vulnerable in here while they are on. Bayard, out the back. See if you can approach them from behind. Our best option may be to take them by surprise. If there are truly only three, this may be our chance to take the offensive before any others arrive."

Bayard blinked out of the room. Breena had a focused look and seemed confused. "I sense... nothing," she said. "I don't know who or what is out there."

Sean pulled the curtains aside to take a quick look outside. He saw three figures, backlit by the headlights of a car and approaching slowly, almost creeping. One seemed to have a light of some kind in their hand.

Kallan looked at Alara and gave a quick nod, which she returned. Suddenly, they were... gone. The door hadn't opened, they simply blinked beyond it. From within, Sean could hear voices raised as the Peripherals, Kallan and Alara from the front and Bayard who had managed to approach silently from the rear, announced themselves with their weapons glinting in the headlights. In response, three voices responded with cries of surprise and alarm. One voice, a female voice, rose above the rest, fairly booming, "Yo, yo, yo!! It's us! Put those things down before you hurt someone!"

Sean recognized the voices and turned all the available lights on, both inside and out. He threw the door open and ran out, with Breena scrambling to keep up. Sean was laughing and smiling, as was Trout, who gave up his search for a weapon and dashed out front. The Peripherals stopped in their tracks, bewildered for just a moment, until everyone took stock of what was happening. Weapons lowered, everyone took a good look around and breathed a sigh of relief. It was not the beginning of an attack. Reinforcements had arrived. The remaining Grumbles had come to town.

CHAPTER 26

Brandy turned to the headlights and waved her arms over her head. "Thanks, Momo! This is the right place!" A bright pink minivan with Pink Tuna Taxi written across the side slowly started to back up and flashed its lights in response.

"Jeez, guys, that was quite a welcome. We're here to help, honest!" Stewart said as the group exchanged greetings and headed back inside.

"Well, I couldn't be happier to see you all," Sean said, "but how did you know where to find us?"

Nick answered him. "He came and told us you may need some help," he said pointing at Kallan. "Don't have to ask us twice."

All eyes turned to Kallan who nodded toward the shop and replied, "Inside. Quickly. I'll explain."

Brandy grabbed Sean as they turned toward The Realm. "Look, Red. Don't you *ever* leave us—leave ME—behind like that again. Yeah, things are weird, but that's when true friends step up. So let us step up! If we didn't apparently need you so much, I'd be tempted to kill you. Jerk."

"I know, I know," Sean stammered. "Things just kept snowballing. One thing led to another, and then another, and before I knew it... it seemed out of control. And dangerous. And... impossible to explain. I felt horrible."

"Yeah, well. No more crap like that. Once a Grumble, always a Grumble, right? It's not just a saying. We mean it."

With that, she grabbed him and gave him a huge hug. Then punched him on the shoulder. Hard.

The other Grumbles had stopped to listen and grinned in response. They gathered, putting arms over each other's shoulders, and then turned toward the shop. The entire group hurried into the store, closed and locked the door behind them.

Sandy greeted her old friends with shock when she saw them come through the door, and they were equally shocked to see her, face painted with symbols and an almost wicked glee in her eyes. Hugs were given all around, exclamations of surprise and disbelief. In answer to the many unspoken questions hanging in the air, Brandy, naturally, spoke first and loudest, saying, "So we were at Culture, just wondering what to do next and how to get in touch with you, when not-so-tall, definitely-not-dark, and pretty-gloomy there appeared at the door. He explained to us what was really happening. Who he was. Where you were, and how dangerous things were about to get for you. We didn't believe him at first, but he disappeared... then reappeared... and we were on board. Needless to say, we caught the next train out and, voila, here we are." She looked pointedly at Trout. "We know full well you think we are Luddites, but you, mister man," she said glaring now at Sean, "need to check your messages."

Sean guiltily pulled out his phone and visibly winced when he saw how many texts and voicemails he had. "Sorry," he mumbled. "Been a little distracted and... well... wasn't really sure how to explain things, but now that you're here, I couldn't be happier." His voice trailed off as he looked around at the Grumbles.

"Yeah, well, we're here now, that's what counts. And... yeah... things are a bit odd at the moment," Stewart piped in.

Breena turned to Kallan and simply said, "Why?"

As the group seated and perched around the main room, Kallan looked awkwardly at his feet and seemed unsure of what to say. His confidence had clearly been shaken with the taking of Odette, and he felt the eyes of everyone on him, judging, second-guessing.

Finally, he spoke. "I realized after Odette," his voice almost caught when he spoke her name, "and I arrived, that there was more to this place than we had anticipated. Knowing that the truck would be longer to arrive with all of you, I took the opportunity to revisit the bar on Forty-fifth Street and fill your friends in"— he glanced at Sean and Trout—"on what was happening. I couldn't shake everything Breena had said about how surprising our new friends were proving to be. With what we were facing, and after seeing how well you carried yourselves in our last encounter, I thought it would be better for you to face this together. You clearly share a strong bond. There is every possibility that we will be outnumbered, and I made the decision that including the rest of your group, and guessing that they also had abilities to offer, would be best for all. I hope you understand." He almost whispered the last few words.

Trout broke the silence with a Montana whoop and shouted, "Yessir, that's what I call using your cranium. Well, done, K-man! Those creepers don't stand a chance with all of us here!"

The group broke into a raucous round of laughter and the air in the store suddenly felt much lighter. Everyone broke into smaller groups, introducing themselves, asking questions, looking through the display cases, pointing at symbols and drawings. Kallan was visibly relieved to see the response and seemed to regain a touch of his confidence, made all the more noticeable when both Bayard and Alara made a point of thanking him for what he'd done. The general air of celebration and merriment quieted when Nick noticed an unfamiliar face appear at the storeroom doorway. "Uh, who's that?" he asked.

Everyone turned to look and Kelphit stepped farther into the room.

"I'm grateful for additional friends. Perhaps you should all say hello to your ailing friend. He may not react, but I believe he is aware of what is going on around him. Please, step through. I'll explain as much as I can."

The new arrivals looked nervously at each other, hesitating. They were hesitant to see what state Ken was in. Finally, Brandy marched to the doorway, turned back to the others, and said, "Get up here. It's just Ken. Sure, he's under some sort of mystical curse and has been stricken mute and maybe deaf, but, hell, any other time we'd be thrilled he couldn't speak." The Grumbles chuckled in response before she took a more measured tone, "He's why we're here. He's still our friend. Let's give him some support."

The others nodded in response and filed through the door.

Entering the room, they all paused when they saw Ken, swaddled in the blanket Kelphit had placed around him. The stones on his chest had cooled to be only warm. Some of the same symbols had been painted on his face, the only part of him that was visible. The Grumbles took up places around him and each muttered a hello and concern for their friend. They hadn't seen him until now, and the reality of the situation set them all back. Stewart in particular seemed visibly upset, while Brandy looked determined, and Nick looked almost dispassionately at their friend as if soaking in new information and coming to conclusions.

"He looks so..." Nick muttered.

"I know," Brandy answered. "But he's in there. And we have to get him back to himself. We *have* to."

Kelphit stood quietly behind them, Sandy by his side, and began to introduce himself and explain what they were seeing. When he mentioned his name, Stewart's head snapped in his direction.

"Did you say your name is Kelphit? he asked.

"I did. Yes."

"My father always told me that we were part Wabanaki. I grew up hearing your name. I... I can't believe you're here. Are you... are you like the others... the Peripherals...?"

"I suppose, from your perspective, yes. We are similar and operate on the same plane, although I'd never met them until now. I welcome any member of the nation," he replied, placing a hand over his heart, and bowing slightly.

"Well... yeah. About that... Turns out my father was, let's just say... mistaken? He's gone now, so I'll never know if he was pulling our collective legs or repeating what someone told him as a child, but I did a DNA test and turns out, we're not Wabanaki, or any nation for that matter." He was clearly disappointed by this.

"Ah. I wonder sometimes if your science steals some of the magic from us all. Well, I welcome you, nonetheless. If you've grown up with our histories, our tales, you are welcome. If you believe you are Wabanaki, and in your heart you follow our ways, you are one of us. I claim you as kinsman. Welcome cousin."

Stewart stood a bit taller after that and went back to examining the markings on Ken.

Kallan appeared at the door. "The sun is down. I believe we must begin moving soon. First, we will travel to the tunnels where Odette was taken, but that is only the first task. After, we will need to find the Dullahan's demesne. I suspect it will be not too far from where we'll be."

The others nodded their understanding, but as they turned to go, Kelphit spoke, "Before you go, I would appreciate if you would give me just a moment. I will speak some words of protection and I believe the presence of you, as his closest friends, will be of help."

"Of course, we will," Sean said, looking to the others for confirmation and seeing them assent quickly. Kelphit lit another bundle of sage and began a low chant in a language none of the others had heard before. The air in the room became charged, as if they were no longer alone. After a moment, Breena, with eyes closed, began a wordless hum, lending her support and her power in the only way she knew. With the addition of her voice, the air fairly crackled with energy.

Sean, without a thought, stepped forward and took her hand, adding his voice to hers and again, the air in the room shifted and seemed to adopt a golden hue that pulsed along with the musical sound filling the room. Stewart moved next, his eyes fixed on Kelphit, as he stepped next to the wise man and added a wordless, deep baritone sound to the growing chord. Sandy appeared at the door, a look of curiosity on her face, but when she took in what was happening, she walked confidently into the room, stood beside Sean, closed her eyes, and added a rich crystalline soprano to the effort.

Trout appeared at the door, his head askew, but with one look he too strode forward, clasped Sandy's hand, and let out a supporting rich bass sound. The golden light now swirled throughout the room, and streaks of blue and green appeared. Brandy looked slowly around the room, incredulous, before even she, with a disbelieving roll of the eyes, took Trout's hand and let out a beautiful alto sound that weaved itself seamlessly into the chord. Nick, a look of detached disbelief on his face, hesitated, and then finally took a half step forward and took Brandy's hand, completing a full circle around Ken lying on the floor. With a shake of his head, he began in a velvety tenor to join the others, quietly at first and then with more determination.

The air crackled around them. Colors streaked throughout the room, expanding until every inch thrummed with hues and sparkled with light. The doorway was suddenly filled with the other Peripherals, with looks of shock and surprise on their faces. Kelphit, using the strength the added voices were lending him, seemed to grow, filling the room from floor to ceiling. Ken, still senseless, seemed to float, first slightly and then noticeably, off the floor, enveloped in a shimmering golden shroud of light. Kelphit finished and knelt on the floor next to Ken, who slowly settled down to the floor. Kelphit looked up at the circle of those around him with a sense of wonder and joy on his face. He took a wavering breath and placed his hand on Ken and nodded.

———

The Grumbles assembled in the main room and stared silently at each other. Brandy broke the silence.

"What the hell was that?" she asked. "We heard all about the things these Peripherals could do, but no one said anything about us getting in on the action. I mean... what was that? What did we do?"

Sean was staring at the floor, unsure of... so many things. "I have no idea... I never expected anything like that, but the one thing I've learned is that none of this will go the way we expected. I had something similar happen with just me and Breena before, but... this was something even bigger."

"Well, I thought we sounded AWESOME!" said Trout with a huge grin stretching his handlebar-ish mustache across his face.

"Can't argue with that," muttered a very stunned Stewart.

"Look, they've spoken to me about the way their cultures value the power of music and music makers... I guess we somehow tapped into that?" said Sean, trying desperately to make sense of events and put his friends at ease.

Kelphit emerged from the back room and approached the group. He seemed tired, but upbeat. "What you did was help me to put a very, very powerful protection around your friend. I won't begin to say I understand how it happened, but that it happened is a very good thing, indeed. For the first time since I arrived, I feel confident that we can heal him and keep him safe."

Breena quietly entered the conversation. "What Sean said is correct. One of the things that drew us to him is our people's belief in the power of music and the storyteller. What we did not expect was to find that apparently you *all* have some residual power along those lines. The proximity to Kelphit and myself seems to have enabled you to tap into that. Believe me, we are as surprised as you are."

Kallan crossed the room to the group and announced that the time had come to leave. Darkness had fallen outside, and he was clearly anxious to attempt to get Odette back. Kelphit excused himself and returned to the back room, mentioning that he owed Trout something before he left.

"Are we all comfortable leaving just Kelphit and Sandy behind to look after Ken?" Alara asked from across the room. "We've seen that our adversaries are very capable of feints and deception. What if they divert here to try to further hurt Ken?"

Stewart stepped forward and said, "I'd like to stay here to help. I came out here to help Ken, and I'd like to see that through. Also, I have a feeling I can learn a few things from Kelphit."

"Very good, Stewart. I think we'd all feel better knowing there were some extra hands here if needed," Breena responded. "That's settled."

Just then, Kelphit appeared from the back room and handed something to Trout. "It's the best I could do in so little time, but here is something, as I promised, to help you tonight. It's simple, but my people have used them for as long as we can remember. It will serve you well."

He handed Trout a simple tomahawk. A wooden shaft, old and hardened with age. At one end, he had tied a sturdy black rock to the handle, lashing it to the wood with strips of leather. One simple rune adorned the handle. It was as basic as could be but felt strong as Trout hefted it and swung it around him slowly.

"Oho! Thank you, good sir! Oh yeah, I got me a Kelphit special! I am beyond ready to take these things out of commission. They are in for a Montana/Wabanaki combo platter tonight!"

Sandy let out a genuinely room-sized laugh and, for just a moment, the mood in the room was lighter. Almost giddy. Then Kallan stepped forward and announced that it was time to go.

The Peripherals gathered by the front door, grim-faced and

determined. Kallan, in particular, looked as if an immense weight was crushing him. Weapons were checked and they turned to each other, communicating silently.

The Grumbles, on the other hand, had assembled near the display countertop farther into the store. They took a moment, looking around at each other. Brandy said, "I have no idea what we're in for or how we got here, but I just want to say that I love each and every one of you idiots. We're all coming back from this, you hear me? Every one of us. You don't, I'll kill you."

She was met with grudging smiles, but the sentiment was appreciated, and they actually finished with a group hug, which was very un-Grumble like. Kelphit looked on from a few feet away before moving in and beginning to paint some runes on Stewart's face. As they broke, Sandy said, "Well, this is not the day I was expecting to have. More action than this town has seen in a while."

"You?!" Stewart replied, "I'm getting my face painted by an ancient medicine man. I'm way out of my comfort zone."

"Liar," Brandy said. "You wore more makeup than that in Act Two, Scene Three. And you loved it."

"Fair point," Stewart replied with a sheepish grin.

"Hopefully, we can take care of business tonight and the town can go back to its snoozing," Nick replied.

The two groups assembled by the door, shaking hands, giving quick hugs, and essentially steeling themselves for what was to come. Breena and Sean stayed close together, an unspoken agreement to face things together.

As they exited the store, the two groups split with Kelphit and his staying in the doorway. At the opening of the door, an enormous round of cawing had kicked off and all eyes were drawn to the roofline. Every inch of space was taken up by an enormous gathering of large crows who began calling at the emergence of the groups.

"A murder of crows. How appropriate. And disturbing," said Nick.

"Quite the contrary," Kelphit answered with a look close to

wonder in his eyes. "Crows play an important part in my people's culture. And specially in the Shinnecock people who have lived on this island for centuries. I suspect this means we have support that we haven't discovered just yet." And then quietly, almost to himself, "I haven't seen anything like this in... so long. Amazing."

The groups split, with the defenders wishing the others well and returning to the store, secure under the protective eyes of the crows above. The rescuers weaved their way through the trees to the awaiting Bronco.

As they walked, Trout remembered the totem Kelphit had given him in the forest and fished it out of his pocket. It was a carving of a bear. A large bear. A grizzly. He smiled to himself, glanced back toward the store at Kelphit, and placed it carefully back in his pocket. "Yessir," he said quietly to himself. "A Montana/Wabanaki special, for sure." He whirled his tomahawk through the air and felt buoyed with confidence as he continued walking.

When they reached the truck, Bayard, who had been conspicuously quiet, and Alara excused themselves to go ahead, meeting the others shortly on the base. They could move faster and quieter alone and would hope to have some information on what to expect by the time the others arrived. The rest piled into the old truck and started on their way. It was a short drive, less than fifteen minutes to the deserted base, but this was sure to be one of the strangest road trips any of them had ever taken.

> # CHAPTER 27

Trout took them through the center of town rather than along the back roads. Perhaps he thought sticking to more populated spaces was good for the moment. Or maybe he was dragging his feet just a bit, leery to start what he knew would be a dangerous night. His thoughts were of his friends more than himself. He had gotten a taste of what they were facing and had come out feeling confident he could hold his own. The other Grumbles, though, were untested and vulnerable. He couldn't stand the thought of losing any of them. Or his new Peripheral friends for that matter.

Many of the shops and restaurants were closed by this time of day. In fact, many were simply closed for the season. But The Point, a local sports bar, shone brightly to their right as they turned onto Route 27 headed east. Village Pizza also remained open in the same direction. With Bayard gone, no one paid it any heed. The rest of downtown slumbered, apart from the venerable Shagwong Tavern on the right as they neared the end of town. Opened in 1936, it now lived a bit of a dual existence. An upscale seafood restaurant that transitioned at night into a grittier dive bar that hearkened back to the days before Montauk had been discovered by celebrities and day traders. There were probably a few old salts in there right now that would come in handy tonight, Trout thought as they cruised past.

On the way out of town, the streetlights gave way to darkness and the Bronco traveled on in a nervous silence. Each occupant alone with their own thoughts. And fears. Breena reached over and took Sean's hand. He squeezed hers lightly and she returned the gesture. Nick looked out the window and took note of the night sky. Free of the light pollution of New York City, and even the little light from Montauk itself, the sky revealed its full wonder. The stars, planets, shooting stars... all shone down on them and proved to be surprisingly bright.

"Well, take a look at that. Don't see that living in the city. In fact, I don't remember the last time I saw anything like it. Almost enough to convince me to move to the country," Nick said with his face to the window.

"You're nuts," Brandy answered. "You're as big a city guy as the rest of us. Broadway doesn't play in the country."

"Still..." Nick responded wistfully.

They passed through Shadmoor State Park on the right. Outlying houses had given way to rugged trees and scrub brush. The parking lot was closed as they drove by, but Sean could have sworn he'd seen some sort of light behind the closed gate. He turned in his seat to get another look but nothing. Whatever it was had gone.

"Sean?" Breena asked as he turned back.

"Thought I saw something but... probably my imagination. Getting jumpy, I guess."

"Well, I see something," Trout announced from the front seat.

On either side of the road were stables offering horseback rides to tourists in season. This time of year, things were much quieter out here. Usually. As the truck neared them, the passengers realized that every horse in the stables had lined the road and was watching them. The Bronco slowed to a crawl, and they eased along. One massive stallion, black as night, stepped forward, gave a loud whinny, and stomped at the ground. Others around him did the same as if in answer.

"Well, that's yet another creepy sight," said Brandy, turning in her seat to watch as the horses disappeared into the night behind them.

"Actually," said Kallan, "like the crows, I suspect that was an exceptionally good sign. I imagine Bayard has already passed this way. We may not be as alone as we fear."

"Ah, well in that case, the more the merrier. Especially since I haven't the slightest idea what we're about to deal with out here," Brandy responded.

"The more the merrier, indeed," answered Kallan, turning his eyes forward again, scanning the road and the shoulders as they traveled on toward Camp Hero.

Back at The Realm, Kelphit, Sandy, and Stewart had settled onto stools around the counter. From time to time, they could hear a rustle from above as their avian guardians moved along the roofline. Other than their scratchings above, the crows were eerily silent.

"I want to thank you for what you said earlier. About belonging," Stewart said haltingly to Kelphit. "I'd always taken that family myth as a disgrace. I felt I'd lost something when I found out we weren't Wabanaki. In just a few words, you managed to restore all of that and more. I don't think I ever realized how much it bothered me."

"I merely said what I believe. You've learned our ways, set your heart to our path... You traveled here to save a friend, knowing full well that you were placing yourself in danger. You have more than earned a place with us. With me."

Stewart, visibly moved, looked away, scanning the items in the display case. "It's interesting that Sean's been calling all of you Peripherals. It seems I've always felt that I'm peripheral, too. In life, always a bit of an outsider. In my career, always close to center stage but never actually in it. Peripheral. Important, but peripheral. I'm not really even sure what I'm trying to say…"

"I understand exactly what you're saying," Sandy spoke up. "I think our little family has all known that feeling. Each of us has gone through some sort of feeling like that. In some ways, I think it brought us together. I mean, hell, I finally felt so peripheral, I up and left to start a store out on the edge of the ocean. Guess I wanted to not be on the edge of anyone else's spotlight anymore."

"I think," said Kelphit, "that what you are describing is understandable, although I believe much of it stems from the way your society has grown. It's also a part of why so many of my kind have withdrawn from you. No one can be the center of every story. Yet your technology has created the illusion that every tiny thing you do is important. Should be viewed, applauded. 'Liked.' But that's impossible. What matters most is to be the center of your own story and to play an important part in the stories of those you love. That must be enough, because that is all there is. Live a good life. The rest… is beyond our control. As it must be."

The trio sat in silence for a few minutes. Sandy and Stewart considering what they had just heard.

Almost as one, they both turned to Kelphit and said, "Thank you."

All three burst out laughing. Turning his attention back to the display case, Stewart asked, "Is that tomahawk you made for Trout really… blessed? Anointed? Whatever you told him? Should I be asking for one of those?"

Kelphit chuckled. "No, that is simply an old rock tied to an old stick. I had not the time to do more. But I wanted him to feel that he was given a talisman. Often, I find the belief is stronger than any enchantment. Your friend Trout, I believe, will be just fine."

The three looked around at each other and then burst out laughing again.

"Well, I guess I won't need one then!" Stewart said.

His last words were almost drowned out as the fluttering from the roof top burst into a full-blown cacophony as hundreds of crows, perched mere feet above them, cried out in alarm.

The Bronco continued east toward Montauk Point. They passed the Seal Haul Out Trail on the left. Trout pointed it out while marveling to himself that it had only been hours ago that he had walked that path. They passed Camp Hero Road, but Trout explained that the back entrance at the end of the street was guarded. Their best entry would be through the main park gate closer to the lighthouse. So, on they drove.

Just a few minutes later, they approached the entrance to the park on the right. The lighthouse, the end of The End, lay ahead of them and shone its light periodically in their direction. Other than that, the stars and moon provided all the light they could hope for, more even. Trout pulled off the main road and toward the park. There was a small guard hut, unmanned and dark, but there was a gate pulled across. Kallan suggested that it would be best if they proceeded on foot to attract less attention. It was unlikely that they would be taking their foes unaware, but the park did have a staff that monitored it, and the last thing they needed was a park ranger or two stumbling into an otherworldly encounter.

Trout found a maintenance road off to the left and pulled a short way down it and around a small curve. The Bronco was invisible from the main entrance there. It would have to do.

They clambered out of the truck. Breena stayed close to Sean. Kallan practically leapt out onto the path, his sword appearing in his hand. Ready. Trout emerged from the driver's side, his tomahawk in hand and made some passes with it in front of him. It was decidedly less impressive than Kallan's sword, but Trout's face held a look of enormous pride and he carried himself with an air of invulnerability which he had a long way to go to earn. The Grumbles piled out, as well. Huddling together, uncertain of themselves, but hoping to make some small difference.

Kallan spoke, "I'll go first. Trout, you bring up the rear. The rest of you should stay near each other. You, humans, Grumbles (gods, I hate that), you will be best served to be together. I suspect you will need to draw strength from each other to make a difference in there. Absolutely no wandering off. If you see something, tell the group. Everything is potentially important."

The group started down the dirt path, turning left onto the main entrance into the park and past the empty guard room. It seemed eerie, sitting alone in the night, protecting no one and nothing. They continued on and came to a right-hand turn that indicated it was the path to the radar installation and the buildings where Odette had been taken.

Kallan spoke quietly, "Let us go forward, first. I hear the ocean and the sign indicates bluffs ahead. It would be good to get a longer view of the area. And if there is water, we may find Alara. It would be good to add her to our number before we approach the abandoned buildings."

They continued straight and came to a rather large parking lot. Apparently, Camp Hero was very popular in the warmer months. Across the lot, the distant sound of the ocean came wafting to them. They approached cautiously, only to find sea cliffs that gave an expansive view of the Atlantic to the east and north. During daylight hours, it would be stunning. Now, in the darkness, it simply yawned in front of them. The moonlight glistened on the water far below, and the lights of a fishing boat winked far out to sea. Shadows cast by passing clouds drifted over the waves, darker spots in an already dim expanse. It seemed serene. Peaceful, even.

Nick pointed to several signs warning hikers to stay clear of the unstable edges of the cliffs. "Hey, folks, just want to point out the signs warning of... you know, falling and death," he said, pointing to a bright red and white sign that said "Caution. Bluff undermined.

Keep Back 25 Feet." He was the only one on the correct side of the sign.

"Well, wouldn't that just be brilliant. Get all worked up to save the world with a group of superhuman beings, and then fall off a cliff before it even gets started," quipped Brandy as she quickly stepped behind the sign.

Trout remained next to Kallan scanning the water. Sean, however, inched backward behind the sign with Breena close by. As he did, he heard something behind him and turned to find Alara emerging from the darkness.

"Your timing is perfect," she said. "We need to begin. Now, before the moon rises too high. Our path is clear all the way to the radar installation, but I don't know what waits within the walls. We must move."

And with that, she turned and began back toward the path that led away from the cliff and toward... what they did not know.

They moved together inland on the path, turning left down a broken road, more of a trail really, that led deeper into the forest. The leaves of early fall swirled, danced, and crackled beneath their feet. The night grew darker the farther they traveled, as the trees crowded in above them, shading them from the starlight. At times, eyes glistened at them from within the woods, watching. Every so often, one or more would lope along besides them through the trees only to veer away after a short while.

Eventually, an empty maintenance building loomed on the left. Utilitarian, it was a square brick structure, out of step with its surroundings. A few park service trucks sat empty next to the outpost. The windows were barren, black, and on another night may have spooked a passing hiker, but on this night the group felt nothing and spared no energy on the space. Their challenges lay ahead and were more than a shiver up the spine from a disused and sad structure.

Brandy stopped to pick up a sturdy stick, swinging it around her before settling down to use it as a hiking aid. She looked at Nick, "Probably best I can do under the circumstances. May come in handy."

"Can't hurt," he answered. He seemed to scan the ground for something similar but found nothing. He stooped and picked up a fist-sized stone. "I got a rock," he joked. The two looked at each other and chuckled. They turned back to the others, hurrying to catch up to the group.

Eventually they turned left and after another short walk, came to a central green. A parking lot sat off to the left, empty now of the tourists' SUVs and hybrids that filled it during the busier months. In the green itself, information boards sat, offering historical nuggets to the curious visitors. Beyond the green loomed three massive buildings behind a large imposing chain-link fence topped with barbed wire. The fence was covered in signs warning to keep out, danger, area monitored, and threats of arrest and fines.

The clearing around the buildings allowed for more light and the area was easier to see and navigate. The closest building was another simple utilitarian structure, although significantly older than the maintenance compound from earlier. It was a rugged and unappealing block that sat by the entrance. A dull, grey-brown color, it stood clearly lifeless and empty. The two buildings beyond it however... were different.

The massive radar installation loomed over all. The radar dish sent scattered shadows across the grounds, a giant malevolent wing that, even shredded by the elements and time, seemed ready to lift into the air carrying the installation away with it. The building itself was the same unattractive color as the gatehouse. Both were covered with graffiti, most of it clearly from the hands of youths proving their bravery by entering and defacing the forbidden space.

But under that disused veneer lay a brooding malevolence. The assembled group knew that there was danger ahead of them, and some credited their discomfort to that knowledge and the proximity of their foes. The more intuitive of the group, though, felt something deeper. Older. Vile things had been done within those walls and the echoes of those things remained. And those echoes likely gave strength to the enemies they were about to face.

Slightly back and to the right of the radar building, lay a house. An old wooden structure that had clearly been some sort of caretaker's residence. It lurked in the background, its empty windows staring down at them. Occasional creaks and rustles came from the interior and those who heard them tried in vain to convince themselves it was "the house settling," but no one really believed that. The house looked as if it belonged in a Hitchcock movie, but the trio of structures in front of them were far more troubling than anything Hollywood had created.

Nick sidled up to Sean as the group paused to decide their next move. "I did some research. The more you know, and all that. That house off to the right is called the Acid House. No one seems to know why, but that can't be good, right?"

"No," Sean answered, "I can't say that sounds too inviting."

"Also, ten years ago, almost to the day, the radar dish reportedly moved ninety degrees to face south. On its own. After being shut down for decades. No clue what that means, but the timing seemed worth noting... and weird."

"That's very strange. Yes, definitely worth noting. I'll mention it to the others." He wondered if these events had been planned for much longer than they'd suspected.

"You know me, big on research," Nick added, before turning aside and disappearing back into his phone's screen. Sean couldn't help but think that not all screen time was bad time. Especially when researching a mysterious, abandoned, possibly paranormal government installation just before breaking into it.

Kallan called the group together and they met by the larger of the information kiosks. "Our only way forward, as far as I can reason, is into the large building and down to the tunnels. That is where I last saw Odette, and it is where I made contact with the Dullahan. It is dark and it is dangerous. And they will certainly be waiting for us. There is no shame should anyone prefer to remain outside. It could even be useful to have some eyes out here to keep watch should anything follow us in..."

Everyone looked around the group, wondering if anyone would speak up. It was Trout that spoke first.

"Well, speaking for myself and I would reckon for my Grumbly friends here, as well, there's just no way we're stepping out now. Find Odette, beat these bad whatever-they-ares, get our buddy Ken back up and running. That's what we came here to do, that's what we're doing."

"Damn straight," Brandy said with determination.

"Hell, yeah," Nick echoed. "I'm screenshotting all the info I need so when I lose service in there, I'll still have something for us to go on. We are so in."

Sean looked around at his friends who had taken such an extreme leap of faith to be here with him and couldn't help but smile. He'd known many people over the years, these were the best he could imagine. He felt a welling up of emotion for each of them and silently vowed to himself that he would make sure they all returned home after this. He reached for Breena's hand, and she responded. Without even looking at her, Sean knew that she understood.

The group proceeded to the main gate of the radar compound. Kallan took the lead, announcing that he knew the way. The steel in his demeanor signaled to the rest that he felt responsible for the current predicament and would not be deterred. At the gate, the lock holding it shut was no match for a quick but firm flick of Kallan's sword. The group silently entered the grounds, and Alara, taking up the rear, closed the gate after they'd passed and propped the doors shut. To any rangers on patrol, all would look normal unless they examined things closely.

"What of Bayard?" Alara whispered to Breena.

"He knows where to find us. I'm sure he's...busy," she responded.

They passed the gatehouse on their right. It sat empty, silent. A shell of what it had once been. Everyone's nerves were on edge, especially the Grumbles, who found themselves in real danger for the first time. Anxious glances flew between them, but their resolve held, and the group climbed the small hill toward the radar installation itself.

Clouds began to cover the stars as they moved into the clearing before to the building. Kallan cast a glance upward and looked meaningfully at Alara and Breena who nodded knowingly back to him. These clouds were unnatural, settling in directly above them and nowhere else. Similar to what they had experienced on the beach in Staten Island. Their presence had been noted. Or more likely, expected.

Kallan led the way into the building, through the vent he and Odette had seen on their last trip here. They passed through the same abandoned rooms, hallways, offices that he had seen the first time. He moved quickly to the stairway leading downward. Nick, Brandy, and Trout were wide-eyed at what they were seeing. Nick muttered bits of information about the history as they proceeded. Facts that he had picked up in his research. It seemed to help keep him calm in the face of this unknown environment. Trout swung his tomahawk in lazy circles next to him, eyes alert. Brandy strode along as if she hadn't a care in the world.

They descended four full floors, finally coming out into the area of abandoned laboratories and cells that Kallan remembered. All was as it had been. Scattered remnants of a bygone decade everywhere. As they looked around them, the group wondered what kind of work had been done here that would leave such a sinister feeling all these years later. The air was heavy, the darkness did its best to swallow any light. Kallan's sword began to glow its icy blue. Alara drew a short sword, curved almost like a scimitar, and carried it aloft in front of her, a faint green glow adding itself to Kallan's. Breena paused and whispered some words in a language that none of the Grumbles recognized. Suddenly, a bright golden ball of light appeared between her hands, and she seemed to shape it into a sphere that, when she released it, floated just above her. Nick, who had just turned on the flashlight feature on his phone, took note of how small it seemed next to these others and powered it down sheepishly.

"Better to save the battery, I guess," he muttered.

Brandy put a hand on his shoulder in support. "Absolutely," she whispered. "Good thinking."

Nick couldn't tell if the sarcasm he sensed was just him being sensitive. He decided to believe that.

They came to the corridor that angled downward. Kallan turned to the group, nodded in that direction, and motioned for everyone to remain quiet. They began the downward hike and as they went the darkness grew... blacker. The walls swallowed any reflection. The lights of the Peripherals seemed diminished, as if something was pushing down on them, trying to extinguish any illumination. Or hope.

Before they reached the bottom, a faint scratching began in the corridor. The group paused, trying to get a bearing on where the sound was coming from but with no success. Alara, in the rear, turned to look behind them, but the darkness swallowed her light, and she could see nothing. It became clear that the sound, now multiplying into many scratchings, was everywhere around them. Kallan motioned for them to continue, knowing that the end of the corridor opened out somewhat and would allow them a better defensive position. In the hallway, single file, they were vulnerable.

They reached the bottom and took up places against one wall, using it to protect their backs. Kallan motioned them into place. Alara, Kallan, and Trout stood at the outer ring of the group. Breena remained close to Sean with Brandy and Nick on either side. Across from them was the large door that Kallan had told them about from his earlier visit. Now, however, it sat firmly closed, no light shining from within.

The scratching noises grew louder. Closer. They seemed to be everywhere at once, but nothing could be seen. And then, as suddenly as they had begun, they stopped. All was silent. For a moment. And then it was not.

CHAPTER 28

Kelphit was the first to react to the cawing of the crows, dashing across the room to make sure that the front door to the store was firmly shut. He glanced at the runes and warnings around it before moving to the windows to do the same with them.

Outside, loud crashes began to echo from all directions. Bellowing, grunting, and snarling began slowly and grew in volume and frequency. Louder and louder, it continued to crescendo until the building itself felt as if it would be shaken apart.

Sandy rushed to the door to the back room, opening it to make sure that Ken was still safe. All was quiet there, so she shut the door, pouring more salt along the floor outside. She turned to the counter and opened a drawer that was partially hidden below. Reaching in, she grabbed three pendants, which were simply crystals affixed to leather strips and tossed one to each of the others while placing one around her neck.

"Staurolite," she announced to them. "Some people call it the Fairy Cross Stone. Helps to protect from dark influences. Good for dealing with the fae realm." Stewart shot her a dubious look and she responded quickly. "Don't give me the doubting Stewart crap. You're the one who decided to stay in a new age shop with us, so... time to get your New Age on. And hey, let's take any advantage we can get, huh?"

Stewart examined the necklace she had thrown him. It was a dull, flat grey, stone that had formed a cross, naturally. He shrugged and placed it around his neck. "No argument here. We can debate the merits of crystal therapy later."

Kelphit looked at his necklace and gave a small smile as he placed it around his neck. As he did so, he brought another necklace out from under his tunic. More ornate than the one he had just received, it almost shone in the light of the room. Sandy saw it and nearly gasped. On it she recognized powerful crystals, some of which were too dear for her to even consider carrying in the store. Hematite, black tourmaline, lapis lazuli, Apache Tear.

"I'm impressed," she said. "You're not messing around."

"I've had quite a long time to gather them. Let's see what's happening outside, yes?" Kelphit answered.

Carefully, he drew back a curtain on one of the windows. He cupped his hand around his eyes to see better. He did not like what he saw.

A grotesque menagerie surrounded the building. Horses, boars, stags, bulls, even some small birds ringed the store. They were all deformed in the most horrible ways. Dead flesh hung from skeletal frames. At odd places, bones poked through skin in ways that should not be possible. The eyes, though. All of the eyes shone with a putrid, yellow light, as if the diseases which had stolen their healthy bodies had infected something much deeper, and glared angrily toward the store and those who were within. But Kelphit saw something worse lurking behind the creatures. A loose circle of tall, pale, spectral figures, dressed only in tattered rags, could be seen on the edge of the glow from the building. They glared back at Kelphit, clearly willing the diseased creatures forward. As one, they raised their hands and pointed not just at the window, but directly at Kelphit. As they did, he noticed that all of them had long, misshapen fingers, and all of those fingers were coaxing the small army to violence. With an otherworldly shrieking, the creatures all began to fling themselves at The Realm.

As they did so, a golden glow, faint at first, then brighter and stronger, sprang up around the structure. Kelphit quickly closed the curtain and turned to his companions. "It seems our foes have enlisted the poor creatures of Plum Island to their cause. I've never seen them gathered together like this."

"Plum Island?" Stewart asked. "Why does that sound familiar?"

"I'll explain later," Sandy answered. "Sounds like we're about to have our hands full."

Kelphit began a low chant in a language neither of the others could understand. As he did, the glow around the building grew still brighter. Sandy rushed to his side and found a wordless tone that fit his chord and added her voice to his. The golden light grew brighter still.

Stewart rushed to the display case and grabbed an ornamental knife from within before joining the other two near the doorway. When Sandy cast a curious glance his way, he shrugged. "Some weapon is better than no weapon. Magic or not," he said. He then placed a hand on Kelphit's shoulder and added his rich baritone to their chord. The noise outside grew. Clawing, stamping, pounding, crying echoed around the tiny building, as the evil assembled outside shrieked to get in. The golden dome of light pulsed and strengthened, but the assault from outside grew. And grew. And the numbers seemed decidedly against the defenders.

<hr>

Deep below the radar installation, the corridor filled with orange light and the group saw that they were surrounded by evil. Wendigo minions clung to the walls, the ceiling, and surrounded them on the floor. All looked recently turned, but bore the hallmark of their master, deep black eyes set far back into their skulls, a grey pallor

that radiated disease and death, some even had small horns beginning to sprout from their foreheads. All had large, angry, gnashing
teeth that they bared as they approached the group. The hallway
they had just come down was filled with an angry shriek as the
Wendigo, the master and creator of these lesser creatures, could be
heard descending toward them. The small space was suddenly
swarming with the monsters. Kallan's sword glowed brighter, and he
lunged, slicing through first one and then another of the lesser
Wendigos. Alara's curved blade joined the fray, slicing the legs out
from another Wendigo before dispatching it with a vicious downward thrust. As this was happening, Breena began to feel her song
rising and the brilliant light Sean remembered so well from the
beach emerged and settled over them as she sang her wordless
notes. The Wendigos recoiled from the light and seemed to burn
wherever it touched them. The small group seemed to be gaining
some breathing room when the Wendigo emerged from the tunnel
and cried out to the others, spurring them to greater anger and rabid
violence.

The Wendigos that had been clinging to the ceiling began dropping into the circle of defenders. The first few were rebuffed by the
dome of light coming from Breena, but their sheer numbers eventually started to break through. The blades flew through the air but
began to lose ground. Trout was swinging his tomahawk in every
direction and the sound of bones breaking followed each of his
swings. His cries of "Montana!" echoed off the walls.

Somehow, Brandy and Nick became detached from the main
group and found themselves quickly surrounded. They attempted to
recreate the chord they had formed back in the store, but only a very
faint glow emerged, and it did little to dissuade the lesser Wendigos
that turned to what they saw as far easier quarry. Brandy waved her
walking stick from the hike through the forest to no avail. Nick found
a brick on the ground and threw it at the tightening circle. It struck a
Wendigo, causing it to recoil then resume its advance with even
more anger. They were losing ground. Quickly.

Sean had added his tenor chord to Breena's, strengthening her light, but now saw his Grumble friends in peril. They were in danger of being overwhelmed and he felt powerless to stop it, a sea of Wendigos between them. He felt frustration, anger, helplessness well up within him. These friends, who had risked everything to be here with him, to save Ken despite having no knowledge of what they were facing, were about to be lost. And yet, Breena clearly needed him to withstand the overwhelming numbers. The other Peripherals were holding their own, but just barely. He felt desperate and torn. Something began to rise in him, something new. Something he could not contain. Just as he thought Brandy and Nick would be lost, a clear, high, immense golden sound erupted from him. It was his voice but was unlike any sound he had ever made. It took shape, a physical manifestation of the notes coming from him, and his golden light absorbed Breena's brilliance, transformed it into part of itself. He rose off the floor, bathed in a nimbus so bright that all, Peripheral, Grumble, and Wendigo alike, were forced to stop what they were doing and look away. As they did, Sean uttered one word, "No," and the room exploded. The lesser Wendigos were literally blown apart, sent sailing up the corridor behind them or into oblivion. The true Wendigo was forced to its knees as Sean's golden light shot toward him in a beam and pushed him relentlessly to the ground. It turned to look up at Sean, curiosity and anger flitting across its grotesque features. It considered Sean for a moment and then broke free and ran quickly to the large doorway on the far side of the room, which opened, bathing the hallway in an ugly orange glow before closing again behind the Wendigo and a handful of its minions who managed to escape. Sean's power, which had been only protective until now, had taken on a new pitch and had struck out, removing all who threatened his friends.

The rest of the group stood frozen in place. Sean, spent, sank to his knees. Breathing hard, he turned to Breena, who returned his look with surprise. Kallan and Alara lowered their blades, clearly caught off guard. Brandy and Nick rushed back toward the others, speechless for the moment.

"Well, that's what I'm talking about!" hooted Trout as he scooped Sean up into a great bear hug. "Just when you think things are about to go south, our boy here just... blew 'em away!"

Breena took Sean's hand to make sure he was all right. He seemed stunned, but otherwise fine as he turned in a circle to make sure everyone was unhurt. "I think we now know why they are so desperate to get to Sean," she said.

At that moment, a storm of bats came shrieking out of the upward corridor. They circled the room above the company before setting into the corners and nooks of the ceiling. Striding out of the hallway came Bayard, draped with bats on either arm and shoulder, his blades drawn and ready.

"Did I miss anything?" he said with his lopsided grin. Then taking stock of the situation, "Well, better late than never. I stopped for reinforcements," he said, "and judging by the Wendigo pieces I passed on the way down, I missed the good part, yes?"

Outside of the shop, the assault grew more fevered. The golden dome around the building held, but barely, and cracks were beginning to appear. Kelphit somehow managed to intensify his effort, as did Sandy and Stewart, but the numbers thrown against them seemed to be insurmountable. Their crow friends returned, and flew with fury at the diseased attackers, but they too were outnumbered, falling in bursts of feathers as hooves and horns tore them from the air. Behind it all, the long-fingered men loomed, gesturing to their hideous menagerie, and flinging them one after another at the beautiful golden dome that was now beginning to flicker.

Stewart disengaged from the others and pushed a bookshelf across the floor to block the doorway. It seemed a futile effort, but better than no effort at all. While he pushed the case into place, a hoof from outside pierced the protection and the window in the door shattered, sending glass crashing inward. Stewart flinched, an angry red cut appearing on his cheek. He finished his task and returned quickly to the others, adding his voice once more to theirs.

Kelphit reached into his pack and brought out a small leather pouch and threw it to Stewart. "A salve," he said. "Make sure to cover that cut. No telling what those creatures are carrying or what they can infect us with..."

Stewart did as he was told and noticed an instant relief as the ointment stopped the bleeding. But outside, the attack was relentless, and the three defenders could feel the beginnings of fatigue creeping into their song.

"I never suspected they would spend such energy on us here," Kelphit said.

"Yeah, I thought we were just watching over the decoy back there," Sandy answered, motioning with her head back toward Ken in the room behind them.

"As did I," Kelphit responded. "We continue to underestimate our adversaries."

Another window off to their left shattered inward and Stewart drew the ornamental dagger, feeling that their time was running out to turn the tide. Kelphit detached himself and approached the doorway, drawing more symbols, this time on the back of the bookcase that Stewart had moved. The golden dome flickered and seemed to grow.

The crows outside magnified their efforts, diving, scratching the infected outside. Suddenly, as if answering some unknown call, they wheeled away. Their cries fell silent, and they seemed to find shelter in nearby trees, abandoning the attack. Clouds, black against the night sky slid in overhead and seemed to settle above the store. Even within the building, the air crackled with energy as the darkness outside found a way to descend over the room, bringing a stillness with it.

Silence fell everywhere. The putrid attackers halted in their efforts. Kelphit sensed a shift and paused in his chant. Sandy and Stewart did the same, following his lead. Finally, the long-fingered men turned to look inland, away from the water toward the interior of the island.

"Oh… oh, this does not feel good," Stewart muttered, and Sandy reached out to take his hand, sharing his sense of foreboding.

Suddenly, the silence was shattered. The black clouds broke with a deafening downpour, lightning filled the sky, and thunder shook the building. Immediately after, a great wind came screaming from the landward side. The trees bent. The crows took to the sky, helplessly riding the gusts away. Away from The Realm, away from its defenders, toward the end of the island.

And still the wind increased. Beyond anything Sandy and Stewart had experienced. The door shook, the windows seemed ready to fly into the night. Kelphit turned his head toward something the others couldn't sense. He strode toward the nearest window and flung the curtains open.

"What are you doing?!" shouted Stewart, running to the window and trying to pull the curtain closed, for what little good it would do. He stopped short in his tracks, looking outside as his mouth dropped open.

Beyond the window, he saw the phantom creatures being swept away. Grotesque boars, bulls, stallions and all their hideous cohorts were being dragged along the ground and carried away. Some held on longer than others. Some were shredded by the shrieking wind and fell to pieces. A small number turned to flee, trying with all they had to escape the fury that was destroying the others. Finally, the long-fingered men, barely able to stand upright themselves, turned to each other and, as if reaching some unspoken decision, they turned their baleful gazes on the store and with a cry of anger and frustration, moved away, allowing the wind to push them far from their target. They, too, were thrust toward the end of the island, very much against their will.

"What the hell..." Sandy said as she approached the window where Stewart and Kelphit stood.

The wind dropped and died almost immediately as soon as all of the attackers had disappeared. The three stood at the window and watched as a mist settled in behind the storm as it passed. Through the mist, they saw movement. They stood, rooted to the spot, and what they were watching came closer.

Suddenly, Kelphit moved toward the door and pushed the bookshelf out of the way. Much easier than it had been for Stewart to drag it, Stewart noted. Kelphit flung the door open and stepped outside. The other two, with a curious glance at each other, followed hesitantly, staying within the doorframe but craning their necks to get a look at whatever had drawn their companion outside.

The movement in the mist intensified and it soon became clear that there were forms, people, moving silently past. A handful at first and then dozens. As they drew closer, they revealed themselves to be barely as tall as children. In fact, Stewart was certain for a moment that they *were* children. Kelphit knew differently and lowered himself to his knee in respect, motioning for the others to do the same.

One of the figures detached itself from the others and moved closer to the three watchers. As the mist cleared, they could see that it was a woman, barely more than three feet tall. It was impossible to tell how old she was, but her eyes were deep and profound and determined. Kelphit covered his heart and bowed his head to her. She did the same to him and then turned to rejoin the others of her kind as they followed the wind to the east.

Sandy and Stewart turned their unspoken questions to Kelphit, who answered without looking at them. "The Little People of Shinnecock lore. Their true name is one that would mean nothing to you."

"Little people? Just when you think it can't get stranger... I always thought of them as Irish... similar?" asked Sandy.

"Similar, yet different. As you will continue to learn, many of what you call myths can be found in cultures everywhere. As in this case. They are essentially the earth's cleaners. They are far more comfortable tending to the soil and growing crops. Maintaining health. If they feel the need to come forth in anger, there is something dire afoot. None of them have been seen in many, many years. Not by me or any of your kind. Our crow friends brought them out, I think. They are caretakers of our earth. Protectors of those who are helpless. We swim in deep waters if they feel the need to appear." He turned a worried gaze on the others. "Our work here is not done. We must protect your friend still but say a silent prayer for the others. Something the likes of which I have never seen is in motion. But our place is here. Keeping watch."

He rose and walked back into the store with the others following him. Once inside, they closed the door, slid the bookshelf back into place and set about retracing the runes and drawings of protection. The night was still young, and they had seen too many surprises already. It seemed danger walked everywhere through Montauk tonight.

CHAPTER 29

"OK, so what the hell just happened?" Brandy asked as the group huddled as far from the glowing doorway as they could squeeze.

"I actually have no idea," Sean answered. He had a confused, almost frightened look on his face. A sheen of sweat covered him. His breathing was slowly returning to normal, but what had happened clearly cost him something.

"I mean, we weren't able to do anything. Nothing like what happened back in the store," Nick muttered. "We were pretty much done for, and then..." He glanced almost warily at Sean, as if seeing his friend as something other than what he'd always known.

"It seems Sean is some sort of keystone, an amplifier. He can absorb others' talents and reflect them back... magnified. He absorbed my own and strengthened it," Breena spoke, teasing her own thoughts out as she spoke the words.

"It certainly explains why our adversaries were so desperate to capture him. If he fell thrall to the Dullahan and it controlled him... there is no telling what damage they could do," Kallan said.

"Well, luckily that didn't happen. Right? And hopefully now that we know, we can get this taken care of and go home—yes?" Nick asked.

"I still have some questions, though," Alara offered.

"No, please, no more questions..." Nick pleaded.

"Yeah, me too," Bayard chimed in. "How has this been hidden for so long?"

"I've been watching Sean for years, so we can't say that we were completely unaware, but I see your point. I never witnessed anything that led me to believe this was possible," Breena said.

Kallan responded, "We're just guessing at this point, but it seems Sean needed a catalyst of some kind. Proximity to someone else with abilities. And clearly the situation here triggered an instinctual response. In an impossible scenario, his power took over."

"Yeah, folks," Sean spoke quietly, while staring at the floor between his feet. "I have absolutely no idea how or why that happened. So, let's not jump to the assumption that I can turn this on and off whenever I feel like it."

The eaves of the store were filled with the fluttering of wings as the crows settled in again to their watch over those within. It was strangely comforting to know they had returned, and Sandy and Stewart allowed themselves to relax ever so slightly, having watched the storm sweep their attackers away. They sat next to each other on the floor in front of the counter. Stewart was questioning Sandy about life in Montauk. Life post-performing. She was more than happy to answer everything, and her enthusiasm for her new life was infectious. Stewart couldn't help but smile in response to her answers while thinking of his own career path. Or lack thereof.

Kelphit made a circuit around the store, reinforcing the windows and doors, applying new drawings where he felt they were needed. He turned to head into the back room to make sure that Ken was comfortable and shielded. As he crossed the floor, the storeroom door opened on its own. He paused. Sandy and Stewart turned at the sound.

In the doorway stood Ken. He was disheveled, wiping his eyes and looking around him, his face full of questions.

"OK, I know you and you," he said pointing at Stewart and Sandy. "But who are you?" he asked, pointing at Kelphit. "And where exactly am I? Because this is definitely not West Forty-fifth Street. Also… can I get a glass of water? I'm parched. It's really hot back there."

The three others reacted quickly, his two friends rushing to him and, as he seemed himself, giving him hugs and looking him over. Kelphit approached more cautiously, obviously wondering why Ken was conscious.

Sandy grabbed him a bottle of water from a small fridge behind the counter and the three settled in to explain things to Ken. And to be sure that Ken was indeed back. Was himself.

In the subterranean tunnels, the group turned as one toward the glowing orange door, as it began to pulse rhythmically. Somehow the hue turned uglier, angrier as the tempo increased. The door itself seemed to bow out with each pulse.

"No rest for the weary," Nick muttered as he scanned the floor for bricks, all too aware that he seemed to be the one with the least means of defending himself.

The door was visibly pulsing along with the light now. Streaks of black winding their way through the orange. Suddenly, and on its own, the door flew inward and shattered against the interior wall. Everyone was on their feet instantly and at the ready, but nothing emerged from the room.

Instead, they heard a woman's voice pierce the sudden silence. "Kallan! No!!" it cried.

"Odette," Kallan said, and was through the door before any of the others could move.

"Kallan, wait!" Bayard shouted, but Kallan was already gone.

Bayard and Alara shot after him and the others formed a group, shielding each other as best they could and followed.

Ken was left with his mouth hanging open after he'd been filled in on the events of the last two days. He wanted to reject it, deny it could have happened, but he looked around himself and couldn't ignore that he was over a hundred miles away from his last conscious memory. He felt drained, but assured the others that he was fine otherwise, with no memory of his time as a captive or the battle on the beach. No memory of the drive out.

"What about Anne?" he asked. "And the kids?"

Stewart answered, assuring him that they'd kept her informed along the way, but had chosen to not fill her in on the... more other-worldly aspects of the situation.

"Probably for the best. I'll have to figure out how to explain when I get back. When can we head back, by the way?"

Kelphit shook his head. "Not yet. Your friends have a very perilous night ahead of them still. Although the fact that you have awakened may be a very good sign, indeed. It's possible they have scored some measure of victory already."

"Well, I sure hope so. And... yes, of course. I'm so sorry. Can I help somehow? Should we go see if they're OK?"

"No," Kelphit answered, warily. "The best thing we can do is remain here and do as we planned. You have only just now woken up. Best to recover here and rest." With that, he found a carved walking stick near the counter and began tracing runes and diagrams along the floor, dropping some dye to embellish certain drawings. He tied one of his totems to the top of the stick and continued marking the floor.

"I'll text Nick and let them know what's happened. If they're underground, he may not get it for a while, but probably a good idea to fill them in," Sandy said, as she typed on her phone.

Ken ambled around the store, picking up items and placing them back. "Nice place you got here, Sand. Business good?"

"Can't complain. Although tonight has taken everything in a decidedly unexpected direction."

"Don't have to tell me about it. I was taking a simple walk to the train, enjoying a little call to my friend MJ, and next thing I know I've been abducted, possessed, driven to the end of The End, and woken up in the care of an ancient indigenous wise man. Woo."

He picked up a long pipe from a shelf. "Peace pipe?" he asked.

"Right the first time," Sandy answered.

Ken got a sly look on his face, shot her a look, and said, "I may have to pick one of these up for myself."

Sandy and Stewart both laughed and shook their heads. He definitely seemed like his old self.

He noticed a mop and bucket stashed in a corner, lifted it up, and examined it. "Let me guess, witch transport?"

"You're thinking a broom, smart guy."

"You're right. Mea culpa. What could I possibly have been thinking?" He lifted the mop, gave a short bow to it, and proceeded to dance across the floor. "Reminds me of my childhood. Used to bore my older relatives with variety shows filled with scintillating acts just like this. Stole it from Gene Kelly. *Let Me Call You Sweetheart*, 1943. Classic. Although I think Gene pulled it off a little better than I can. Wow. I really feel great..."

"Guess we were all performers from the start. Some more than others..." Stewart responded as Ken waltzed around the showroom. The others looked on with smiles. Even Kelphit seemed to enjoy watching the old friends banter and reminisce. A welcome shift from the extreme anxiety that they had all been through for the last day. None of them even noticed the tap-tapping of first a single crow, and then others, as they settled on the windowsills outside and pecked the glass to gain their attention.

With Kallan in front, the group charged into the chamber. What they were greeted with was a hellscape that none of them could have imagined. Opposite the door, the far half of the room was on fire. Angry orange flames rippled the length of the walls, settled on the floor like an agonizing tide, and licked along the ceiling. In the midst of it, the Dullahan sat on the bench of a wagon, drawn by two spectral horses. His detached head was held high in one hand, staring balefully at the new arrivals, while his other hand waved his whip menacingly. Bayard and Trout recognized them to be the same as the Plum Island horse they had encountered at Seal Haul Out. The Wendigo stood to the side of the wagon on the floor, a handful of lesser Wendigos that had survived Sean's revelation seethed and writhed nearby, torn between wanting to tear into the flesh of the living in front of them and terror at the power that they had just witnessed.

The Dullahan rose from his seat, fixed Kallan with a withering glare, and slowly dismounted from the wagon. As he did so, he revealed what was behind him. Odette was suspended off the floor of the cart, engulfed in orange and purple flames. Her arms were stretched out to her sides and her feet were shackled to the flooring. She flailed back and forth, pain pulling her teeth back from her lips in an agonizing scream that never found the air to burst forth. How she still lived was beyond the comprehension of her friends.

Kallan stepped forward, locking his eyes on her. She watched him, the cords of her muscles straining in vain against her bonds. Her situation was hopeless. Escape was impossible. Kallan paused, desperate to find a solution and fearing that the only one was the worst he could imagine. He nodded to her and she, with a look of gratitude, gave the slightest of nods in return. If rescue was hopeless, release would be the only alternative. They both acknowledged that. Slowly, Kallan withdrew Odette's spear from behind him where he had carried it since her abduction. He held it, almost delicately, and bowed his head in a soft prayer, willing the spear to fly true and serve its purpose. Then, in one fluid motion, and without pause lest he lose his nerve, he reared back and hurled the spear directly at Odette.

The group collectively let out a strangled reaction, tears jumping to the eyes even of those who hadn't yet met her. The idea of her end coming at the point of her own spear, even while seemingly the most merciful of outcomes, felt too cruel to bear.

The spear flew true, straight at Odette. And then something unexpected happened. The spear sailed past the laughing Dullahan and when it reached its master in the bed of the wagon, it stopped dead, turning parallel to her, and slid gently into her outstretched hand. As soon as she felt its familiar cold shaft, she flicked her wrist ever so slightly and the razor-sharp spear sheared through the bonds holding her in place. One arm, then another, and finally, with the slightest touch, her feet. She was free and with a cry of rage like none heard before, she launched herself out of the wagon toward her friends. As she did, her spear slashed, almost faster than the eye could follow and both gruesome stallions collapsed, empty flesh no longer animated. She rolled quickly to her feet and took her place next to Kallan, who clasped her forearm with a look of greatest relief on his face. She was drained, but free and full of anger.

The Wendigo screamed in frustration, and its minions echoed its cry, but the Dullahan looked on calmly, its empty gaze flashing black, and the macabre smile that stretched across its face seemingly grew. It took a half step forward and said simply, "The End is near." One more step toward them and then it spoke, "Kenneth Michael O'Carroll."

Suddenly, the chamber became a whirl of activity. Kallan and Odette charged forward but were too late. The Dullahan once again grasped its cloak and, grabbing the Wendigo, covered them both with it. The flames from the wagon exploded outward and collapsed backward, creating a swirling gateway that fell in upon itself, taking the two of them with it. The room was plunged into darkness, quickly dispelled by Breena's light, but their chief adversaries were gone, and they found themselves facing a blank wall.

The abandoned lesser Wendigos howled in anger and fear but were quickly dispatched by the Peripherals' blades. Unfortunate souls lost to an evil they'd never known existed until they had fallen victim to it.

Breena looked at the others with panic in her voice. "We were wrong. So wrong, all along. He spoke Ken's name. Ken was never a feint or a mistake. He was a trap. He must have some sort of power like you, Sean. But he's been unleashed on our friends. If it's even a fraction of what yours is... Far from here and in a town filled with unsuspecting innocents..."

Bayard and Odette slipped out immediately without a word. "Even they may not be fast enough to save them. And if Ken has access to his power while under their control, or can somehow tap into Kelphit's, there's no telling what can happen," Breena said.

Kallan stepped forward and placed a hand on Breena's shoulder. "They must deal with that. We know where the evil ones fled. We know where we must go."

Alara answered from behind them. "The End."

CHAPTER 30

K en had finished his mop dance and sat down on a stool near the counter, winded. "Guess that possession took more out of me than I realized," he huffed.

Kelphit busied himself behind the counter, unseen by Ken. He moved slowly toward the storeroom door, drawing new runes until they filled nearly every inch of space.

"You think you might be overdoing it there, friend?" Sandy asked Kelphit, looking askance at her floor. "Actually, you know what? No, knock yourself out. Can't be too protected and it might even be good for business."

At that point, many things happened at once. The tapping of the crows had been growing in volume and urgency until two of the windows cracked open and the air filled with dozens of crows circling the room.

As that happened, Ken stood, cocked his head as if hearing something the others could not. His eyes flashed red once and then turned black. His back arched, his face a rictus of pain, and he unleashed a cry of rage, anger, confusion... The dead stare he turned to the others was full of hunger. His desire for flesh all but written on him and his friends no longer anything but a way to satisfy this sudden burning inside. His voice began to hum, and with it a charge began to fill the air.

Kelphit struck his rune-covered staff on the floor, and as he spoke in a language only he could understand, a brilliant green light shot from the end of the staff toward Ken, who lashed out and sent Stewart flying across the room, skidding to a stop near the far wall. Ken had taken a deep breath and was about to unleash something more—a shout, a song, a forgotten word—but whatever he had planned died in his throat as Kelphit's green light encircled his head and stretched across his mouth, sealing it closed with an other-worldly verdant mask. As Ken struggled, he looked down and realized that the runes that had seemed randomly placed around the floor encircled him and glowed, constricting him where he was. He could not move.

The crows now numbered in the hundreds and the air was filled with the rustle of their wings and their low croaking as they swirled and dove around Ken, further imprisoning him where he stood. His black eyes darted from side to side, looking for escape. But there was none to be had. He was soon bound so tightly, by rune, and staff, and bird, that he was motionless, radiating anger and violence that, at least for now, had no release.

Kelphit was breathing hard, the strain showing as he fought to maintain control over Ken. Sandy helped Stewart to his feet, and they joined Kelphit, laying their hands on his shoulders and adding their voices to his effort. It was a pale light they provided, far from the brilliance that the entire group had created earlier, but it buffered Kelphit, and he seemed to regain greater control over the situation.

When Bayard and Odette blinked into the room moments later, fearing that they would find the worst and ready for violence, they skidded to a halt. The scene that greeted them would have been unimaginable if they hadn't experienced the last two days together. Ken hovered an inch or two above the floor, imprisoned by concentric runic circles that spread throughout the store. His head was shrouded by a brilliant green halo that had gripped his mouth shut firmly. Sandy and Stewart were backing Kelphit, adding a chord that shimmered a pale yellow and ran through the green cocoon. Around it all, the crows of Montauk dove and circled Ken, a living enclosure to make certain that, should Kelphit or the others falter, Ken would have no means of escape without passing through their dervish of beaks, and talons, and wings.

Bayard grinned. "Well, that is an entirely new kind of birdcage. Literally. A cage of birds. I like it."

Back at the radar installation, the group raced back along the corridors they'd taken on the way in. Kallan led the way, much lighter now that Odette had been rescued and he had a final destination ahead. The others followed, silent, worried about what was happening to their friends back at the store. After a few minutes, they emerged into the crisp night air. The bats that had followed Bayard into the tunnels streamed into the night around them, swirled momentarily above their heads, and then vanished into the night. The sky above was dappled with clouds and a white-as-cream moon that danced through them. Black clouds gathered to the east, showing them where they must go next.

Alara gestured Kallan over to her. "I must go ahead," she said. "We need to know what to expect, and our human friends will take longer, but need protection. I can find what we need by myself."

Kallan, with a glance at Sean, answered, "I'm not entirely sure it's they that need the protection anymore. Yes, go. But be very wary. We can't afford to lose you just when we've gotten Odette back."

"No worry there. I have many friends near the water. Only they will know I'm there." With that, she slipped silently into the night. There one moment. The next, not.

"Do you ever get used to that?" Brandy asked Trout.

"Well, I doubt it. Not yet, anyway," he answered with a shake of his head.

"OK, good to know."

Nick checked his phone as soon as they reached the clearing. "Hey, folks, I have a text saying that Ken woke up a little while ago... He seems fine!" he happily announced. "No, wait, strike that. Not long after, he was taken over again... Kelphit and the others restrained him, something about birds? I'm very confused..."

At that moment Odette blinked in. Seeing the confusion in the group, she filled them in on all that had happened at the store, up to the point where she and Bayard had helped them maneuver Ken and his green sarcophagus into the back room where he had been sealed in with further runes and enchantments. "The situation is well in hand now. Kelphit anticipated what was about to happen and captured the possessed," she glanced at Sean, "Sorry, captured your friend, as soon as the transformation occurred. He is more than capable of holding him until things are resolved." The group nodded in understanding and relief that one burden, at least, had been resolved. "However," she continued, "the only remedy for... Ken, is to dispatch the Wendigo. Permanently. Otherwise, the curse will remain, and he will never be safe. Nor will those around him."

"Well, that seems to work out just fine," Trout answered. "I have every intention of sending that piece of nasty back to where it came from. For good."

"Get in line, mountain man," Brandy spoke stepping forward. "I have the very same plan."

"Yeah, well, I have an enchanted tomahawk and you have a walking stick, so maybe you should just keep behind me for this one, short stuff." Trout grinned and patted her on the head which didn't exactly sit well with Brandy, who gave him a less than gentle punch to the shoulder.

Odette approached Nick and Brandy. "That reminds me," she addressed them. "At Kelphit's suggestion, I brought each of you one of these. They may be useful if you find yourself in a difficult situation. But as a last resort only. Your best chance of success is to stay together." She drew from her belt two medium-sized war clubs. They were both replicas of ancient weapons, roughly a foot and a half long. Carved out of a single piece of a hardwood, they utilized a burl, or irregular growth on a branch, to form a large ball on one end, used to strike an enemy. There were ribs carved along the back of the handle, placed there to trap a foe's weapon if one tried to strike the bearer. Both had runes along the shaft. Nick reached out and took one, examining it closely and giving it a practice swing. He noticed that his had a fish carved into the handle with a silver spike protruding from the ball at the end, clearly an artist's embellishment as it looked out of place with the rest of the club. Brandy had accepted the other and noted that hers had a snake on the handle and a similar silver spike.

Trout took it all in, glanced at his tomahawk and shook his head. "Would ya look at us. Can't think of many things less intimidating than a bunch of middle-aged musical theatre nerds running around the woods swinging clubs and trying to look tough."

The others took stock of each other. Nodded in agreement and chuckled. But the laughter was tense and short-lived.

Kallan noticed that Odette had turned her back to the group and was looking out into the dark forest. He strode to her, ready to task her with safeguarding the more vulnerable Grumbles on their way to the lighthouse. He was surprised as he neared her, to see her shoulders heave and heard a quiet sob before she realized he was approaching. He drew her farther from the others and faced her.

"What is it?" he asked, and the question was earnest. He couldn't imagine what could reduce Odette, the most resolute and fierce of them, to such raw emotion.

"Kallan... don't. Just leave me alone for a moment," she responded, turning her face away.

"No," he replied. "We're here, now, near the end... whatever that may be. We need each other more than ever. I need you. Talk to me."

"Don't you see?" she answered, the pain catching at the edge of her voice as she struggled to speak. "I'm not what I've always believed. They took me. Me! I thought I was unbeatable. I thought I was fierce. I was the one others could rely on, and in the end, I'm none of those things. I was weak. Helpless."

"No," said to her. "You've got it all wrong. You're the only one among us who could have survived that. Your strength saw you through. What you went through would have ended any of the rest of us."

She looked at him with questions in her eyes. She wanted to believe what he said, wanted to find some piece of the self she thought she had always been, but doubt had taken hold of her. For the first time ever.

"I just don't know," she said quietly. "I never... *never*... thought anything like that was possible. And, Kallan, they took me someplace else. Another dark place far from here. There was water. It was dark. I remember cypress trees. It must have been far to the south. This is bigger than we know."

"That is concerning, obviously. But we must stay focused. One thing at a time. Nothing will matter if we're defeated here tonight. But trust me. You will be stronger because of what happened. And we need you. More than ever before. I have never trusted anyone as much as I trust you. After what you've been through, you will fight harder and more fiercely than ever. You know the cost of them winning, and you will never let it happen. To us. To the others."

She stared at him a moment longer. Hesitant. And then Kallan did something no one would have expected. He reached out to Odette and wrapped her in an embrace. Long and heartfelt. She stiffened at first, resisting. Such shows of emotion were a weakness, admitting vulnerability. Gradually, she relaxed. She sagged into him, and quiet tears fell on his shoulder. Her defenses down for the first time in... a very long time. After long moments, she drew herself up to her full height, put her shoulders back, and held him at arm's length.

"Thank you," she said quietly. Together they turned back to the group and rejoined them.

Watching all of this, the group stood hushed and turned quickly away as the two made their way back.

Breena took Sean's hand. "It seems being close to your kind has changed us in ways I didn't foresee. I never thought I would see anything like that. Remarkable."

As Kallan and Odette approached, he barked to them again that time was short, and they must move. They all turned to go, but sensed that something had shifted. For the better.

They retraced their steps through the forest back to the clearing where they had first looked out over the ocean. As they emerged into the clearing, a fierce wind kicked in blowing east toward the end of the island, where the dark clouds from earlier had grown black and seemed to roil in the sky, not blowing in any direction but sitting in one place, whipping the sea. Every few moments, the beam from the lighthouse arced the sky, lighting the clouds and throwing a faint glare upon the sea below. It was a slow-motion strobe effect that revealed something new each time the lamp circled around. They could see whitecaps even from this distance, and Sean, having been there before, knew the exposed point of land past the lighthouse would be treacherous.

"We can walk along the coast to the point from here. It's probably quicker than heading back out to the main road, but mind the unstable cliffs," Nick said as he examined the map he'd called up on his phone.

And so they did. Quickly but cautiously moving on a well-worn trail that wound around and toward Montauk Point. The trail's frequent use gave proof to the fact that locals and tourists alike paid little attention to the warnings posted every few feet.

Sean's heart was racing. He could hear nothing but the scream of the wind and, far below, what he guessed to be the waves crashing into the island, chipping it away more fervently tonight than they usually had in the millennia-long battle they had waged against the land. The crisp night air did little to dry the perspiration that broke out on his brow and he that felt inching down his spine. He knew it was adrenaline and fear that were responsible. Reaching out, he felt Breena's hand slide into his as they wound along the trail. In that moment, nothing could have given him more comfort than knowing she was there.

Nick was reading again from his phone's screen, the glow bathing has face in an almost otherworldly blue light. "I can't quite figure out when high tide is out here. The sites each seem to say something different. Best I can estimate, we should be getting there just as high tide is coming in. Should be some crazy surf..." Before he could finish his last sentence, he stumbled. Looking up from his screen he was temporarily blinded, seeing only the ghostly halo in front of him where the phone had been. Off balance, he pitched to the right, toward the cliff, and began to go over.

Just as it seemed nothing could stop him from falling down the more than eighty feet to the rocky shore below, Kallan was there in less than the blink of an eye. He held out his arm, which Nick grabbed frantically, while he latched onto Nick's shirtfront with his other hand, drawing him up and fairly throwing him toward safety and the brush behind them.

"Thanks," Nick muttered, pushing himself up from the ground and checking himself for anything worse than the embarrassment that now rose to color his face.

"Best to put your telephone away now, I think. Aside from the obvious, the screen will begin to draw unwanted attention. They know we're coming, but no need to give too much away."

Nick quickly powered down his phone and put it in his pocket. Slowly his, and everyone else's, eyes adjusted to the night again and they pushed on, Nick's pulse racing a bit more than the others'.

As they turned a corner on the cliffs, the lighthouse itself came into view. The beach just past it, their destination, still lay hidden, and their cliff trail began a descent that would take them around the light itself and onto the exposed tip of the island. The water was streaked white with foam, and the waves pounded the shore relentlessly. Steeling their nerve, the group continued on, trying to mirror the unrelenting tempo of the sea. Faint shadows raced just below the surface of the waves, streaming toward the beachhead, their wakes adding to the maelstrom as sky and sea seemed poised to shatter the edge of The End.

Back at The Realm, relative calm had been restored. Stewart lingered by the front door, still barricaded with the bookshelf. Sandy sat on her stool behind the counter, facing the door to the back room. Kelphit had stationed himself by that door, leaning against it as if by placing himself there he could hold back the evil inside should it try again to break free. From the door, a brilliant green seeped from around the edges, bathing the room in an ironically healthy, almost springlike glow. From beyond the storeroom door, an occasional muffled cry could be heard, but the glow remained strong and undimmed.

Bayard strode about the rest of the room, picking out items and books, commenting on those that seemed familiar. And those he thought to be ridiculous. A dozen crows had perched upon him, on his shoulders, his arms, one even had helped itself to the crown of his head and seemed quite content. So, too, did Bayard, who from time to time, looked at one of the birds and showed them something he found of interest on the store shelves.

"It seems to me," he said finally, turning to the others, "that you have things well in hand here. Is that fair to say?"

Kelphit pushed himself off the doorframe, laid his staff across the doorway, and turned. "Yes, friend. We will face no more danger from this lesser Wendigo. His fate is now in the hands of your friends."

"In that case, and if there are no objections," he responded, looking to the others, "I think I'll be better put to use where the final confrontation will take place." The others nodded their assent. "Very good. I'll leave a few of my friends here to help keep an eye on things. They will warn you—and me—if I should be needed here. Please believe me when I say that I will do everything I can to make sure your friend in back is returned to himself safely. And the rest of our friends, as well. Stay vigilant."

And with that he was gone, slipping out of the store and into the night presumably toward the eastern end. Many of the crows took flight and left through the windows they had broken on the way in.

"Wait..." Sandy began, but he was gone. "Not really sure how I'll be getting all of these birds out of here when this is over. And... they're making a mess everywhere. Those windows are going to expensive, too."

At that moment, the green glow pulsed and was accompanied by another loud, muffled cry from the what-had-been-Ken.

"Let's just hope that's the biggest worry we have when all is said and done," said Stewart, eyeing the storeroom nervously.

Kelphit made a sound of agreement and took up his place by the door, reclaiming his staff and tracing some of the protective drawings anew.

Outside, the night had grown conspicuously quiet. The three took up their stations again, and the crows, sitting throughout the store, watched on in silence.

CHAPTER 31

The group trudged on, slowly making their way down toward the bottom of the cliffs. Toward the beach. The sounds of the wind and the waves kept them from hearing what was ahead, hidden still behind the rocky ledges that lay below the light. To their left as they slowly descended, the light flashed out into the night. As quickly as it shone, it seemed to be swallowed by the gathering darkness and then was gone altogether, as it spun away from them and cast its light north, and then west, and then back to them southward and east. With each revolution, it revealed an ocean that became angrier and angrier. The waves hitting the beach and outcrops were growing stronger, throwing spray high into the air and leaving an unnatural, oily mist that seemed to cling to everything.

They rounded the headland below the lighthouse, still a dozen feet or so above the beach, winding their way along the trail that in happier times was used by tourists and fishermen. Tonight though, the spray made the stones slick, and they slowed, trying to pick their way carefully along the gentle slope to the rocky beach. The shore past the light slowly came into view and the strobing light revealed a scene that stopped them all in their place.

The Wendigo and the Dullahan stood at the water's edge, facing inland. Lesser Wendigos encircled them, already replacing those lost in the tunnels. They snarled and snapped hungry jaws, tethered to their master but clearly wanting to chase down and consume anything they could find. The Dullahan held his head down by his waist while, with his other hand, he flicked his macabre whip idly, an occasional snap from it riding the winds to the group. The water behind them seethed with movement, and upon closer inspection, the group could see the surf filled with Kelpies, their black hooves churning the water angrily.

Farther out still, not one but three Oniare, the great horned serpent they had encountered in their battle on Staten Island, prowled the deeper waters, at times raising their heads out of the sea to scream their rage into the night.

All of their enemies had gathered here. This had been the plan all along. To draw the group out to this exposed spit of land. To catch them between the rocky cliffs and the wild ocean. To finally put an end to whatever had drawn them together. To eliminate or enslave Sean. And Ken. And anyone else who placed themselves in the way.

As the group paused to take in the assorted creatures who aimed to destroy them, movement to the north caught their attention. A host of infected and decaying animals, those that had, unknown to this group, laid siege to The Realm, streamed onto the beach. The long-fingered men, their grotesque shepherds, marched them into place by the Wendigo and the Dullahan, where they stopped, pawing the rocks at their feet, and adding their tortured voices to the cacophony that rose into the wind.

"Oh, you have got to be kidding me," Brandy muttered. "What the hell are those things?"

"Oh, those poor creatures..." Breena whispered, her voice pained by the sight of what had been done to the creatures.

"Their eyes are yellow!" Trout nearly shouted. "It's like a nightmare. More victims of Plum Island."

"Yeah, they seem horrible, but what about the guys behind

them? Who the hell are they and what happened to *them*? Their hands..." Sean's voice trailed off, not finding adequate words to describe what he was seeing.

The group all turned their attention to the men and noticed the same things... their hands. Long, deformed, twisted fingers hung loosely at their sides. They shared a skeletal, diseased countenance that, even at this distance, felt unclean. Unhealthy. Dangerous. Deadly.

It was Nick who broke the silence first. "Well, I'll be damned. Didn't think that was really a thing." He quickly explained the history of Plum Island and its proximity to where they now stood. "There were rumors of a long-fingered man found on the island. Possibly an experiment gone wrong, possibly... well, no one knew. I guess we're about to find out more about them than we would want to."

Brandy turned to him quizzically. "When did you become an expert on weird goings-on near Long Island? Have you ever even been here before?"

"OK, first, no I haven't, but while you were napping on the way out here, I googled every single thing I could find out about the area. I'll fill you in on some the other things I learned when we're not about to fight for our lives. Sound good?"

"Yeah, whatever. Geek," Brandy retorted before patting Nick on the shoulder and muttering "good job" under her breath.

Sean noticed that Breena had grown horribly pale, barely seeming able to keep on her feet. He helped her to a nearby rock and eased her down to sit. He knelt by her, taking her hand, and gently kneading it. "What is it? What can I do to help?" he asked.

"Oh, Sean. Nothing. It's just... so much hate. Anger. Rage. Violence. It's a lot for someone who feels things the way I do. We do. How can you take it?"

"I do feel it. I guess I'm just focused on Ken. And making sure no one else gets hurt. It's all new to me still. I'm not sure what to do with all of this."

"I know. I wish we could have eased you in slowly, somehow. But that wasn't an option open to us."

Behind them, Trout looked out over the assembled adversaries on the beach. "Wow, it's a 'greatest hits' of all the nasties that have tried to take us out over the past couple days."

"It was all a trap. From the moment they took your friend on the street to this moment. Each attack was a feint, testing us, gauging our strength. This place. The portal in the tunnels, Plum Island, evil from cultures that should not be in league. It all brought us here. The End, indeed," said Kallan.

"Friends, attention," Odette said, indicating the beach below them.

As they turned their attention to the shore below, they realized that it had grown silent. Every creature below had stilled their voice and turned to see the small party gathered on the rocks above them. Not only had they grown silent, but they had also grown still. No hooves worried the stones below their feet. Long fingers were still at their sides. The Oniare drifted beyond the surf, only their horns and eyes visible above the water. The Kelpies bobbed in the waves closer to the beach. Even the Wendigo, with its leering angry gash of a mouth, had ceased its wild screams and turned to face them.

Each member of the group felt that the malicious focus was turned to them, specifically. Felt the sting of it and, deep within, a wriggling scratching sensation. Fear. Even Kallan and Odette, who had known true fear very rarely in their long years, looked shaken. And that feeling grew stronger in each of them as the Dullahan lifted its own head high above its body, turning the empty eyes toward them, and spoke. Not aloud, although even the howling wind had fallen still for the moment, but within them. His whispered, rasping voice sounding as evil, as malevolent, as sinister, as his visage was to their eyes.

"To the traitors and their human pets, we see you and are pleased you have chosen to meet your demise here, where we've been leading you. You have with you one who we could not allow to exist. He is a magnifier, a prism, for the power of others. We have not seen his like in millennia. But much has changed since the last one. The age of men has run its course, and his appearance has hastened that end. It was close already. We have watched as you, apologists for them, have hidden away. Letting them run rampant across the earth. Our kind, the balance to your cowardice and coddling, has chosen now to restore order as it should be. No more will they spread their death and destruction. No more will they poison the water, the air, the creatures that walk amongst them. We will reclaim our place. You can stand with us or be swept aside. There will be places for you. Serving us and our mission. But all who stand with the selfish, arrogant humans must pay the price.

"This one, the one who can focus the power of others, threatens not only the future we will create, but our very existence. We have hidden ourselves for too long. Allowed you to dictate where and how we live. We will no longer accept that, with or without him. To you, Tuatha, leave now and live. Or stay and die. We care not which."

The group stood, silent, as the Dullahan lowered its head and stopped speaking. At that moment, the wind resumed, the waves gained intensity, and those gathered on the beach resumed their cries, with even greater volume.

"Well, guess that answers a lot of our questions," Sean said, finally. "I can't allow any of you to take this risk. It's me they want. Let me go face them. The rest of you can still leave..."

"Sean," Kallan answered, "you know we can't and won't do that. This creature, this Dullahan, has lived in darkness and evil. That is its nature. It lies as easily as it breathes. And you heard what it said. It wants to end mankind. You, your friends, all of you are in danger while they," he pointed to the shore, "are intent on changing the balance of the world."

"I mean, he does have a few points," Brandy spoke up. "Men have done a lot of crappy things. Just look at what we did to those poor creatures down there, from that island. They're hideous. We did that."

Breena gripped Brandy's shoulders and looked directly into her face. "Yes, men did that. That has always been one of the most vexing things about mankind. Your capacity for both good and evil. You, meaning all of you, have done horrible things throughout your history. And we have watched, at times appalled, or saddened, or angry. But we have also watched you create unimaginable beauty in the world. We've seen your capacity for love, and sacrifice, and inspiration. You contain all of that within you. We don't. We tend to a good and bad spectrum. One or the other. There is less grey in our world. You live in the middle. In the uncertainty."

She looked around the group. "But make no mistake. Those creatures have crawled from the evil side of our realms. There is no uncertainty in them. They exist to destroy. To pull down and eradicate anything that they don't understand. Or control."

She turned to Sean. "No, we won't leave you. I won't. Where they see a threat to themselves, we see opportunity. You being here, with strength we've not seen in so long, doesn't frighten us. It excites us. We see possibilities. At long last, a chance to bring all the peoples of this world together, where they should always have been. The one place we do agree with them is that things must change. But we see a chance to share this world with you. To make it better.

"They know only chaos. Carnage," she continued. "That takes no courage. Or talent. Or vision. But to create," she looked at the Grumbles around her, "that requires strength. It is why I've said that we still value the singers, the poets, the writers. Because they choose to put something of themselves into the world, sometimes at great personal cost. Something that asks you to be vulnerable. It is especially powerful coming from you who know that your time on the earth is limited. But you choose to leave a piece of yourself in the hope that it will make things better for those who come after. Creation, not destruction, is the world I want to live in."

Odette stepped forward to be next to Breena, and in her usual brusque manner said, "No, Sean, we will not leave. They are evil. We are not. It's that simple."

Kallan spoke next. "We will fight with you, Sean. We have much to learn from you still. And we can never surrender to the darkness they espouse. It goes against everything we've ever believed. We can no more become forces of chaos than they can become forces for good. It is who we are. And, what's more, they know that. They sought you out to destroy you. We sought you out to befriend you."

A voice came from above them and they all turned, startled. Bayard had blinked onto the rocks above them. "This is all quite touching, and I'm moved to see you all confessing your undying respect and devotion to each other, but can we save some of it until after we clean that beach up?"

Trout laughed loudly. "Him," he said, pointing up at Bayard. "He's my favorite. No offense intended," he added for the other Peripherals. "Let's take care of some business."

Brandy spoke up, "Yup, time to make the donuts. I'm in the line of fire either way, so let's get to it."

Breena looked to Sean and mouthed "Donuts?" He grinned and told her he'd explain later.

Before he blinked out again, Bayard announced, "I've brought some more friends. I'll clear those poor deformed creatures first. You take care of the rest."

"How will we know when it's time?" Nick asked.

"Trust me, you'll know. Just be ready." And he was gone again.

Kallan called the group to him as he leaned against a large boulder, facing down toward the shoreline and keeping an eye on the assembled creatures arrayed against them. "We need to have a plan, be disciplined. Everything they've done has been to draw us here, so we must expect them to have laid a trap of some sort. My sense is that, while they once wanted to control Sean, at this point they'd be just as happy to destroy him."

"But more than that," answered Sean, "they want to destroy all of us," he gestured to his friends. "Suddenly this feels a lot more important than just what may happen to me."

"Very true," said Kallan. "Further, they want to eliminate all who stand with you. Given that, we should be seeing this as much more than just protecting Sean. We must stop this movement of theirs. If it reaches others of like mind, beyond this beach…"

"It cannot," Odette spoke. "We must end this now. Completely."

"To that end, Odette and I will approach first. Breena, you and Sean follow us at some distance. Humans, stay by them. It seems you work best together," Kallan explained. "We can only trust that Bayard will reveal himself when the time is right. The element of surprise should work to our advantage. He'll be surprising us, as well, apparently."

"What about Alara?" Nick asked. "What can we expect from her?"

"Alara will likely approach from the sea. If we are fortunate, perhaps she will prevent them from escaping in that direction."

"That's a pretty big 'if' there," Brandy said.

"OK, OK," Trout chimed in. "We get it. Big Peripheral fighter folk go first. Tip of the spear, so to speak. We plow in after, hoping to drive a wedge. Sean and the rest of us will hopefully tap into whatever it is we've been able to create together. With Breena, of course. Right? Let's get to it." He hefted his tomahawk and felt an unfamiliar weight in his pocket. The totem from Kelphit. He lifted it out to take a look and saw the roughhewn figure of a bear. He grinned to himself and placed it back in his pocket feeling taller and stronger. More confident. He growled under his breath, "Montana mauling time."

"Time indeed," Kallan answered, and added with a glance to Trout, "For Montana?"

"You know it, dude. Let's finish this so you can see firsthand just how much you'll love it."

Jostling into a rough formation as Kallan had outlined, the group started down the rest of the path, the few short yards to the rock-strewn beach.

"I'm nervous," Sean whispered to Breena. "What if I can't do anything when I'm needed? I don't know how to make it happen."

"Trust, Sean. Stay near me. Think of what's at stake. And trust."

They rounded a large rock formation that had been shielding them from the open beach and stopped. Struck by not only the vicious wind lashing them unimpeded now, but the sight of what faced them.

Dozens, perhaps hundreds, of creatures glared at them. The long-fingered men were in a ring behind the horrible Plum Island creatures. Behind them, the Wendigo howled with mindless rage. Surrounded by its remaining minions, it was now driven by the consuming hunger that ruled its kind. Farther back still, with the water swirling around his feet, the Dullahan took it all in, while the sea behind him thrashed with his allies.

The Dullahan silently raised its head in its hands, and as one the long-fingered men lifted their spindly hands and the grotesque menagerie they herded began a dash up the beach.

Kallan and Odette in the fore raised their weapons and began a controlled march toward the advancing horde. Sean reached out and felt Breena take his hand. Her voice, rising bright and clean, enveloped him and the other Grumbles, who looked nervously to each other and raised their weapons, which now seemed horribly insufficient. Only Trout looked confident, carving the air in front of him with what he believed was his blessed tomahawk.

As the creatures looked ready to overwhelm the small group on the beach, a great cry rose from the north and Bayard appeared, riding the large stallion that Sean had seen in the stables on the drive out from town. Bayard rode bareback and his swords carved the air to either side, a wide grin on his face as the wind whipped his auburn hair back. He raised his arms as if in celebration, and it was then his surprise became clear. Behind him, hooves pounding the rocky beach, poured the remaining horses from the stables. Dozens streaming around the headland from the north. With them appeared many of the natural creatures of the island: stags, foxes, and swarming the air above and behind them were crows. Hundreds of crows. And bats, diving, flitting, swerving through the night. At times, large, elegant shadows sliced through the night air. Osprey had joined the fray. Healthy, whole, pure nature had stepped forward to purge the unclean and unnatural from the shore, recognizing the threat posed to the order of things. They descended on the misshapen creatures and drove through them cleanly. Bayard's blades dispatched the infected left and right. With each unclean creature he defeated, he watched as their bodies turned to dust and were blown away by the screaming wind. And with each departure, he muttered a low prayer for the eternal rest of the creature so distorted by men and abused by the evil creatures controlling them this night. The horses pounded them beneath their hooves and the stags brandished their antlers, giving flight to the horrors who were caught off guard.

Kallan and Odette saw the advantage and charged forward as Bayard and his host swept the beach clear, leaving the long-fingered men exposed. Spear and sword came crashing down over and over. The men, seemingly defenseless having thrown all of their focus to the malformed attackers under their sway, gave ground backing into the sea. Soon they met the lesser Wendigos and, caught between the advancing Peripherals and the assembled "allies," they floundered and began to stream south and west, away from the fight.

The Wendigo, however, gave not an inch and screamed into the night. Those in its thrall leapt forward, as if released from a cage, and snapped their livid jaws, attempting to catch hold of any living thing to slake the overwhelming hunger that drove them forward.

Knowing that even a small wound from the jaws of the Wendigos could prove fatal to their allies, Kallan and Odette held steady and were pained to see a handful of the horses and stags fall victim to the flashing teeth, quickly dispatched and fallen upon by the ravenous beasts.

Just as the Wendigos seemed to wane in their attack, distracted by their victims on the beach, the water behind them seethed and exploded as a phalanx of Kelpies, assuming human form as they emerged from the water, seethed forward.

Odette and Kallan gave some ground and found themselves backing into the light that Breena had sent forth. Gaining confidence and strength from its brilliance, they paused to catch their breath and steel themselves to advance again. Sean was having trouble matching his music to Breena's. The battle raged around them, but he couldn't find a focus, feeling overwhelmed by the chaos everywhere he looked.

Trout stepped forward, beyond the light that was being thrown, and confronted a Kelpie as it moved, leaving a trail of damp vegetation behind it. Trout reared back and with enormous force, brought his tomahawk down on the crown of the Kelpie as it stretched its scaled arms forward. It screamed and collapsed to the ground, turning to drag itself back to the seeming safety of the water.

"Dan Trout," called Kallan, "avoid the Wendigo bites. The slightest could mean your end."

"Don't need to tell me twice," Trout called back, and chose another Kelpie to target while shouting with an almost feral growl.

Nick and Brandy realized that Sean was struggling and rushed to his side. They joined their voices with Breena's and the light brightened a bit and extended itself. Where Wendigos or Kelpies came close, they cried out in pain and shielded their eyes from the brilliance, unable to face the purity of what shone down on them.

Bayard and his host of creatures wheeled around and readied themselves for another charge through the ranks of their enemies. As he saw the fallen horses and stags, he howled in anger and dove back into the fight.

Sean had begun to panic. Nothing he did summoned any of the strength he had wielded in the tunnels. He glanced to either side and saw Nick and Brandy contributing what they could to the song, but he knew that they were in danger as long as he added nothing. The more he fought to join, the less he accomplished, and his frustration started to get the better of him. He looked at Breena, radiant in her song and bathed in the perfect light, and he felt shame and anger take root. He knew he could do it, but he had no idea how.

Kelpies continued to rise from the waves, streaming onto the rocks. Joining with the lesser Wendigos, who had recovered from the initial shock of Bayard's charge, they all turned their attention to the brilliant globe of light and the four figures within. They adapted to the light, and with the urging of their masters, the Wendigo and the Dullahan, threw themselves forward, fear of failing their masters greater than the pain they felt in the presence of the uncontaminated glow.

At this point, a great disturbance drew attention to the surf line in the water. It surged and seethed, looking as if it were boiling, but the truth became quickly apparent. Between the Oniare and the shore, a cordon of Undines, the beautiful, luminous water elementals last seen by the group in the waters of New York Harbor, placed itself to head off the giant serpents and their path to the shore. Their song set up a barrier within the water and the sea creatures found themselves unable to approach closer, forced farther away from the battle and into deeper water.

Next, Alara emerged from the water. Striding purposefully forward, she drew her curved blade, and approached the Kelpies and the Wendigos from behind. As she moved onto the rocks, the water behind her swarmed with seals, larger and more engaged than those normally seen lazing in the waters off the point. As they reached shallower waters, they shed their skins, much like taking off a large cloak, and revealed themselves to be the legendary Selkies, of ancient mythology, changing into human form and marching behind Alara into the fray. Normally seen and heard of only in other parts of the world, it was surprising to see so many here, so far from home. Dozens. More than that.

Trout recognized a few from his time at the Seal Haul Out with Bayard and raised his tomahawk in salute. Bayard's reaction was much grander, as he jumped to his feet atop the stallion he rode and cried aloud to them a greeting in a language none of the Grumbles had ever heard. With renewed vigor, he dropped back onto the steed and threw himself at the remaining creatures in front of him before turning his attention to the Wendigos.

The Kelpies were no match for the Selkies, especially taken unawares from behind and with Alara's vicious sword carving a path through them. The Selkies grabbed them and dragged them bodily back into the sea where they were with tossed aside or dispatched with terrible force.

The tide of battle seemed to be turning, and Breena, with the help of Brandy and Nick, had shifted from a defensive position to moving slowly down the beach in the direction of the Dullahan. Sean, still struggling to contribute, fell slightly behind, desperate to find a way to tap into the reserves he knew he had.

Unnoticed in the melee, the Wendigo itself had circled behind Breena's orb and approached the lagging Sean. When Sean stumbled on a stone, Breena's power moved on and left him exposed. It was only for the briefest of moments, but it was all the Wendigo needed. Sean scrambled to his feet and found himself cut off from his friends by the gaping maw of the Wendigo. He stood, uncertain which direction to turn, and the Wendigo dealt him a backhanded blow that sent him flying even farther away from his allies. He crashed into one of the large boulders at the back of the beach and fell to his knees, the breath knocked out of him. He turned to the Wendigo, no fight in him as he flailed, trying to summon some power.

Many things happened at once. Bayard saw Sean's dilemma and urged his horse in that direction, a cry on his lips, telling Sean he was on his way. Kallan and Odette both paused in their assault, turning to see Sean, trapped by the Wendigo with no escape in sight. Alara also saw what was happening, but a mass of Kelpies and Selkies lay between her and Sean. She was helpless to assist.

The two closest to Sean and the Wendigo were Brandy and Nick, who were slightly behind Breena as she had moved forward. They turned, and with both crying out to Sean, immediately turned in his direction with no hesitation or fear for their own safety. As they emerged from the protection of Breena's song, they paused slightly, hefting their largely ceremonial war clubs. Without a word to each other, they launched themselves toward the Wendigo. Nick dashed in from the right, while Brandy came at it from the opposite side. Their motions, in concert with each other, saw them draw back and swing with all their might at the massive Wendigo in front of them. From either side, their clubs caught the Wendigo, who was entirely focused on Sean, unaware. The silver spikes on both clubs drove deep into the torso, one at the shoulder the other lower toward the waist. More than the open wounds, the touch of the silver itself affected the beast. It writhed in agony and clawed where the sterling tips had pierced. The metal snapped off and remained in the wounds when the war clubs were drawn back, sending the Wendigo into spasms of anguish. The creature tried to whirl toward its attackers, but the damage was done. The pure silver coursed through the contaminated creature's body. It screamed, arching its back, and flailing with its claws and gnashing its teeth. Nick grabbed Sean, pulling him to safety, while Brandy dropped and rolled out of the way with surprising agility. The Wendigo whirled, now with its back to the boulder where it had trapped Sean. It cried out, screaming to the Dullahan for aid. It looked to the sky. The countless stars, now starting to shine through the receding clouds, looked impassively down, as this ancient evil that had walked the earth longer than anyone could know pounded the stone behind it in frustration, anger, and finally fear, as it felt itself slip away from the corporeal world. Its final sound was little more than a whimper, as it felt the desperation it had inflicted on so many for so long. And with that, it collapsed, sighed, and turned to dust before floating to the north and eventually out over the sea.

CHAPTER 32

Back at The Realm, the light from behind the storeroom door flashed once, brilliantly, and was gone. Kelphit turned to Stewart and Sandy, arched an eyebrow, and took one step closer to the door. From below, the light remained out, and all was silent within.

Sandy moved toward Kelphit, her hand raised, and implored, "Don't. This is how they got us last time. Let's just wait for word from the others."

Stewart, moving up behind her, nodded in agreement and held his ornamental dagger out. His hand shook, but he remained by Sandy, near the door.

As they paused, Kelphit with a look of concentration on his face, they heard a small voice from within. "Um... guys... little help, here?"

Examining the runes of protection around the doorway, the wise man cocked his head with curiosity. "Sandy, could you check the window, please?"

She crossed the room and very slowly drew the curtain back just a touch. After a moment, she opened it wider, and then wider still. She turned to the others.

"Nothing," she said. "Absolutely nothing. Not sure what's different, but it's... quiet. But, like, a good quiet."

Kelphit nodded his head and turned once more to the door. With just the slightest of pauses, he reached out and slowly swung the door open.

The room was dark, only a pale green luminescence cast about the walls and ceiling. Ken was within, suspended within the green enclosure into which he'd been placed. His toes just barely brushing the floor.

"Well, I think I'm really back this time. I feel a *lot* worse than before, but something is different. I mean... something more than this glowing green coffin thing you put me in. Help a guy out?"

Nick grabbed Sean by the shoulders and turned him so that he could see his face. "Are you OK?" he asked, concern etched in every line of his face.

Sean was winded. Scared. But he nodded that he was fine and started to get to his feet. Nick grabbed an arm and helped when Sean stumbled slightly. Brandy rushed over, taking stock of her friend, making sure he was unharmed.

"Thank you," Sean muttered. "Didn't think I was getting out of that one."

"That makes two of us, Ginge," Brandy responded.

"Three," added Nick.

Sean was spared, but the battle raged on and as the others' attention had turned to the Wendigo's assault, it gave a brief opening to the attackers. What was left of them. The long-fingered men that remained rallied the diseased to their sides and threw them back into the fight. The Kelpies, sensing an opening, also renewed their attack on the defenders.

The Dullahan paced back and forth behind his horde, screaming in anger, and urging them forward. He noted the death of the

Wendigo but spared little thought for it. There was no love between them, merely fear and a common purpose. In fact, it raged more at the loss of the lesser Wendigos who, now freed from the control of their dispatched master, stopped attacking entirely. They turned in place, confused, and fled from the beach, many already reverting to their previous physical form. Bewildered, they raced from the violence that swirled around them, hoping to find a way to whatever home they had known before.

In all of this, Breena found herself exposed. Brandy and Nick had dropped from her song when they turned toward Sean, so she stood alone facing the renewed violence of the attackers. While they were fewer than they had been, they were still numerous and threatened to overwhelm her as she felt her strength waning.

Sean saw what was happening to her and shrugged Nick's helping hands from him, racing headlong into the thickest of the fighting. He felt fear and desperation coursing through him as he saw Breena begin to fall under the concerted effort to break her. His self-doubt and hesitation disappeared, and he paused to catch his breath. His voice burst from him, forming a pure golden light arcing into the sky creating a dome of brilliance that settled over himself, Breena, Nick, and Brandy. As it did so, it detonated outward, throwing all who had threatened Breena dozens of yards through the air. For a moment, night turned to day and the beach grew hot, as if the midday sun was beating down on it. Just as quickly as it began, the dome withdrew, creating a protective shield over and around Sean and the others. Many of the attackers lay motionless after, and those who could, hurried toward the water, back to the perceived safety of the Dullahan.

Everyone else, both good and evil, stopped what they were doing and stared at Sean, who crouched next to Breena beneath the protection he had created. He was oblivious to everything but her, while every other eye was fixed on him, understanding that what they had seen marked an enormous shift. The power he had unleashed was greater than any of them had ever witnessed. Or had even imagined.

The few remaining long-fingered men melted away, the last thing seen of them their pale, deathly hands disappearing behind rocks or over outcroppings, retreating like mercury slipping away and sounding a last scratching as their yellow, distorted nails receded. With them gone, the remaining Plum Island creatures became lost, bellowing and confused. Bayard began the grim task of dispatching them as mercifully as possible with his blades, wishing them each a lasting peace.

The tide of battle had turned, and the end seemed in sight. The Kelpies were in a full rout, roiling the water around the Dullahan as they streamed back into the ocean, ignoring its cries to remain and fight. The Undines' song, perhaps taking note of the glorious explosion of sound and light from Sean, strengthened and pushed the Oniare increasingly farther out to sea, until finally they turned and dove into the depths with not even a cry or scream to mark their retreat.

Suddenly, at the last, the top of the bluffs teemed with small figures, barely the size of children. A small woman, leading them, stepped forward and with a low chant, wove a pattern in the air before her which grew in tempo. The others at her back joined her and a great breeze cascaded over the cliff edge and blew the remaining clouds overhead away. The sky, now clear and bright with stars, shone down on the rubble left on the shore. It seemed to shine brightest over Sean and his golden dome of light, glittering and sparkling through his song.

And now, alone, the Dullahan remained. Still defiant, it cracked its whip overhead and screamed at the approaching figures. The Peripherals led the way, blades and spear gleaming in reflected light from above and from Sean. Still the Dullahan looked wildly around, as if there may be some last ally to snatch victory back that had seemed so close just minutes ago. No one appeared.

Sean now rose from Breena's side and walked slowly down to the water. The Dullahan frantically looked for an escape. There seemed to be none. It sank to the ground in what seemed to be defeat, abandoned. But as the others approached, in a last desperate and spiteful act, it rose suddenly and cracked its whip out to its attackers. It arced through the air and aimed for Odette, the one it had held prisoner, determined to finish what it had started with her.

But as it did, the others launched into action. Bayard rushed forward and used his two blades to catch the whip in mid-strike. Trout leapt to Bayard's side and used his tomahawk to drive the whip to the ground, where Odette used her spear to pin it in place. Alara, approaching from the water, swung her blade and severed the whip from its gruesome handle and it fell, steaming and useless into the water, where it writhed snakelike for a moment and then sank. Kallan walked toward the Dullahan, sword raised, and struck out, toward the head that was held by the greying, lank hair in the other hand. That head, with its dead black eyes, leering smile, and deathly pallor... fell. And as it did, Sean, from behind the others reared back and aimed his voice in that direction, a beam of light flashing toward the Dullahan. The head, now suspended over the waves, wailed in pain as the golden light grabbed hold of it and sent it careening away. On and on it flew, until it was no longer visible, disappearing over the waves. Its cry dwindling into nothingness.

What remained of the Dullahan flailed in the shallows, its arms swung back and forth searching in vain for the head that now was long gone. Before any of the assembled could react, it swirled its cloak, and dissolved into a black mist, absorbing all light, a blight on the clear night sky and golden light everywhere else. It rose quickly and raced out over the water, stopping briefly past the waves, barely visible.

As it did, all those present heard the familiar and terrifying rasp of its voice filling their minds.

"You think you have won. You think this is finished. You are wrong. Others will see the threat posed to our order and join the fight. Others will see the balance we've maintained for so long is imperiled and will join our struggle. Many already have. Many more will. Be warned. And trust not the humans. They will betray you."

And with that, the mist flew out to sea, heading north and east and within mere seconds was gone. The beach fell silent. The silence that falls when violence reaches its end.

CHAPTER 33

The group looked at each other, torn between being heartened at the victory and chilled by the warning. The Grumbles, self-conscious, were afraid that the Peripherals would abandon them. The Peripherals were chilled at the thought of more violence ahead. All felt the itch of doubt deep within.

The silence was broken when Trout quietly murmured, "Pa-pow! Magic Tomahawk."

The tension was broken, and everyone laughed, allowing relief to win the moment. In that instant, mistrust of each other vanished. Seemed impossible.

Brandy turned to Trout. "You really are a gargantuan idiot." But her eyes were full of laughter, and she gave him a fond punch to the stomach. "But I'm glad you're our idiot."

Kallan went to the cliff top and spoke to the Little People while the others took stock of the scene by the water. Breena drew Sean away and took his hands.

"Thank you," she said. "I wouldn't have survived that without you."

"Well, to be fair, you wouldn't have been in danger if it weren't for me. I froze. I was helpless..."

"When it mattered most, you were anything but helpless." She placed her forehead on his and they stood like that for a moment. Quiet.

The friends lay scattered where they had dropped at the conclusion of the battle. Taking stock of each other, it was remarkable that there were no serious injuries. Scratches and bruises seemed inconsequential given all that they'd been through. No one, not even the Peripherals, seemed able to muster the strength to stand, and so they lay back, drained.

Kallan returned to the group and announced that the Little People would see to it that the beach was returned to its normal state. No one would ever know what had happened there.

"Why do you keep calling them 'Little People'? Don't you have a name for them?" Nick asked.

"Yes. But I decided that Little People would be easier than Makiaweesug," he answered.

"Ah. Good call," Nick agreed.

"They tend to the earth and are adept at the healing arts. Word of warning, though, don't stare at them. They think it's rude. And you don't want them to be offended by you. Believe me."

"Yeah, I don't want anyone angry at me for a good while now," Brandy chimed in.

Kallan lowered himself to a nearby boulder, joining the others in their exhaustion. The adrenaline was ebbing, and exhaustion took hold. As tired as they were, they knew they needed to move. Early fishermen would arrive soon, and all evidence of the battle needed to be gone, including them. They watched as the Little People busied themselves on the beach, restoring order to the scene.

"So... can we get out of here?" Trout asked. "I'm exhausted and, if I remember correctly, I'm still paying for a beachfront hotel room."

As they headed up the path toward the lighthouse, they turned to see the beach being swept clean. The leader of the Little People was standing in the shallows looking out to sea. Sean followed her gaze and saw a massive figure doing the same in the water, sweeping away all evidence of the battle.

Breena noticed where he was looking. "Her husband. They're quite a unique couple. To say the least. I suspect we had more help oceanside than we knew."

"I believe you are correct," Alara said with a glance toward the giant in the surf. "My guess is he had something to do with that."

Shaking his head in wonder, Sean turned to follow the rest up and away. Each step he took felt heavy and he realized how weary he was. How weary they all were.

It was a long walk back to the Bronco, which was still parked by the entrance to Camp Hero. All the Peripherals, other than Breena, excused themselves to go ahead, planning to go to The Realm to let Kelphit and the others know what had happened. They all agreed to meet at the rooms in the Royal Atlantic. It seemed a lifetime ago that they had been there. In some ways it had been.

The remaining five walked on in silence. Breena and Sean hand in hand. Trout leading the way. Brandy and Nick bringing up the rear, with Nick nose-first in his phone's screen and Brandy keeping him on the path. From time to time, Nick would mutter "Huh" or "Really?" as he read.

Eventually, they reached the truck, climbed slowly in, and Trout pointed it westward on Route 27 and toward town. As they passed the riding stables along the way, all the horses were safely and quietly back in their pastures. The large black stallion stood alone at the fence as they passed and bowed its head.

They were shocked when they arrived at the hotel in less than ten minutes. What had happened on the beach felt so very far away from the quiet little town. The town lay silent, everyone tucked safely at home. It seemed impossible, and yet...

Out of the truck, they dragged themselves up the stairs to the rooms and, noticing that the light was on in one of them, Trout opened that door, and they filed inside. Brandy was last and as she closed the door behind her, she saw the entire group, including Sandy, Stewart, Kelphit and a very haggard-looking Ken, standing inside and spilling onto the balcony.

"Hi, honeys, I'm home," she said, and fell face-first onto the nearest bed.

CHAPTER 34

The Grumbles each took to a bed, filling the two rooms. Sandy excused herself to go back to her own home for some rest. They all agreed to meet first thing in the morning. While they rested, the Peripherals, including Kelphit, sat on the balconies, quietly discussing what had happened on the beach and at the store. Eventually, as the conversation waned and the Peripherals fell into silence and stared out over the sea, Breena began a low song. Had any of the Grumbles been awake, they would not have recognized the language. Or the tune. She sang of peace, and love, and loss. Quietly, the other Peripherals joined in. One by one. As they did, they reached out to each other. A hand on a shoulder here. Fingers intertwined there. They found hope and healing in their music and a soft glow rose around them, seen by none but themselves.

The sun broke over the ocean all too soon, and the light streaming in through the sliders to the outside eventually woke each of the sleepers in turn. One by one, they wandered out to stand at the railing, surrounded by the Peripherals. No one said a word as the sun slid over the horizon, filling the sky with brilliant orange, and purple, and finally golden yellow, painting a brilliant swath across the water that seemed to reach directly toward them.

Eventually, Kelphit broke the silence. "We have done well to come through the night. I fear that we have not heard the last of these threats. I will return to the tunnels, today, to make sure that the portal there is closed. And each time I return here, I will renew my work there, but I cannot be here constantly. My work takes me to other places where I am needed. But rest assured, I will keep watch here, as and when I can."

Alara stirred in the corner. "I will stay here. To call this my home. I will watch over this area. I will protect it," she said quietly.

Breena went to her. "Are you sure? What about your home, your family?"

"My family has made it very clear that I am not needed there. I feel I *am* needed here. And honestly, it feels more home to me already than anywhere else I've known. There is something about it that speaks to me. Maybe because it's remote. Maybe it's the water everywhere. Maybe it's that I think I can make a difference. Maybe it's that I hope some of the good I did here will help erase the shame I was made to feel back home... or maybe I just need some peace."

"It does ease my worries to know you will be here, as well. I do hope that, between the two of us, it is peaceful here for some time. And it will be nice to look forward to seeing you," Kelphit said to Alara.

Kallan spoke next. "Odette and I have decided to return to our people to inform them of what has happened here. From what we heard, our victory here may be short lived. The Dullahan is not finished. Even if we close the portal here, there may be others he knows of nearby. If so, he could reappear almost anywhere. We must prepare."

From the doorway, Nick spoke hesitantly. "So... I was doing some reading last night and something caught my attention. Not too far from the point, one of the shoals has a name unlike any of the others. I thought… it might be worth mentioning?"

"What is the name?" Breena asked.

"See that's the thing. Everything else out there seems to have pretty innocuous names. Endeavor, Little Gull, Cartwright… but this one, north of the point, pretty much the direction that thing took off in, and not overly far from Plum Island, is called Cerberus," he said haltingly, "as in the three-headed dog that's the guardian of the underworld? It stood out. That seemed… notable."

The Peripherals looked amongst themselves. Concern etched on their faces. "Well done, Nick. It is worth mentioning. And it is concerning. We'll investigate," Odette replied.

"Well, I've got nothing waiting for me back home. I'll head out later to take a look. Let's hope it's just nothing more than an unusual name," said Bayard.

Sandy, who had arrived a few minutes earlier and had been listening from within the room, popped her head out through the doorway, next to Nick. "Well, I have to say I'm thrilled some of you folks will be around for a bit. I don't think I could go back to the way it was before. Also, I have a small boat you," she said, gesturing to Bayard, "can use to reach the shoal if you'd like."

Bayard grinned. "A boat. How quaint. That sounds positively… delightful. And in return, I will answer all those questions you have before I go."

"Perfect. Everybody wins!" Sandy crowed.

Kelphit leaned forward in his seat. "I believe nothing here will ever be quite the same again. In fact, I dare say none of you will ever be the same again, either. Sandy, rest assured that I will see you each time I am near," he told her.

"And I think you'll see me very often," said Alara.

Trout approached Kelphit and shook his hand firmly. "Thanks, man. That magic tomahawk saved my hide more than once. I owe you."

Kelphit grinned, and with a glance at Sandy and Stewart, said simply, "I am so glad it served its purpose."

"OK, OK... I'm starving," Brandy announced. "Can we humans get something to eat?"

Odette and Kallan made their farewells. Thanking each Grumble for their part in what had happened. They both stopped at Sean.

Odette grasped his forearm, one warrior to another. "I do believe I will see you again, Sean. You... these last two days... have been remarkable."

Kallan was next, placing his hands on Sean's shoulders. "I fear our work together is not done. Do not let your guard down. Stay vigilant. This is not finished. Hopefully, if my people allow me to see this through, I will see you again."

Sean nodded and smiled grimly at the two. Surprised that he felt a catch in his throat at the goodbye. His face flushed and he looked down in embarrassment. In that moment, they slipped out. When he looked up, they were gone.

Bayard said his goodbyes next. Embraces went to each of the Grumbles. "Trout, I look forward to Montana."

"It's a promise, my friend," Trout answered. "You'll never want to leave."

Well," answered Bayard, "that would be a first for this wanderer. That might be pleasant, I think..." Next, he went to Sean. "Stay safe, my friend. You are not done with me yet." He turned to hide the emotion in his eyes. "I'll let you all know if I find a three-headed dog in the ocean!" With that, he was gone.

Alara let everyone know that she would see them again the next time they came to town. She thanked each profusely before heading down to the beach to take a look around her new home. From the balcony, they saw her walking east, eyes scanning the sea.

Sean, with a look to Breena, told the other Grumbles he would catch up with them in a few minutes.

"Yeah, yeah," Brandy answered. "We'll be at…" she shot a questioning look to Trout.

"John's," he answered.

"John's," she said. "I'm starving, so make it quick." She winked at him as they all headed out to breakfast, leaving Sean and Breena alone on the balcony, the rising sun giving both of them a golden sheen. Ken cast a curious look back at them as he left.

"I'll fill you in," Nick said on the way down the stairs.

Sean turned to her. "Breena," he began," I don't know what to say. Are you really going back?"

"I have to, Sean. My family needs to hear what we have learned. They expected this to be nothing, a useless task for the most useless among them. They have to be warned."

"You're not useless. That is the last thing you are," he protested.

They sat, silent for a moment. Both trying to find words.

"I can't imagine you gone. After all of this. I don't understand any of it… least of all what we are to each other."

"I don't know either, Sean. I do know we are linked… somehow. I suspect, if we traced your line back far enough, we would find some Tuatha in you. But as for us," she trailed off, "I just don't know."

"That's possible?" he asked. "Tuatha and human…"

"It was. Many millennia ago. It has not happened for as long as we can remember, and that's a very long time. I think, for now, we should just take comfort that we will see each other again. Of that, I am sure."

"Yeah. OK. That makes sense… I guess," he spoke, although he wanted to say something more.

"Trust me, Sean. We'll see each other soon."

She stood and pulled him to his feet. He hugged her, gently at first and then holding her tighter, as if he could keep her there if he just held on long enough. She returned the embrace and leaned her head against his. Then she pulled away, touched his face, smiled... and was gone.

As he walked over to John's to meet the others, he stopped by the office of the Royal Atlantic and extended one of the rooms another night. He wasn't ready to go back to the city. Not ready to put this behind him just yet.

He walked into John's and saw the Grumbles had pushed two tables together to fit everyone. They had left a chair for him nearest the door, and he slid wearily into it, across from Trout and next to Brandy, who touched his shoulder and gave him a reassuring pat, letting him know that she understood.

Stewart was speaking to Sandy, telling her that he hoped to come out for an extended stay soon. "I almost hope I don't get a show just yet. I'd like to spend some more time with Kelphit. I feel like I learned so much in one night. What could a week do for me?"

"You're welcome anytime, you know that. You handled yourself well last night. He'll be happy to see you," she told him. "And I'll be happy for the company, too."

Sean ordered and soon the food came. The table was full of chatter, each wanting to tell the others of the incredible things they had experienced the night before. Plates clattered, forks and knives clinked, and glasses were raised in toast to each other. They toasted with coffee and orange juice and shouted "Trout!" while making their silly fish-on-a-hook gesture.

If Sean and Ken were a bit more reticent than the others, everyone chalked it up to them having been through things that they could not imagine.

As they finished, Sean told them he'd extended a room for the night and invited anyone to stay who wanted.

"I'd love to, but I need to get back to Anne. I called last night to let her know I'd be back. I have absolutely no idea what I'm going to tell her..." said Ken.

"I usually recommend the truth, but in this case... I think you're on your own," said Stewart with a clap on Ken's back.

"Thanks so much. Very helpful," he responded, with more bite than any had expected.

Brandy, Nick, and Stewart also made their excuses, needing to get back for appointments and, in Brandy's case, to put the saintly Mick's mind at ease.

"I have no idea how that man stays married to you," Nick said.

"Honestly, neither do I. But don't you ever tell him I said that," she grinned.

Nick then announced he was going to the countryside in New Jersey to look at a house. "Been thinking about a change of pace. Live on a lake. Maybe write a book. Get a dog."

"Shut up. We'll never see you again! You'll be bored in a week," Brandy declared.

"Maybe," Nick responded. "Just seemed time for something new."

"Do what you gotta do. As my mom says, no one but you knows how tight your shoes are," Trout announced supportively.

The group stopped to look at him and then broke out laughing. Even Sean and Ken joined in.

"Well, your first book can be about the last two days," Stewart suggested.

"Trust me," Nick responded, "I've been taking notes."

"Well," Trout said looking at Sean. "I'm happy to spend another day here if it's OK. Looks like it's just me and you, in that case. The way we started."

"Hey, jerkface," Sandy said slapping Trout on the arm. "I live here, so it's not just you two. I'll meet you at the brewery later. I have to clean up my shop a bit. Crow feathers everywhere. Four o'clock?"

Trout laughed and agreed, as the group headed back to the hotel. The next train wasn't until afternoon, so they had some time still to enjoy the view from the balcony. And that's exactly what they did.

Early afternoon rolled around, and Trout piled the departing Grumbles into the Bronco to drive them the five minutes to the train station. As they pulled out of the parking lot, Brandy pressed her face to the window and motioned to Sean that he should call her when he got back to the city. And if he didn't, she would… punch him, apparently. Trout saw them off at the train with a promise of meeting in the city before the end of the week. He then climbed back into the suddenly too quiet truck and wound his way back to the hotel.

He entered the room and found Sean on the balcony, staring out to sea. "How you doing?" he asked.

"Not really sure, honestly," Sean replied. "It's quiet. Too quiet, now. So much so fast and now… what?"

"I get it. I do. The city always felt claustrophobic to me. Probably why I talk about Montana so much. Sorry about that, by the way. I know it can get annoying."

Sean waved that away and tutted at Trout to let him know that wasn't true. As they both looked out over the waves, they saw some seals, flashing through a shoal of fish just past the waves. They watched spellbound.

"Do you think they're…?" Trout started.

"I have no idea. But I'll never look at them the same way again, whatever they are."

"I hear that," Trout answered.

They rested a bit, then walked the beach. Nodding to the odd beachcombers they passed. There were precious few of them as the colder nights were moving in and driving the visitors out. A golden retriever ran past, off its leash, then stopped to come back for a pat or two from them as its person hurried up, apologizing for the interruption.

"No, not at all," Trout answered. "He's been looking for a fellow ginger since he got here," he said indicating Sean. They made small talk for a moment and then moved on in opposite directions on the sand.

Later, they met Sandy at Montauk Brewing. It was surprisingly busy, and they were not surprisingly exhausted, so they got some growlers to bring back to the hotel. It was pumpkin ale season, and Sean loved it, no matter what beer purists had to say on the subject. They picked up some food at The Point on the way back, and what started as the most unusual of days twenty hours ago, ended up in the most relaxing and enjoyable way they could have wished.

They laughed, and ate, and drank, and shared stories until Sandy announced she needed to head home before she fell asleep in her chair. Trout walked her down to her car and, upon returning, announced that he, too, was done and headed to sleep.

As he headed back into the room, Trout stopped and looked back at Sean. "I guess we're all Peripherals now. It's a helluva thing we just went through. One helluva thing."

"That's putting it mildly. Grumbles *and* Peripherals forever," Sean answered.

Sean wished him good night and stayed on the balcony. The brilliant sun of the morning now replaced by a bright opal moon. He sipped his beer and remembered that he hadn't checked his phone all day. He pulled it out of his pocket and was surprised to see over a dozen messages, mostly unimportant.

He laughed out loud when he read one of the last ones. He had been offered the job from the audition just a few days ago. The one that he thought had gone so poorly. Another message from Brandy let him know that she had gotten an offer, too. Show business. You just never know. Somehow, it didn't seem quite as important now.

Out on the ocean, the lights of the freighters and fishing boats far out on the horizon winked and crept slowly along. Business as usual. For them.

Sean began to sing something quietly to himself, and realized it was a song from his childhood. One he hadn't thought of in a very long time. One his father had first sung to him. He let it carry him away and he lost himself in the notes. Just for a moment. He breathed deeply. Something flashed in the corner of his eye. He didn't turn to it. Instead, he gazed out over the ocean and smiled. And sang on.

The Peripherals will ride again.

If you enjoyed this book, please take a moment to visit Amazon and provide a short review. Every reader's voice is important for the continued life and growth of a book or series.
Look for Book Two soon and keep up to date on all things Peripherals at

www.markaldrich.net

where you can also sign up for a mailing list. Rest assured it will be used sparingly and only for announcements about the series.

GLOSSARY

THE PERIPHERALS

Breena is a name of Gaelic/Irish origin and means "fairy palace" or "fairy place." It also can denote nobility, particularly of the faery realm.

Bayard, the horse, first appears in a twelfth-century French chanson, where it was described as having the power of carrying many people at once and understanding human speech. Eventually, the horse was gifted to Charlemagne and escaped.

Bayard also appeared in Bullfinch's Mythology and numerous French epic poems.

By the late thirteenth century, Bayard had come to be accepted as describing any horse with a reddish-brown coat.

Alara is a water fairy from Turkic and Siberian mythologies. Her beauty and youth are said to depend on proximity to water. She has the ability to make people capable of true love by removing hate and greed from their hearts. She has been known to grant wishes to the heartbroken, often through bioluminescent algae in water, a shooting star, or simply appearing herself.

Kallan is an ancient Celtic/Scottish name, meaning warrior. Here, he is imagined as being an elf of the Scottish Gude Fairies, who are inclined to help mankind.

Odette is a female name from the ancient High German and means "wealth." An alternate meaning is "elfin spear," which inspired this character. The name is most widely known for being a character in Tchaikovsky's Swan Lake, although that has no bearing on the character here.

Kelphit (aka Gwelab'bot, Turn Over, Father of Medicine) was known for teaching others the healing arts and herbalism. His origins lie with the Wabanaki Tribe and in the Mi'kmaq Tribe he is associated with the changing of the seasons.

PLACES

Fort Wadsworth is accurately described here. It lies under the Verrazzano-Narrows Bridge and today is a park containing both the old fort and a beach that nestles next to Staten Island's South Beach. It is a favorite spot for hiking, fishing, swimming, and sightseeing. They do, indeed, bring goats in each year to control the vegetation.

Camp Hero is also described here with very little embellishment. The history is accurate, as is the inspiration it provided for many books, movies, and television shows. The theories on the experiments done there are many and have been written about extensively.

Plum Island does exist and has been the subject of conspiracy theories and conjecture for years. It is both a former Animal Disease Center and a former military installation. It has appeared numerous times in pop culture from *The Silence of the Lambs* to *What We Do in the Shadows* and many others. The legends/myths of the Montauk Monster and Long-Fingered Man have been topics of speculation for years. It remains entirely owned by the US government and is still shrouded in secrecy.

CREATURES

All of the creatures referenced are adapted from the mythologies referenced. The Dullahan, Wendigo, Oniare, Undines, Kelpies, and Selkies appear throughout the mythologies of their cultures.

I have chosen to include numerous local businesses that do exist. Beer Culture, Royal Atlantic, Montauk Brewing, The Point, Shag-wong, Blade + Salt, and Liar's Saloon are all establishments that you can visit the next time you're in Manhattan or Montauk. I've long advocated supporting local businesses as a way to foster community development and growth, so I am happy to continue that encouragement here.

Update: The venerable Liar's Saloon, one of the vestiges of "old Montauk", closed during the spring of 2022. Its fate remains unclear, a prime example of why I feature local establishments whenever possible. I'll have my fingers crossed for them.

Acknowledgments

No book is ever the product of just the author, and The Peripherals is certainly no exception. I began this book, both as an expression of creativity and ideas that had been percolating for quite some time, but also after encouragement and support from both family and friends.

No list of people to thank could possibly begin anywhere but with my family. They have been the rocks on which a decades-long acting career was built, and their boundless patience and thoughtfulness saw me through this project in ways I never could have imagined when I sat down and penned the first words. Thank you to my mother, Ida, who has always encouraged me to explore boundaries, and then push past them. My brother, Stephen Aldrich, and sister, Cindy Vollmer, stood in as beta readers, design consultants, voices of reason when things seemed difficult, and voices of celebration when things seemed to be going well. My debt to them extends far beyond this book, but I will happily take this chance to thank them.

Thanks to my editor, Chris Urie, who balanced encouragement with constructive ideas and this first-time author is very grateful.

Gretchen Douglas, proofreader extraordinaire (and so much more), provided invaluable insight both grammatically, logically, and thematically. I am forever grateful for the keen eye she brought to the project. It is a better book because of her.

Thanks, also, to Chris Sorensen for his excellent cover design. Somehow, he put into visuals what I had only imagined. Also, thanks to Chris for his formatting of this book. His The Messy Man series of books is wonderfully terrifying.

A heartfelt thank you to all of my beta readers, who took this new venture seriously and offered excellent ideas, corrections, suggestions, and encouragement. Stephen Aldrich, Cindy Vollmer, Robin Lee-Thorp, Christen Cain, John E. Brady, James Ludwig, Kevin Carolan, Bekah Church, Amy Lingley, Chris Sorensen, Nick Sullivan. Thank you, a thousand times.

I must single out Nick Sullivan for going far beyond the task of beta reading. He has offered thoughts on everything from grammar to theme to the many moving parts of getting a book into the world. Further, his journey to becoming an author in part inspired my own. Thank you. Thank you. Thank you. His The Deep series of books is one of my favorite action/adventure series.

As a first-time author, I will take this chance to thank a certain few teachers who impacted me and planted the seeds of this book and a love for writing many years ago. Tom Watson, Ken Link, and Brian Nelson, all of whom unlocked a love of language, inspired creativity, and believed that, no matter the age of a student, they should be treated as if their ideas and aspirations are to be nurtured, encouraged, and valued. Teachers change lives every day. They changed mine.

Lastly, my wife Jennifer, for believing in and pushing me. For trusting that I had something to say and that it should be said. For being there. Always.

To all of these, I offer my deepest thanks.

Lastly, I thank you, the readers, for taking this journey with me. I've always told stories, whether on a stage, a screen, or a page. None of it would have been possible without people like you willing to come along. Thank you for loving stories.

About the Author

Mark Aldrich was born in Massachusetts and raised in Virginia. Most of his adult life he has made New York City his home while traveling extensively as an actor and singer. He has appeared in television, film, and theatre, including Broadway and many of the world's most famous stages. However, some of his favorite performances were given in village pubs late at night on the wild West Coast of Ireland.

Mark has written extensively for web publications, periodicals, and industry journals. After helping to tell others' stories on stage, he decided to commit some of his own to the page. *The Peripherals* marks his debut novel and combines his love of history, travel, folk-lore, music, and his decades-long knowledge of the inner workings of live theatre and the artists working there.

Please feel free to follow and keep in touch at markaldrich.net and @marktheginger on Instagram and Twitter.